THE WORLD INSIDE

ROBERT SILVERBERG's many novels include *The Alien Years*; the most recent volume in the Majipoor Cycle, *The King of Dreams*; the bestselling Lord Valentine trilogy; and the classics *Dying Inside* and *A Time of Changes*. He has been nominated for the Nebula and Hugo awards more times than any other writer; he is a five-time winner of the Nebula and a five-time winner of the Hugo. In April 2004, he received the prestigious title of Grand Master from the Science Fiction and Fantasy Writers of America.

"Where Silverberg goes today, the rest of science fiction will follow tomorrow."
—Isaac Asimov

"One of science fiction's modern masters... his words and his work have shaped the whole direction of the field."
—*Chicago Sun-Times*

"Done Silverberg's way, science fiction is a fine art."
—Associated Press

THE ROBERT SILVERBERG COLLECTION
published by ibooks

Sailing to Byzantium
Science Fiction 101: Where to Start
Cronos
Nightwings
Dying Inside
Up the Line
The Man in the Maze
Shadrach in the Furnace

ALSO AVAILABLE

Science Fiction: The Best of 2001
Fantasy: The Best of 2001
Science Fiction: The Best of 2002
Fantasy: The Best of 2002
Robert Silverberg
and Karen Haber, Editors

THE WORLD INSIDE

ROBERT SILVERBERG

ibooks
new york
www.ibooks.net

DISTRIBUTED BY SIMON & SCHUSTER, INC.

For Ejler Jakobsson

A Publication of ibooks, inc.

An ibooks, inc. Book

ibooks, inc.
24 West 25th Street
New York, NY 10010

The ibooks World Wide Web Site Address is:
http://www.ibooks.net

ISBN 0-7434-8723-0
First ibooks, inc. printing September 2004
10 9 8 7 6 5 4 3 2 1

Printed in the U.S.A.

We were born to unite with our fellow-men and to join in community with the human race.

—Cicero

De finibus, IV

Of all animals, men are the least fitted to live in herds. If they were crowded together as sheep are they would all perish in a short time. The breath of man is fatal to his fellows.

—Jean-Jacques Rousseau

Emile, I

1

Here begins a happy day in 2381. The morning sun is high enough to touch the uppermost fifty stories of Urban Monad 116. Soon the building's entire eastern face will glitter like the bosom of the sea at daybreak. Charles Mattern's window, activated by the dawn's early photons, deopaques. He stirs. God bless, he thinks. His wife yawns and stretches. His four children, who have been awake for hours, now can officially start their day. They rise and parade around the bedroom, singing:

God bless, god bless, god bless!
God bless us every one!
God bless Daddo, god bless Mommo, god bless you and
me!
God bless us all, the short and tall,
Give us fer-til-i-tee!

They rush toward their parents' sleeping platform. Mattern rises and embraces them. Indra is eight, Sandor is seven, Marx is five, Cleo is three. It is Charles Mattern's secret shame that his family is so small. Can a man with only four children truly be said to have reverence for life? But Principessa's womb no longer flowers. The medics have declared that she will not bear again. At twenty-seven she is sterile. Mattern is thinking of taking in a second woman. He longs to hear the yowls of an infant again; in any case, a man must do his duty to god.

Sandor says, "Daddo, Siegmund is still here."

The child points. Mattern sees. On Principessa's side of the sleeping platform, curled against the inflation pedal, lies fourteen-year-old Siegmund Kluver, who had entered the Mattern home several hours after midnight to exercise his rights of propinquity. Siegmund is fond of older women. He has become quite notorious in the past few months. Now he snores; he has had a good workout. Mattern nudges him. "Siegmund? Siegmund, it's morning!" The young man's eyes open. He smiles at Mattern, sits up, reaches for his wrap. He is quite handsome. He lives on the 787th floor and already has one child and another on the way.

"Sorry," says Siegmund. "I overslept. Principessa really drains me. A savage, she is!"

"Yes, she's quite passionate," Mattern agrees. So is Siegmund's wife, Mamelon, according to what Mattern has heard. When she is a little older, Mattern plans to try her. Next spring, perhaps.

Siegmund sticks his head under the molecular cleanser. Principessa now has left the bed. Nodding faintly to her husband, she kicks the pedal and the platform deflates swiftly. She begins to program breakfast. Indra, reaching forth a pale, almost transparent little hand, switches on the screen. The wall blossoms with light and color. "Good morning," says the screen heartily. "The external temperature, if anybody's interested, is 28°. Today's population figure at Urbmon 116 is 881,115, which is + 102 since yesterday and + 14,187 since the first of the year. God bless, but we're slowing down! Across the way at Urbmon 117 they've added 131 since yesterday, including quads for Mrs. Hula Jabotinsky. She's eighteen and has had seven previous. A servant of god, isn't she? The time is now 0620. In exactly forty minutes Urbmon 116 will be honored by the presence of Nicanor Gortman, the visiting sociocomputator from Hell, who can be recognized by his distinctive outbuilding costume in crimson and ultraviolet. Dr. Gortman will be the guest of the Charles Matterns of the 799th floor. Of course we'll treat him with the same friendly blessmanship we show one another. God bless Nicanor Gortman! Turning now to news from the lower levels of Urbmon 116—"

Principessa says, "Hear that, children? We'll have a guest, and we must be blessworthy toward him. Come and eat."

When he has cleansed himself, dressed, and breakfasted, Charles Mattern goes to the thousandth-floor landing stage to meet Nicanor Gortman. As he rises through the building to the summit, Mattern passes the floors on which his brothers and sisters and their families live. Three brothers, three sisters. Four of them younger than he, two older. All quite successful. One brother died, unpleasantly, young. Jeffrey, Mattern rarely thinks of Jeffrey. Now he is passing through the floors that make up Louisville, the administrative sector. In a moment he will meet his guest. Gortman has been touring the tropics and is about to visit a typical urban monad in the temperate zone. Mattern is honored to have been named the official host. He steps out on the landing stage, which is at the very tip of Urbmon 116. A force-field shields him from the fierce winds that sweep the lofty spire. He looks to his left and sees the western face of Urban Monad 115 still in darkness. To his right, Urbmon 117's eastern windows sparkle. Bless Mrs. Hula Jabotinsky and her eleven littles, Mattern thinks. Mattern can see other urbmons in the row, stretching on and on toward the horizon, towers of super-stressed concrete three kilometers high, tapering ever so gracefully. It is a thrilling sight. God bless, he thinks. God bless, god bless, god bless!

He hears a cheerful hum of rotors. A quickboat is landing. Out steps a tall, sturdy man dressed in high-spectrum garb. He must surely be the visiting sociocomputator from Hell.

"Nicanor Gortman?" Mattern asks.

"Bless god. Charles Mattern?"

"God bless, yes. Come."

Hell is one of the eleven cities of Venus, which man has reshaped to suit himself. Gortman has never been on Earth before. He speaks in a slow, stolid way, no lilt in his voice at all; the inflection reminds Mattern of the way they talk in Urbmon 84, which Mattern once visited on a field trip. He has read Gortman's papers: solid stuff, closely reasoned. "I particularly liked 'Dynamics of the Hunting Ethic,'" Mattern tells him while they are in the dropshaft. "Remarkable. A revelation."

"You really mean that?" Gortman asks, flattered.

"Of course. I try to keep up with the better Venusian journals. It's so fascinating to read about alien customs. Such as hunting wild animals."

"There are none on Earth?"

"God bless, no," Mattern says. "We couldn't allow that! But I love gaining insight into different ways of life."

"My essays are escape literature for you?" asks Gortman.

Mattern looks at him strangely. "I don't understand the reference."

"Escape literature. What you read to make life on Earth more bearable for yourself."

"Oh, no. Life on Earth is quite bearable, let me assure

you. There's no need for escape literature. I study off-world journals for *amusement*. And to obtain a necessary parallax, you know, for my own work," says Mattern. They have reached the 799th level. "Let me show you my home first." He steps from the dropshaft and beckons to Gortman. "This is Shanghai. I mean, that's what we call this block of forty floors, from 761 to 800. I'm in the next-to-top level of Shanghai, which is a mark of my professional status. We've got twenty-five cities altogether in Urbmon 116. Reykjavik's on the bottom and Louisville's on the top."

"What determines the names?"

"Citizen vote. Shanghai used to be Calcutta, which I personally prefer, but a little bunch of malcontents on the 778th floor rammed through a referendum in '75."

"I thought you had no malcontents in the urban monads," Gortman says.

Mattern smiles. "Not in the usual sense. But we allow certain conflicts to exist. Man wouldn't be man without conflicts, eh? Even here. Eh?"

They are walking down the eastbound corridor toward Mattern's home. It is now 0710, and children are streaming from their apartments in groups of three and four, rushing to get to school. Mattern waves to them. They sing as they run along. Mattern says, "We average 6.2 children per family on this floor. It's one of the lowest figures in the building, I have to admit. High-status people don't seem to breed well. They've got a floor in Prague—I think it's 117—that averages 9.9 per family! Isn't that glorious?"

"You are speaking with irony?" Gortman asks.

"Not at all." Mattern feels an uptake of tension. "We

5

like children. We *approve* of breeding. Surely you realized that before you set out on this tour of—"

"Yes, yes," says Gortman, hastily. "I was aware of the general cultural dynamic. But I thought perhaps your own attitude—"

"Ran counter to norm? Just because I have a scholar's detachment, you shouldn't assume that I disapprove in any way of my cultural matrix. Perhaps you're guilty of projecting your own disapproval, eh?"

"I regret the implication. And please don't think I feel the slightest negative attitudes in relation to your matrix, although I admit your world seems quite strange to me. Bless god, let us not have strife, Charles."

"God bless, Nicanor. I didn't mean to seem touchy."

They smile. Mattern is dismayed by his show of irritability.

Gortman says, "What is the population of the 799th floor?"

"805, last I heard."

"And of Shanghai?"

"About 33,000."

"And of Urbmon 116?"

"881,000."

"And there are fifty urban monads in this constellation of houses?"

"Yes."

"Making some 40,000,000 people," Gortman says. "Or somewhat more than the entire human population of Venus. Remarkable!"

"And this isn't the biggest constellation, not by any means!" Mattern's voice rings with pride. "Sansan is bigger, and so is Boshwash! And there are several larger ones in Europe—Berpar, Wienbud, I think two others. With more being planned!"

"—A global population of—"

"—75,000,000,000," Mattern cries. "God bless! There's never been anything like it! No one goes hungry! Everybody happy! Plenty of open space! God's been good to us, Nicanor!" He pauses before a door labeled 79915. "Here's my home. What I have is yours, dear guest." They go in.

Mattern's home is quite adequate. He has nearly ninety square meters of floor space. The sleeping platform deflates; the children's cots retract; the furniture can easily be moved to provide play area. Most of the room, in fact, is empty. The screen and the data terminal occupy two-dimensional areas of wall that in an earlier era had to be taken up by bulky television sets, book-cases, desks, file drawers, and other encumbrances. It is an airy, spacious environment, particularly for a family of just six.

The children have not yet left for school; Principessa has held them back, to meet the guest, and so they are restless. As Mattern enters, Sandor and Indra are struggling over a cherished toy, the dream-stirrer. Mattern is astounded. Conflict in the home? Silently, so their mother will not notice, they fight. Sandor hammers his shoes into his sister's shins. Indra, wincing, claws her brother's cheek. "God *bless,*" Mattern says sharply. "Somebody wants to go down the chute, eh?" The children gasp. The toy drops. Everyone stands at attention. Principessa looks up, brushing a lock of dark hair from her eyes; she has been busy with the youngest child and has not even heard them come in.

Mattern says, "Conflict sterilizes. Apologize to each other."

7

Indra and Sandor kiss and smile. Meekly Indra picks up the toy and hands it to Mattern, who gives it to his younger son, Marx. They are all staring now at the guest. Mattern says to Gortman, "What I have is yours, friend." He makes introductions. Wife, children. The scene of conflict has unnerved him a little, but he is relieved when Gortman produces four small boxes and distributes them to the children. Toys. A blessfull gesture. Mattern points to the deflated sleeping platform. "This is where we sleep," he explains. "There's ample room for three. We wash at the cleanser, here. Do you like privacy when voiding waste matter?"

"Please, yes."

"You press this button for the privacy shield. We excrete in this. Urine here, feces there. Everything is reprocessed, you understand. We're a thristy folk in the urbmons."

"Of course," Gortman says.

Principessa says, "Do you prefer that we use the shield when we excrete? I understand some outbuilding people do."

"I would not want to impose my customs on you," says Gortman.

Smiling, Mattern says, "We're a post-privacy culture, naturally. But it wouldn't be any trouble for us to press the button, if–" He falters. A troublesome new thought. "There's no general nudity taboo on Venus, is there? I mean, we have only this one room, and–"

"I am adaptable," Gortman insists. "A trained sociocomputator must be a cultural relativist, of course!"

"Of course," Mattern agrees, and he laughs nervously.

Principessa excuses herself from the conversation and

sends the children, still clutching their new toys, off to school.

Mattern says, "Forgive me for being overobvious, but I must bring up the matter of your sexual prerogatives. We three will share a single platform. My wife is available to you, as am I. Within the urbmon it is improper to refuse any reasonable request, so long as no injury is involved. Avoidance of frustration, you see, is the primary rule of a society such as ours, where even minor frictions could lead to uncontrollable oscillations of disharmony. And do you know our custom of nightwalking?"

"I'm afraid I—"

"Doors are not locked in Urbmon 116. We have no personal property worth guarding, and we all are socially adjusted. At night it is quite proper to enter other homes. We exchange partners in this way all the time; usually wives stay home and husbands migrate, though not necessarily. Each of us has access at any time to any other adult member of our community."

"Strange," says Gortman. "I'd think that in a society where there are so many people living so close together, an exaggerated respect for privacy would develop, rather than a communal freedom."

"In the beginning we had many notions of privacy. God bless, they were allowed to erode! Avoidance of frustration must be our goal, otherwise impossible tensions develop. And privacy is frustration."

"So you can go into any room in this whole gigantic building and sleep with—"

"Not the whole building," Mattern says, interrupting. "Only Shanghai. We frown on nightwalking beyond one's own city." He chuckles. "We do impose a few little restrictions on ourselves, you see, so that our freedoms don't pall."

Gortman turns toward Principessa. She wears a loinband and metallic cup over her left breast. She is slender but voluptuously constructed, and even though her childbearing days are over she has not lost the sensual glow of young womanhood. Mattern is proud of her, despite everything.

Mattern says, "Shall we begin our tour of the building?"

They go toward the door. Gortman bows gracefully to Principessa as he and Mattern leave. In the corridor, the visitor says, "Your family is smaller than the norm, I see."

It is an excruciatingly impolite statement, but Mattern is able to be tolerant of his guest's faux pas. Mildly he replies, "We would have had more children, but my wife's fertility had to be terminated surgically. It was a great tragedy for us."

"You have always valued large families here?"

"We value life. To create new life is the highest virtue. To prevent life from coming into being is the darkest sin. We all love our big bustling world. Does it seem unendurable to you? Do we seem unhappy?"

"You seem surprisingly well adjusted," Gortman says. "Considering that—" He stops.

"Go on."

"Considering that there are so many of you. And that you spend your whole lives inside a single colossal building. You never do go out, do you?"

"Most of us never do," Mattern admits. "I have traveled, of course—a sociocomputator needs perspective, obviously. But Principessa has never left the building. I believe she has never been below the 350th floor, except when she was taken to see the lower levels while she was in school. Why should she go anywhere? The secret of our happiness is to create self-contained villages of five or six floors within the cities of forty floors within the urbmons of a thousand floors. We have no sensation of being overcrowded or cramped. We know our neighbors; we have hundreds of dear friends; we are kind and loyal and blessworthy to one another."

"And everybody remains happy forever?"

"Nearly everybody."

"Who are the exceptions?" Gortman asks.

"The flippos," says Mattern. "We endeavor to minimize the frictions of living in such an environment; as you see, we never deny one another anything, we never thwart a reasonable desire. But sometimes there are those who abruptly decide they can no longer abide by our principles. They flip; they thwart others; they rebel. It is quite sad."

"What do you do with flippos?"

"We remove them, of course," Mattern says. He smiles, and they enter the dropshaft once again.

Mattern has been authorized to show Gortman the entire urbmon, a tour that will take several days. He is a little apprehensive; he is not as familiar with some parts of the structure as a guide should be. But he will do his best.

"The building," he says, "is made of superstressed concrete. It is constructed about a central service core two hundred meters square. Originally, the plan was to have fifty families per floor, but we average about 120 today, and the old apartments have all been subdivided into single-room occupancies. We are wholly self-sufficient, with our own schools, hospitals, sports arenas, houses of worship, and theaters."

"Food?"

"We produce none, of course. But we have contractual access to the agricultural communes. I'm sure you've seen that nearly nine tenths of the land area of this continent is used for food production; and then there are the marine farms. Oh, we have plenty of food on this planet, now that we no longer waste space by spreading out horizontally over good land."

"But aren't you at the mercy of the food-producing communes?"

"When were city-dwellers not at the mercy of farmers?" Mattern asks. "But you seem to regard life on Earth as an affair of fang and claw. Actually the ecology of our world is neatly in mesh. We are vital to the farmers—their only market, their only source of manufactured goods. They are vital to us—our only source of food. Reciprocal indispensabilities, eh? And the system works. We could support many billions of additional people. Someday, god blessing, we will."

The dropshaft, coasting downward through the building, glides into its anvil at the very bottom. Mattern feels the oppressive bulk of the whole urbmon over him, and is vaguely surprised by the intensity of his distress; he tries not to show that he is uneasy. He says, "The foundation of the structure is four hundred meters deep. We are now at the lowest level. Here we generate our power." They cross a catwalk and peer into an immense generating room, forty meters from floor to ceiling, in which sleek green turbines whirl. "Most of our power is obtained," he points out, "through combustion of compacted solid refuse. We burn everything we don't need, and sell the residue as fertilizer. We have auxiliary generators that work on accumulated body heat, also."

"I was wondering about that," Gortman murmurs. "What you do with the heat."

Cheerily Mattern says, "Obviously 800,000 people within one sealed enclosure will produce an immense thermal surplus. Some of this heat is directly radiated from the building through cooling fins along the outer surface. Some is piped down here and used to run the generator. In winter, of course, we pump it evenly through the building to maintain temperature. The rest of the excess heat is used in water purification and similar things."

They peer at the electrical system for a while. Then Mattern leads the way to the reprocessing plant. Several hundred school-children are touring it; silently the two men join the tour.

The teacher says, "Here's where the urine comes down, see?" She points to gigantic plastic pipes. "It passes through the flash chamber to be distilled, and the pure water is drawn off here—follow me, now—you remember from the flow chart, the part about how we recover the chemicals and sell them to the farming communes—"

Mattern and his guest inspect the fertilizer plant, too, where fecal reconversion is taking place. Gortman asks a number of questions. He seems deeply interested. Mattern is pleased; there is nothing more significant to him than the details of the urbmon way of life, and he had feared that this stranger from Venus, from a place where men live in private houses and walk around in the open, would regard the urbmon way as repugnant or hideous.

They go onward. Mattern speaks of air-conditioning,

the system of dropshafts and liftshafts, and other such topics.

"It's all wonderful," Gortman says. "I couldn't imagine how one little planet with 75,000,000,000 people could even survive, but you've turned it into—into—"

"Utopia?" Mattern suggests.

"I meant to say that, yes," says Gortman.

Power production and waste disposal are not really Mattern's specialties. He knows how such things are handled here, but only because the workings of the urbmon are so enthralling to him. His real field of study is sociocomputation, after all, and he has been asked to show the visitor how the social structure of the giant building is organized. Now they go up, into the residential levels.

"This is Reykjavik," Mattern announces. "Populated chiefly by maintenance workers. We try not to have too much status stratification, but each city does have its predominant populations—engineers, academics, entertainers, you know. My Shanghai is mostly academic. Each profession is clannish." They walk down the hall. Mattern feels edgy in this low level, and he keeps talking to cover his nervousness. He describes how each city within the urbmon develops its characteristic slang, its way of dressing, its folklore, and heroes.

"Is there much contact between cities?" Gortman asks.

"We try to encourage it. Sports, exchange students, regular mixer evenings. Within reason, that is. We don't have people from the working-class levels mixing with those from the academic levels, much. It would make everyone unhappy, eh? But we attempt to get a decent flow between cities of roughly similar intellectual level. We think it's healthy."

"Wouldn't it help the mixing process if you encouraged intercity nightwalking?"

Mattern frowns. "We prefer to stick to our propinquity groups for that. Casual sex with people from other cities is a mark of a sloppy soul."

"I see."

They enter a large room. Mattern says, "This is a newlywed dorm. We have them every five or six levels. When adolescents mate, they leave their family homes and move in here. After they have their first child they are assigned to homes of their own."

Puzzled, Gortman asks, "But where do you find room for them all? I assume that every room in the building is full, and you can't possibly have as many deaths as births, so—how—?"

"Deaths do create vacancies, of course. If your mate dies and your children are grown, you go to a senior citizen dorm, creating room for the establishment of a new family unit. But you're correct that most of our young people don't get accommodations in the building, since we form new families at about two percent a year and deaths are far below that. As new urbmons are built, the overflow from the newlywed dorms is sent to them. By lot. It's hard to adjust to being expelled, they say, but there are compensations in being among the first group into a new building. You acquire automatic status. And so we're constantly overflowing, casting out our young, creating new combinations of social units—utterly fascinating, eh? Have you read my paper, 'Structural Metamorphosis in the Urbmon Population'?"

"I'm afraid I haven't encountered it," Gortman replies. "I'll be eager to look it up." He glances around the dorm.

A dozen couples are having intercourse on a nearby platform. "They seem so young," he says.

"Puberty comes early among us. Girls generally marry at twelve, boys at thirteen. First child about a year later, god blessing."

"And nobody tries to control fertility at all?"

"*Control fertility?*" Mattern clutches his genitals in shock at the unexpected obscenity. Several copulating couples look up, amazed. Someone giggles. Mattern says, "Please don't use that phrase again. Particularly if you're near children. We don't—ah—think in terms of control."

"But—"

"We hold that life is sacred. Making new life is blessed. One does one's duty to god by reproducing." Mattern smiles, feeling that he sounds too earnest. "To be human is to meet challenges through the exercise of intelligence, right? And one challenge is the multiplication of inhabitants in a world that has seen the conquest of disease and the elimination of war. We could limit births, I suppose, but that would be sick, a cheap, anti-human way out. Instead we've met the challenge of overpopulation triumphantly, wouldn't you say? And so we go on and on, multiplying joyously, our numbers increasing by three billion a year, and we find room for everyone, and food for everyone. Few die, and many are born, and the world fills up, and god is blessed, and life is rich and pleasant, and as you see we are all quite happy. We have matured beyond the infantile need to place layers of insulation between man and man. Why go outdoors? Why yearn for forests and deserts? Urbmon 116 holds universes enough for us. The warnings of the prophets of doom have proved hollow. Can you deny that we are happy here? Come with me. We will see a school now."

* * *

The school Mattern has chosen is in a working-class district of Prague, on the 108th floor. He thinks Gortman will find it especially interesting, since the Prague people have the highest reproductive rate in Urban Monad 116, and families of twelve or fifteen are not at all uncommon. Approaching the school door, Mattern and Gortman hear the clear treble voices singing of the blessedness of god. Mattern joins the singing; it is a hymn he sang too, when he was their age, dreaming of the big family he would have:

> *And now he plants the holy seed.*
> *That grows in Mommo's womb,*
> *And now a little sibling comes—*

There is an unpleasant and unscheduled interruption. A woman rushes toward Mattern and Gortman in the corridor. She is young, untidy, wearing only a flimsy gray wrap; her hair is loose; she is well along in pregnancy. "Help!" she shrieks. "My husband's gone flippo!" She hurls herself, trembling, into Gortman's arms. The visitor looks bewildered.

Toward her there runs a man in his early twenties, haggard, eyes bloodshot. He carries a fabricator torch; its tip glows with heat. "Goddamn bitch," he mumbles. "Allatime babies! Seven babies already and now number eight and I gonna go off my *head*!" Mattern is appalled. He pulls the woman away from Gortman and shoves the dismayed visitor through the door of the school.

"Tell them there's a flippo out here," Mattern says. "Get help, fast!" He is furious that Gortman should witness so atypical a scene, and wishes to take him away from it.

The trembling girl cowers behind Mattern. Quietly, Mattern says, "Let's be reasonable, young man. You've spent your whole life in urbmons, haven't you? You understand that it's blessed to create. Why do you suddenly repudiate the principles on which—"

"Get the hell away from her or I gonna burn you too!"

The young man feints with the torch, jabbing it straight at Mattern's face. Mattern feels the heat and flinches. The young man swipes past him at the woman. She leaps away, but she is clumsy with girth, and the torch slices her garment. Pale white distended flesh is exposed, with a brilliant burn-streak slashed across it. She cups her jutting belly and falls, screaming. The young man jostles Mattern out of the way and prepares to thrust the torch into her side. Mattern tries to seize his arm. He deflects the torch; it chars the floor. The young man, cursing, drops it and throws himself on Mattern, pounding frenziedly with his fists. "Help me!" Mattern calls. "Help!"

Into the corridor erupt dozens of schoolchildren. They are between eight and eleven years of age. They continue to sing their hymn as they pour forth. They pull Mattern's assailant from him. Swiftly, smoothly, they cover him with their bodies. He can dimly be seen beneath the flailing, thrashing mass. Dozens more rush from the schoolroom and join the heap. A siren wails. A whistle blows. The teacher's amplified voice booms, "The police are here! Everyone off!"

Four men in uniform have arrived. They survey the situation. The injured woman lies groaning, rubbing her burn. The insane man is unconscious; his face is bloody and one eye appears to be destroyed. "What happened?" a policeman asks. "Who are you?"

"Charles Mattern, sociocomputator, 799th level, Shanghai. The man's a flippo. Attacked his pregnant wife with the torch. Attempted to attack me."

The policemen haul the flippo to his feet. He sags, dazed, battered, in their midst. The police leader says, rattling the words into one another, "Guilty of atrocious assault on woman of childbearing years currently carrying unborn life, dangerous countersocial tendencies, menace to harmony and stability, by virtue of authority vested in me I pronounce sentence of erasure, carry out immediately. Down the chute with the bastard, boys!" They haul the flippo away. Medics appear and cluster about the fallen woman. The children, once again gaily singing, return to the classroom. Nicanor Gortman looks stunned and shaken. Mattern seizes his arm and whispers fiercely, "All right, so those things happen sometimes. I don't deny it. But it was a billion to one against having it happen where you'd see it! It isn't typical! It isn't typical!"

They enter the classroom.

The sun is setting. The Western face of the neighboring urban monad is streaked with red. Nicanor Gortman sits quietly at dinner with the members of the Mattern family. The children, voices tumbling in chaotic interplay, chatter of their day at school. The evening news comes on the screen; the announcer mentions the unfortunate event on the 108th floor. "The mother was not seriously injured," he says, "and no harm came to her unborn child. Sentence on the assailant has been carried out and a threat to the security of the whole urbmon has thus been eliminated." Principessa murmurs, "Bless god." After dinner Mattern requests copies of his most recent technical papers from the data terminal and gives the whole sheaf to Gortman to read at his leisure. Gortman thanks him energetically.

"You look tired," Mattern says.

"It was a busy day. And a rewarding one."

"Yes. We really covered ground, didn't we?"

Mattern is tired too. They have visited nearly three dozen levels already; he has shown Gortman town meetings, fertility clinics, religious services, business offices, all on this first day. Tomorrow there will be much more to see. Urban Monad 116 is a varied, complex community. And a happy one, Mattern tells himself firmly. We have a few little incidents from time to time, but we're *happy*.

The children, one by one, go to sleep, charmingly kissing Daddo and Mommo and the visitor good night and running across the room, sweet nude little pixies, to their cots. The lights automatically dim. Mattern feels faintly depressed; the unpleasantness on 108 has spoiled what was otherwise an excellent day. Yet he still thinks that he has succeeded in helping Gortman see past the superficialities to the innate harmony and serenity of the urbmon way. And now he will allow the guest to experience for himself one of their most useful techniques for minimizing the interpersonal conflicts that could be so destructive to their kind of society. Mattern rises.

"It's nightwalking time," he says. "I'll go. You stay here...with Principessa." He suspects that the visitor would appreciate some privacy.

Gortman looks uneasy.

"Go on," Mattern says. "Enjoy yourself. People don't deny pleasure to people, here. We weed the selfish ones out early. Please. What I have is yours. Isn't that so, Principessa?"

"Certainly," she says.

Mattern steps out of the room, walks quickly down the corridor, enters the dropshaft, and descends to the 770th floor. As he gets out he hears sudden angry shouts, and he stiffens, fearing that he will become involved in another nasty episode, but no one appears. He walks on. He passes the black door of a chute access and shivers a little, and he cannot avoid thinking of the young man with the fabricator torch, and what has become of him. And then, without warning, there swims up from memory the face of the brother he had once had who had gone down that same chute, the brother one year his senior, Jeffrey, the whiner, the stealer, Jeffrey the selfish, Jeffrey the unadaptable, Jeffrey who had had to be given to a chute. For an instant Mattern is sickened and dizzied. He starts to fall, and wildly seizes a doorknob to steady himself.

The door opens. He goes in. He has never been a nightwalker on this floor before. Five children lie asleep in their cots, and on the sleeping platform are a man and a woman, both younger than he is, both asleep. Mattern removes his clothing and lies down by the woman's left side. He touches her thigh, then her small cool breast. She opens her eyes and he says, "Hello. Charles Mattern, 799."

"Gina Burke," she says. "My husband Lenny."

Lenny awakens. He sees Mattern, nods, turns over, and returns to sleep. Mattern kisses Gina Burke lightly on the lips. She opens her arms to him. He trembles in his need, and sighs as she receives him. God bless, he thinks. It has been a happy day in 2381, and now it is over.

2

The city of Chicago is bounded on the north by Shanghai and on the south by Edinburgh. Chicago currently has 37,402 people, and is undergoing a mild crisis of population that will have to be alleviated in the customary manner. Its dominant profession is engineering. Above, in Shanghai, they are mostly scholars; below, in Edinburgh, computer men cluster.

Aurea Holston was born in Chicago in 2368 and has lived there all of her life. Aurea is now fourteen years old. Her husband, Memnon, is nearly fifteen. They have been married almost two years. God has not blessed them with children. Memnon has traveled through the entire building, but Aurea has scarcely ever been out of Chicago. Once she went to visit a fertility expert, an old midwife down in Prague, and once she went up to Louisville, where her powerful uncle, an urban administrator, lives. Many times she and Memnon have been to their friend Siegmund Kluver's apartment in Shanghai. Other than that she has not seen much of the building. Aurea does not really care to travel. She loves her own city very much.

Chicago is the city that occupies the 721st through the 760th floors of Urban Monad 116. Memnon and Aurea Holston live in a dormitory for childless young couples on the 735th floor. The dorm is currently shared by thirty-one couples, eight above optimum.

"There's got to be a thinning soon," Memnon says.

"We're starting to bulge at the seams. People will have to go."

"Many?" Aurea asks.

"Three couples here, five there—a slice from each dorm. I suppose Urbmon 116 will lose about two thousand couples. That's how many went the last time they thinned."

Aurea trembles. "Where will they go?"

"They tell me that the new urbmon is almost ready. Number 158."

Her soul floods with pity and terror. "How horrid to be sent somewhere else! Memnon, they *wouldn't* make us leave here!"

"Of course not. God bless, we're valuable people! I have a skill rating of—"

"But we have no children. That kind goes first, doesn't it?"

"God will bless us soon." Memnon takes her in his arms. He is strong and tall and lean, with rippling scarlet hair and a taut, solemn expression. Aurea feels weak and fragile beside him, although in fact she is sturdy and supple. Her crown of golden hair is deepening in tone. Her eyes are pale green. Her breasts are full and her hips are broad. Siegmund Kluver says she looks like a goddess of motherhood. Most men desire her and night-walkers come frequently to share her sleeping platform. Yet she remains barren. Lately she has become quite sensitive about that. The irony of her wasted voluptuousness is not lost on her.

Memnon releases her and she walks wearily through the dormitory. It is a long, narrow room that makes a right-angle bend around the central service core of the urbmon. Its walls glow with changing inlaid patterns of blue and gold and green. Rows of sleeping platforms, some deflated, some in use, cover the floor. The furniture is stark and simple and the lighting, though indirectly suffused from the entire area of the floor and the ceiling, is bright almost to harshness. Several view screens and three data terminals are mounted on the room's eastern wall. There are five excretion areas, three communal recreation areas, two cleanser stations, and two privacy areas.

By unspoken custom the privacy shields are never turned on in this dormitory. What one does, one does before the others. The total accessibility of all persons to all other persons is the only rule by which the civilization of the urbmon can survive, and in a mass residence hall such as this the rule is all the more vital.

Aurea halts by the majestic window at the dormitory's western end, and stares out. The sunset is beginning. Across the way, the magnificent bulk of urban Monad 117 seems stained with golden red. Aurea follows the shaft of the great tower with her eyes, down from the landing stage at its thousandth-floor tip, down to the building's broad waist. She cannot see, at this angle, very far below the 400th floor of the adjoining structure.

What is it like, she wonders, to live in Urbmon 117? Or 115, or 110, or 140? She has never left the urbmon of her birth. All about her, to the horizon, sprawl the towers of the Chipitts constellation, fifty mighty concrete piles, each three kilometers high, each a self-contained entity housing some 800,000 human beings. In Urbmon 117, Aurea tells herself, there are people who look just like us. They walk, talk, dress, think, love, just like ourselves. Urbmon 117 is not another world. It is only the building next door. We are not unique. We are not unique. We are not unique.

Fear engulfs her.

"Memnon," she says raggedly, "when the thinning time comes, they're going to send us to Urbmon 158."

Siegmund Kluver is one of the lucky ones. His fertility has won him an unimpeachable place in Urbmon 116. His status is secure.

Though he is just past fourteen, Siegmund has fathered two children. His son is called Janus and his newborn daughter has been named Persephone. Siegmund lives in a handsome fifty-square-meter home on the 787th floor, slightly more than mid-way up in Shanghai. His specialty is the theory of urban administration, and despite his youth he already spends much of his time as a consultant to the administrators in Louisville. He is short, finely made, quite strong, with a large head and thick curling hair. In boyhood he lived in Chicago and was one of Memnon's closest friends. They still see each other quite often; the fact that they now live in different cities is no bar to their friendship.

Social encounters between the Holstons and the Kluvers always take place at Siegmund's apartment. The Kluvers never come down to Chicago to visit Aurea and Memnon. Siegmund claims there is no snobbery in this. "Why should the four of us sit around a noisy dorm," he asks, "when we can get together comfortably in the privacy of my apartment?" Aurea is suspicious of this attitude. Urbmon people are not supposed to place such a premium on privacy. Is the dorm not a good enough place for Siegmund Kluver?

Siegmund once lived in the same dorm as Aurea and Memnon. That was two years ago, when they all were newly married. Several times, in those long-ago days, Aurea yielded her body to Siegmund. She was flattered by his attentions. But very swiftly Siegmund's wife became pregnant, qualifying the Kluvers to apply for an apartment of their own, and the progress he was making in his profession permitted him to find room in the city of Shanghai. Aurea has not shared her sleeping platform with Siegmund since he left the dormitory. She is distressed by this, for she enjoyed Siegmund's embraces, but there is little she can do about it. The chance that he will come to her as a nightwalker is slight. Sexual relationships between people of different cities are currently considered improper, and Siegmund abides by custom. He may nightwalk in cities above his own, but he is not likely to go lower.

Siegmund now is evidently bound for higher things. Memnon says that by the time he is seventeen he will be, not a specialist in the theory of urban administration, but an actual administrator, and will live in lofty Louisville. Already Siegmund spends much time with the leaders of the urbmon. And with their wives as well, Aurea has heard.

He is an excellent host. His apartment is warm and agreeable, and two of its walls glisten with panels of one of the new decorative materials, which emits a soft hum keyed to the spectral pattern its owner has chosen. Tonight Siegmund has turned the panels almost into the ultraviolet and the audio emission is pitched close to the supersonic; the effect is to strain the senses, pushing them toward their maximum receptivity, a stimulating challenge. He has exquisite taste in handling the room's scent apertures too: jasmine and hyacinth flavor the air. "Care for some tingle?" he asks. "Just in from Venus.

Quite blessworthy." Aurea and Memnon smile and nod. Siegmund fills a large fluted silver bowl with the costly scintillant fluid and places it on the pedestal-table. A touch of the floor pedal and the table rises to a height of 150 centimeters.

"Mamelon?" he says. "Will you join us?"

Siegmund's wife slides her baby into the maintenance slot near the sleeping platform and crosses the room to her guests. Mamelon Kluver is quite tall, dark of complexion and hair, elegantly beautiful in a haggard way. Her forehead is high, her cheekbones prominent, her chin sharp; her eyes, alert and glossy and wide-set, seem almost too big, too dominant, in her pale and tapering face. The delicacy of Mamelon's beauty makes Aurea feel defensive about her own soft features: her snub nose, her rounded cheeks, her full lips, the light dusting of freckles over tawny skin. Mamelon is the oldest person in the room, almost sixteen. Her breasts are swollen with milk; she is only eleven days up from childbed, and she is nursing. Aurea has never known anyone else who chose to nurse. Mamelon has always been different, though. Aurea is still somewhat frightened of Siegmund's wife, who is so cool, so self-possessed, so mature. So passionate too. At twelve, a new bride, Aurea found her sleep broken again and again by Mamelon's cries of ecstasy, echoing through the dormitory.

Now Mamelon bends forward and puts her lips to the tingle bowl. The four of them drink at the same moment. Tiny bubbles dance on Aurea's lips. The bouquet dizzies her. She peers into the depths of the bowl and sees abstract patterns forming and sundering. Tingle is faintly intoxicating, faintly hallucinogenic, an enhancer of vision, a suppressant of inner disturbance. It comes from certain musky swamps in the lowlands of Venus; the serving Siegmund has offered contains billions of alien microorganisms, fermenting and fissioning even as they are digested and absorbed. Aurea feels them spreading out through her, taking possession of her lungs, her ovaries, her liver. They make her lips slippery. They detach her from her sorrows. But the high is also a low; she gets through the early visionary moments and emerges tranquil and resigned. A spurious happiness possesses her as the last coils of color slide behind her eyelids and disappear.

After the ritual of drinking, they talk. Siegmund and Memnon discuss world events: the new urbmons, the agricultural statistics, the rumor of a spreading zone of disurbanized life outside the communes, and so forth. Mamelon shows Aurea her baby. The little girl lies within the maintenance slot, drooling, gurgling, cooing. Aurea says, "What a relief it must be not to be carrying her any longer!"

"One enjoys being able to see one's feet again, yes," Mamelon says.

"Is it very uncomfortable, being pregnant?"

"There are annoyances."

"The stretching? How can you puff up that way and stand it? The skin like going to burst any minute." Aurea shudders. "And everything getting pushed around inside your body. Your kidneys rammed up into your lungs, that's how I always think of it. Pardon me. I guess I'm exaggerating. I mean, I don't really know."

"It's not that bad," says Mamelon. "Though of course it's strange and a little bothersome. Yet there are positive aspects. The moment of birth itself—"

"Does it hurt terribly?" Aurea asks. "I imagine it would.

29

Something that big, ripping through your body, popping right out of your—"

"Gloriously blessful. One's entire nervous system awakens. A baby coming out is like a man going in, only twenty times as thrilling. It's impossible to describe the sensation. You must experience it for yourself."

"I wish I could," says Aurea, downcast, groping for the last shreds of her high. She slips a hand into the maintenance slot to touch Mamelon's child. A quick burst of ions purifies her skin before she makes contact with little Persephone's downy cheek. Aurea says, "God bless, I want to do my duty! The medics say there's nothing wrong with either of us. But—"

"You must be patient, love." Mamelon embraces Aurea lightly. "Bless god, your moment will come."

Aurea is skeptical. For twenty months she has surveyed her flat belly, waiting for it to begin to bulge. It is blessed to create life, she knows. If everyone were as sterile as she, who would fill the urbmons? She has a sudden terrifying vision of the colossal towers nearly empty, whole cities sealed off, power failing, walls cracking, just a few shriveled old women shuffling through halls once thronged with happy multitudes.

Her one obsession has led her to the other one, and she turns to Siegmund, breaking into the conversation of the men to say, "Siegmund, is it true that they'll be opening Urbmon 158 soon?"

"So I hear, yes."

"What will it be like?"

"Very much like 116, I imagine. A thousand floors, the usual services. I suppose seventy families per floor, at first, maybe 250,000 people altogether, but it won't take long to bring it up to par."

Aurea clamps her palms together. "How many people will be sent there from here, Siegmund?"

"I'm sure I don't know that."

"There'll be some, won't there?"

Memnon says mildly, "Aurea, why don't we talk about something pleasant."

"Some people will be sent there from here," she persists. "Come on, Siegmund. You're up in Louisville with the bosses all the time. *How many?*"

Siegmund laughs. "You've really got an exaggerated idea of my significance in this place, Aurea. Nobody's said a word to me about how Urbmon 158 will be stocked."

"You know the theory of these things, though. You can project the data."

"Well, yes." Siegmund is quite cool; this subject has a purely impersonal interest for him. He seems unaware of the source of Aurea's agitation. "Naturally, if we're going to do our duty to god by creating life, we've also got to be sure that there's a place for everyone to live," he says. Hand flicks a vagrant lock of hair into place. Eyes glow; Siegmund loves to lecture. "So we go on building urban monads, and, naturally, whenever a new urbmon is added to the Chipitts constellation, it has to be stocked from the other Chipitts buildings. That makes good genetic sense. Even though each urbmon is big enough to provide an adequate gene-mix, our tendency to stratify into cities and villages within the building leads to a good deal of inbreeding, which they say isn't healthy for the species on a long-term basis. But if we take five thousand people from each of fifty urbmons, say, and toss them together into a new urbmon, it gives us a pooled gene-mix of 250,000 individuals that we didn't have before. Actually, though, easing population pressure is the most urgent reason for erecting new buildings."

"Keep it clean, Siegmund," Memnon warns.

Siegmund grins. "No, I mean it. Oh, sure, there's a cultural imperative telling us to breed and breed and breed. That's natural, after the agonies of the pre-urbmon days, when everybody went around wondering where we were going to put all the people. But even in a world of urban monads we have to plan in an orderly way. The excess of births over deaths is pretty consistent. Each urbmon is designed to hold 800,000 people comfortably, with room to pack in maybe 100,000 more, but that's the top. At the moment, you know, every urbmon more than twenty years old in the Chipitts constellation is at least 10,000 people above maximum, and a couple are pushing maximum. Things aren't too bad yet in 116, but you know yourselves that there are trouble spots. Why, Chicago has 38,000—"

"37,402 this morning," Aurea says.

"Whatever. That's close to a thousand people a floor. The programed optimum density for Chicago is only 32,000, though. That means that the waiting list in your city for a private apartment is getting close to a full generation long. The dorms are packed, and people aren't dying fast enough to make room for the new families, which is why Chicago is offloading some of its best people to places like Edinburgh and Boston and—well, Shanghai. Once the new building is open—"

Aurea says, steely-voiced, "How many from 116 are going to be sent there?"

"The theory is, 5,000 from each monad, at current levels," Siegmund says. "It'll be adjusted slightly to

compensate for population variations in different buildings, but figure on 5,000. Now there'll be about a thousand people in 116 who'll volunteer to go—"

"Volunteer?" Aurea gasps. It is inconceivable to her
that anyone will *want* to leave his native urbmon.

Siegmund smiles. "Older people, love. In their twenties
and thirties. Bored, maybe stalemated in their careers,
tired of their neighbors, who knows? It sounds obscene,
yes. But there'll be a thousand volunteers. That means
that about 4,000 more will have to be picked by lot."

"I told you so this morning," Memnon says.

"Will these 4,000 be taken at random throughout the
whole urbmon?" Aurea asks.

Gently Siegmund says, "At random, yes. From the
newlywed dorms. From the childless."

At last. The truth revealed.

"Why from us?" Aurea wails.

"Kindest and most blessworthy way," says Siegmund.
"We can't uproot small children from their urbmon
matrix. Dorm couples haven't the same kind of community ties that we—that others—that—" He falters, as if
recognizing for the first time that he is not speaking of
hypothetical individuals, but of Aurea and her own
calamity. Aurea starts to sob. He says, "Love, I'm sorry.
It's the system, and it's a good system. Ideal, in fact."

"Memnon, we're going to be *expelled!*"

Siegmund tries to reassure her. She and Memnon have
only a slim chance of being chosen, he insists. In this
urbmon thousands upon thousands of people are eligible
for transfer. And so many variable factors exist, he
maintains—but she will not be consoled. Unashamed, she
lets geysers of raw emotion spew into the room, and then
she feels shame. She knows she has spoiled the evening

for everyone. But Siegmund and Mamelon are kind about
it, and Memnon does not chide her as he hurries her out,
into the dropshaft, down fifty-two floors to their home
in Chicago.

That night, although she wants him intensely, she turns
her back on Memnon when he reaches for her. She lies
awake listening a long time to the gasps and happy
groans of the couples sprawled on the sleeping platforms
about her, and then sleep comes. Aurea dreams of being
born. She is down in the power plant of Urban Monad
116, 400 meters underground, and they are sealing her
into a liftshaft capsule. The building throbs. She is close
to the heat-sink and the urine-reprocessing plant and
the refuse compactors and all the rest of the service gear
that keeps the structure alive, all those dark, hidden
sectors of the urbmon that she had to tour when she was
a schoolgirl. Now the liftshaft carries her up, up through
Reykjavik where the maintenance people live, up through
brawling Prague where everyone has ten babies, up
through Rome, Boston, Edinburgh, Chicago, Shanghai,
even through Louisville where the administrators dwell
in unimaginable luxury, and now she is at the summit
of the building, at the landing stage where the quickboats
fly in from distant towers, and a hatch opens in the
landing stage and Aurea is ejected. She soars into the
sky, safe within her snug capsule while the cold winds
of the upper atmosphere buffet it. She is six kilometers
above the ground, looking down for the first time on the
entire urbmon world. So this is how it is, she thinks. So
many buildings. And yet so much open space!
    She drifts across the constellation of towers. It is early
spring, and Chipitts is greening. Below her are the tapered
structures that hold the 40,000,000+ people of this urban

cluster. She is awed by the neatness of the constellation, the geometrical placement of the buildings to form a series of hexagons within the larger area. Green plazas separate the buildings. No one enters the plazas, ever, but their well-manicured lawns are a delight to behold from the windows of the urbmon, and at this height they seem wondrously smooth, as if painted against the ground. The lower-class people on the lower floors have the best views of the gardens and pools, which is a compensation of sorts. From her vantage point high above, Aurea does not expect to see the details of the plazas well, but her dreaming mind suddenly gives her an intense clarity of vision and she discerns small golden floral heads; she smells the tang of floral fragrance.

Her brain whirls as she engorges herself on the complexities of Chipitts. How many cities at twenty-five to an urban monad? 1,250. How many villages at seven or eight to a city? More than 10,000. How many families? How many nightwalkers now prowling, now slipping into available beds? How many births a day? How many deaths? How many joys? How many sorrows?

She rises effortlessly to a height of ten kilometers. She wishes to behold the agricultural communes that lie beyond the urban constellation.

She sees them now, stretching to the horizon, neat flat bands of green bordered in brown. Seven eighths of the land area of the continent, she has been told endlessly, is used for the production of food. Or is it nine tenths? Five eighths? Twelve thirteenths? Busy little men and women oversee the machines that till the fertile fields. Aurea has heard tales of the terrible rites of the farming folk, the bizarre and primitive customs of those who must live outside the civilized urban world. Perhaps that is all fantasy; no one she knows has ever visited the communes. No one she knows has ever set foot outside Urban Monad 116. The courier pods trundle endlessly and without supervision toward the urbmons, carrying produce through subterranean channels. Food in; machinery and other manufactured goods out. A balanced economy. Aurea is borne upward on a transport of joy. How miraculous it is that there can be 75,000,000,000 people living harmoniously on one small world! God bless, she thinks. A full room for every family. A meaningful and enriching city life. Friends, lovers, mates, children.

Children. Dismay seizes her and she begins to spin.

In her dizziness she seems to vault to the edge of space, so that she sees the entire planet; all of its urban constellations are jutting toward her like spikes. She sees not only Chipitts but also Sansan and Boswash, and Berpar, Wienbud, Shankong, Bocarac, every gathering of mighty towers. And also she sees the plains teeming with food, the former deserts, the former savannas, the former forests. It is all quite wonderful, but it is terrifying as well, and she is uncertain for a moment whether the way man has reshaped his environment is the best of all possible ways. Yes, she tells herself, yes; we are servants of god this way, we avoid strife and greed and turmoil, we bring new life into the world, we thrive, we multiply. We multiply. We multiply. And doubt smites her and she begins to fall, and the capsule splits and releases her, leaving her bare body unprotected as it tumbles through the cold air. And she sees the spiky tips of Chipitts' fifty towers below her, but now there is a new tower, a fifty-first, and she drops toward it, toward a gleaming bronzed needle-sharp summit, and she cries out as it penetrates her and she is impaled. And she wakes, sweating and shaking, her tongue dry, her mind dazed by a vision beyond her grasp, and she clutches Memnon, who murmurs sleepily and sleepily enters her.

They are beginning now to tell the people of Urban Monad 116 about the new building. Aurea hears it from the wallscreen as she does her morning chores in the dormitory. Out of the patterns of light and color on the wall there congeals a view of an unfinished tower. Construction machines swarm over it, metal arms moving frantically, welding arcs glimmering off octagonal steel-paneled torsos. The familiar voice of the screen says, "Friends, what you see is Urbmon 158, one month eleven days from completion. God willing, it'll shortly be the home of a great many happy Chipittsians who will have the honor of establishing first-generation status there. The news from Louisville is that 802 residents of your own Urbmon 116 have already signed up for transfer to the new building, as soon as—"

Next, a day later, comes an interview with Mr. and Mrs. Dismas Cullinan of Boston, who, with their nine littles, were the very first people in 116 to request transfer. Mr. Cullinan, a meaty, red-faced man, is a specialist in sanitary engineering. He explains, "I see a real opportunity for me to move up to the planning level over in 158. I figure I can jump eighty, ninety floors in status in one hell of a hurry." Mrs. Cullinan complacently pats her middle. Number ten is on the way. She purrs over the immense social advantages the move will confer on her children. Her eyes are too bright; her upper lip is thicker than the lower one and her nose is sharp. "She looks like a bird of prey," someone in the dorm comments. Someone else says, "She's obviously miserable here. Hoping to grab rungs fast over there." The Cullinan children range from two to thirteen years of age. Unfortunately, they resemble their parents. A runny-nosed girl claws at her brother while on screen. Aurea says firmly, "The building's better off without the lot of them."

Interviews with other transferees follow. On the fourth day of the campaign, the screen offers an extensive tour of the interior of 158, showing the ultramodern conveniences it will offer. Thermal irrigation for everybody, superspeed liftshafts and dropshafts, three-wall screens, a novel programing system for delivery of meals from the central kitchens, and many other wonders, representing the finest examples of urban progress. The number of volunteers for transfer is up now to 914.

Perhaps, Aurea thinks giddily, they will fill the entire quota with volunteers.

Memnon says, "The figure is fake. Siegmund tells me they've got only ninety-one volunteers so far."

"Then why—"

"To encourage the others."

In the second week, the transmissions dealing with the new building now indicate that the number of volunteers has leveled off at 1,060. Siegmund admits privately that the actual figure is somewhat less than this, although surprisingly not much less. Few additional volunteers are expected. The screen begins gently to introduce the possibility that conscription of transferees will be necessary. Two management men from Louisville and a pair of helix adjusters from Chicago are shown discussing the need for a proper genetic mix at the new building. A moral engineer from Shanghai speaks about the importance of being blessworthy under all circumstances. It is blessworthy to obey the divine plan and its representatives on Earth, he says. God is your friend and will not harm you. God loves the blessworthy. The quality of life in Urbmon 158 will be diminished if its initial population does not reach planned levels. This would be a crime against those who have volunteered to go to 158. A crime against your fellow man is a crime against god, and who wants to injure *him*? Therefore it is each man's duty to society to accept transfer if transfer is offered.

Next there is an interview with Kimon and Freya Kurtz, ages fourteen and thirteen, from a dorm in Bombay. Recently married. They are not about to volunteer, they admit, but they wouldn't mind being conscripted. "The way we look at it," Kimon Kurtz declares, "it could be a great opportunity. I mean, once we have some children, we'd be able to find top status for them right away. It's a brand new world over there—no limits on how fast you can rise, no one in the way. The readjustment of going over would be a little nudgy at first, but we'd be jumping soon enough. And we'd know that our littles wouldn't have to enter a dorm when they got old enough to marry. They could get rooms of their own without waiting, even before they had littles too. So even though we're not eager to leave our friends and all, we're ready to go if the wheel points to us." Freya Kurtz, ecstatic, breathless, says, "Yes. That's right."

The softening-up process continues with an account of how the conscriptees will be chosen: 3,878 in all, no more than 200 from any one city or thirty from any one dorm. The pool of eligibles consists of married men and women between the ages of twelve and seventeen who have no children, a current pregnancy not being counted as a child. Selection will be by random lot.

At last the names of the conscripts are released.

The screen's cheerful voice announces, "From Chicago's 735th floor dormitory the following blessworthy ones have been chosen, and may god give them fertility in their new life:

"Brock, Aylward and Alison.

"Feuermann, Sterling and Natasha.

"Holston, Memnon and Aurea—"

She will be wrenched from her matrix. She will be torn from the pattern of memories and affections that defines her identity. She is terrified of going.

She will fight the order.

"Memnon, file an appeal! Do something, fast!" She kneads the gleaming wall of the dormitory. He looks at her blankly; he is about to leave for work. He has already said there is nothing they can do. He goes out.

Aurea follows him into the corridor. The morning rush has begun; the citizens of 735th-floor Chicago stream past. Aurea sobs. The eyes of others are averted from her. She knows nearly all of these people. She has spent her life among them. She tugs at Memnon's hand. "Don't just walk out on me!" she whispers harshly. "How can we let them throw us out of 116?"

"It's the law, Aurea. People who don't obey the law go down the chute. Is that what you want? To end up contributing combustion mass to the generators?"

"I won't go! Memnon, I've always lived here! I—"

"You're talking like a flippo," he says, keeping his voice low. He pulls her back inside the dormitory. Staring up, she sees only cavernous dark nostrils. "Pop a pill, Aurea. Talk to the floor consoler, why don't you? Stay calm and let's adjust."

"I want you to file an appeal."

"There is no appeal."

"I refuse to go."

He seizes her shoulders. "Look at it rationally, Aurea. One building isn't that different from another. We'll have some of our friends there. We'll make new friends. We—"

"No."

"There's no alternative," he says. "Except down the chute."

"I'd rather go down the chute, then!"

For the first time since they were married, she sees him regarding her contemptuously. He cannot abide irrationality.

"Don't heave nonsense," he tells her. "See the consoler, pop a pill, think it through. I've got to leave now."

He departs again, and this time she does not go after him. She slumps on the floor, feeling cold plastic against her bare skin. The others in the dorm tactfully ignore her. She sees fiery images: her schoolroom, her first lover, her parents, her sisters and brothers, all melting, flowing across the room, a blazing trickle of acrid fluid. She presses her thumbs to her eyes. She will not be cast out. Gradually she calms. I have influence, she tells herself. If Memnon will not act, I will act for us. She wonders if she can ever forgive Memnon for his cowardice. For his transparent opportunism. She will visit her uncle.

She strips off her morning robe and dons a chaste gray girlish cloak. From the hormone chest she selects a capsule that will cause her to emanate the odor that inspires men to act protectively toward her. She looks sweet, demure, virginal; but for the ripeness of her body she could pass for ten or eleven years of age.

The liftshaft takes her to the 975th floor, the throbbing heart of Louisville.

All is steel and spongeglass here. The corridors are spacious and lofty. There is no rush of people through the halls; the occasional human figure seems incongruous and superfluous, though silent machines glide on unfathomable errands. This is the abode of those who administer the plans. Designed to awe; calculated to overwhelm; the permissible *mana* of the ruling class. How comfortable here. How sleek. How self-contained. Rip away the lower 90 percent of the building and Louisville would drift in serene orbit, never missing a thing.

Aurea halts outside a glistening door inlaid with moiré-generating stripes of bright white metal. She is scanned by hidden sensors, asked to name her business, evaluated, shunted into a waiting room. At length her mother's brother consents to see her.

His office is nearly as large as a private residential suite. He sits behind a broad polygonal desk from which protrudes a bank of shimmering monitor dials. He wears formal top-level clothes, a cascading gray tunic tipped with epaulets radiating in the infrared. Aurea feels the crisp blast of heat from where she stands. He is cool, distant, polite. His handsome face apears to have been fashioned from burnished copper.

"It's been many months, hasn't it, Aurea?" he says. A patronizing smile escapes him. "How have you been?"

"Fine, Uncle Lewis."

"Your husband?"

"Fine."

"Any littles yet?"

Blurting. "Uncle Lewis, we've been picked to go to 158!"

His plastic smile does not waver. "How fortunate! God bless, you can start a new life right at the top!"

"I don't want to go. Get me out of it. Somehow. Anyhow." She rushes toward him, a frightened child, tears flowing, knees melting. A force-field captures her when she is two meters from the outer rim of his desk. Her breasts feel it first, and as they flatten painfully against the invisible barrier she averts her head and injures her cheek. She drops to her knees and whimpers.

He comes to her. He lifts her. He tells her to be brave, to do her duty to god. He is kind and calm at first, but as she goes on protesting, his voice turns cold, with a hard edge of irritation, and abruptly Aurea begins to feel unworthy of his attention. He reminds her of her obligations to society. He hints delicately that the chute awaits those who persist in abrading the smooth texture of community life. Then he smiles again, and his icy blue eyes meet hers and engulf them, and he tells her to be brave and go. She creeps away. She feels disgraced by her weakness.

As she plunges downward from Louisville, her uncle's spell ebbs and her indignation revives. Perhaps she can get help elsewhere. The future is crashing around her, falling towers burying her in clouds of brick-black dust. A harsh wind blows out of tomorrow and the great building sways. She returns to the dorm and hastily changes her clothing. She alters her hormone balance too. A drop or two of golden fluid, sliding down to the mysterious coils of the female machinery. Now she is clad in iridescent mesh through which her breasts, thighs, and buttocks are intermittently visible, and she exudes an odor of distilled lust. She notifies the data terminal that she requests a private meeting with Siegmund Kluver of Shanghai. She paces the dorm, waiting. One of the young husbands comes to her, eyes gleaming. He grasps her haunch and gestures toward his sleeping platform.

"Sorry," she murmurs. "I'll be going out." Some refusals are allowed. He shrugs and goes away, pausing to glance back at her in a wistful way. Eight minutes later word comes that Siegmund has consented to meet with her in one of the rendezvous cubicles on the 790th floor. She goes up.

His face is smudged and memoranda bulge in his breast pocket. He seems cross and impatient. "Why did you pull me away from my work?" he asks.

"You know Memnon and I have been—"

"Yes, of course." Brusquely. "Mamelon and I will be sorry to lose your friendship."

Aurea attempts to assume a provocative stance. She knows she cannot win Siegmund's aid merely by making herself available; he is hardly that easily swayed. Bodies are easily possessed here, career opportunities are few and not lightly jeopardized. Her aims are trivial. She feels rejection flowing out of the minutes just ahead. But perhaps she can recruit Siegmund's influence. Perhaps she can lead him to feel such regret at her departure that he will aid her. She whispers, "Help us get out of going, Siegmund."

"How can I—"

"You have connections. Amend the program somehow. Support our appeal. You're a rising man in the building. You have high friends. You can do it."

"No one can do such a thing."

"Please, Siegmund." She approaches him, pulls her shoulders back, unsubtly lets her nipples come thrusting through her garment of mesh. Hopeless. How can she magic him with two pink nubs of stiff flesh? She moistens her lips, narrows her eyes to slits. Too stagy. He will laugh. Huskily she says, "Don't you want me to stay? Wouldn't you like to take a turn or two with me? You know I'd do anything if you'd help us get off that list. *Anything!*" Face eager. Nostrils flaring, offering promise of unimaginable erotic delights. She will do things not yet invented.

She sees his flickering momentary smile and knows that she has oversold herself; he is amused, not tempted, by her forwardness. Her face crumples. She turns away.

"You don't want me," she mutters.

"Aurea, please! You're asking the impossible." He catches her shoulders and pulls her toward him. His hands slip within the mesh and caress her flesh. She knows that he is merely consoling her with a counterfeit of desire. He says, "If there was any way I could fix things for you, I would. But we'd all get tossed down the chute." His fingers find her body's core. Moist, slippery, despite herself. She does not want him now, not this way. With a wriggle of her hips she tries to free herself. His embrace is mere kindness; he will take her out of pity. She pivots and stiffens.

"No," she says, and then she realizes how hopeless everything is, and she yields to him only because she knows that there will never be another chance.

Memnon says, "I've heard from Siegmund about what happened today. And from your uncle. You've got to stop this, Aurea."

"Let's go down the chute, Memnon."

"Come with me to the consoler. I've never seen you acting this way before."

"I've never felt so threatened."

"Why can't you adjust to it?" he asks. "It's really a grand chance for us."

"I can't. I can't." She slumps forward, defeated, broken.

"Stop it," he tells her. "Brooding sterilizes. Won't you cheer up a bit?"

She will not give way to chiding, however reasonable the tone. He summons the machines; they take her to the consoler. Soft rubbery orange pads gently grasping her arms all the way through the halls. In the consoler's office she is examined and her metabolism is probed. He draws the story from her. He is an elderly man, kind, gentle, somewhat bored, with a cloud of white hair rimming a pink face. She wonders whether he hates her behind his sweetness. At the end he tells her, "Conflict sterilizes. You must learn to comply with the demands of society, for society will not nurture you unless you play the game." He recommends treatment.

"I don't want treatment," she says thickly, but Memnon authorizes it, and they take her away. "Where am I going?" she asks. "For how long?"

"To the 780th floor, for about a week."

"To the moral engineers?"

"Yes," they tell her.

"Not there. Please, not there."

"They are gentle. They heal the troubled."

"They'll change me."

"They'll improve you. Come. Come. Come."

For a week she lives in a sealed chamber filled with warm, sparkling fluids. She floats idly in a pulsing tide, thinking of the huge urbmon as a wondrous pedestal on which she sits. Images soak from her mind and everything becomes deliciously cloudy. They speak to her over audio channels embedded in the walls of the chamber. Occasionally she glimpses an eye peering through an optical fiber dangling above her. They drain the tensions and resistances from her. On the eighth day

Memnon comes for her. They open the chamber and she is lifted forth, nude, dripping, her skin puckered, little beads of glittering fluid clinging to her. The room is full of strange men. Everyone else is clothed; it is dreamlike to be bare in front of them, but she does not really mind. Her breasts are full, her belly is flat, why then be ashamed? Machines towel her dry and clothe her. Memnon leads her by the hand. Aurea smiles quite often. "I love you," she tells Memnon softly.

"God bless," he says. "I've missed you so much."

The day is at hand, and she has paid her farewells. She has had two months to say good-bye, first to her blood kin, then to her friends in her village, then to others whom she has known within Chicago, and at last to Siegmund and Mamelon Kluver, her only acquaintances outside her native city. She has rewound her past into a tight coil. She has revisited the home of her parents and her old schoolroom, and she has even taken a tour of the urbmon, like a visitor from outbuilding, so that she may see the power plant and the service core and the conversion stations one final time.

Meanwhile Memnon has been busy too. Each night he reports to her on that day's accomplishments. The 5,202 citizens of Urban Monad 116 who are destined to transfer to the new structure have elected twelve delegates to the steering committee of Urbmon 158, and Memnon is one of the twelve. It is a great honor. Night after night the delegates take part in a multiscreen linkage embracing all of Chipitts, so that they can plan the social framework of the building they are going to share. It has been decided, Memnon tells her, to have fifty cities of twenty floors apiece, and to name the cities not after the vanished cities of old Earth, as has been the general custom, but rather after distinguished men of the past: Newton, Einstein, Plato, Galileo, and so forth. Memnon will be given responsibility for an entire sector of heat-diffusion engineers. It will be administrative rather than technical work, and so he and Aurea will live in Newton, the highest city.

Memnon expands and throbs with increased importance. He cannot wait for the hour of transfer to arrive. "We'll be really influential people," he tells Aurea exultantly. "And in ten or fifteen years we'll be legendary figures in 158. The first settlers. The founders, the pioneers. They'll be making up ballads about us in another century or so."

"And I was unwilling to go," Aurea says mildly. "How strange to think of myself acting like that!"

"It's an error to react with fear until you perceive the true shape of things," Memnon replies. "The ancients thought it would be a calamity to have as many as 5,000,000,000 people in the world. Yet we have fifteen times as much and look how happy we are!"

"Yes. Very happy. And we'll always be happy, Memnon."

The signal comes. The machines are at the door to fetch them. Memnon indicates the box that contains their few possessions. Aurea glows. She glances about the dorm, astonished by the crowdedness of it, the crush of couples in so little space. We will have our own room in 158, she reminds herself.

Those members of the dorm who are not leaving form a line, and offer Memnon and Aurea one final embrace.

Memnon follows the machines out, and Aurea follows Memnon. They go up to the landing stage on the thousandth floor. It is an hour past dawn and summer sunlight gleams in shining splotches on the tips of Chipitts' towers. The transfer operation has already begun; quickboats capable of carrying 100 passengers each will be moving back and forth between Urbmons 116 and 158 all day.

"And so we leave this place," Memnon says. "We begin a new life. Bless god!"

"God bless!" cries Aurea.

They enter the quickboat and it soars aloft. The pioneers bound for Urbmon 158 gasp as they see, for the first time, how their world really looks from above. The towers are beautiful, Aurea realizes. They glisten. On and on they stretch, fifty-one of them, like a ring of upraised spears in a broad green carpet. She is very happy. Memnon folds his hand over hers. She wonders how she could ever have feared this day. She wishes she could apologize to the universe for her foolishness.

She lets her free hand rest lightly on the curve of her belly. New life now sprouts within her. Each moment the cells divide and the little one grows. They have dated the hour of conception to the evening of the day when she was discharged by the consoler's office. Conflict indeed sterilizes, Aurea has realized. Now the poison of negativeness has been drained from her; she is able to fulfill a woman's proper destiny.

"It'll be so different," she says to Memnon, "living in such an empty building. Only 250,000! How long will it take for us to fill it?"

"Twelve or thirteen years," he answers. "We'll have few deaths, because we're all young. And lots of births."

She laughs. "Good, I hate an empty house."

The quickboat's voice says, "We now will turn to the

southeast, and on the left to the rear you can catch a last glimpse of Urbmon 116."

Her fellow passengers strain to see. Aurea does not make the effort. Urbmon 116 has ceased to concern her.

3

They are playing tonight in Rome, in the spishy new sonic center on the 530th level. Dillon Chrimes hasn't been that far up in the building in weeks. Lately he and the group have been doing the grime stint: Reykjavik, Prague, Warsaw, down among the grubbos. Well, they're entitled to some entertainment too. Dillon lives in San Francisco, not so lofty himself. The 370th floor; the heart of the cultural ghetto. But he doesn't mind that. He isn't deprived of variety. He gets around, everywhere from the bottom to the top in the course of a year, and it's only a statistical anomaly that it's been nothing but bottoms up for a while. The odds are he'll be blowing Shanghai, Chicago, Edinburgh, that crowd, in the month to come. With all those clean long-limbed lovelies to spread for him after the show.

Dillon is seventeen. More than middle height, with silken blond hair to his shoulders. Traditional, the old Orpheus bit. Crystalline blue eyes. He loves staring at them in a round of polymirrors, seeing the icy spheres intersect. Happily married, and three littles already, god bless! His wife's name is Electra. She paints psychedelic tapestries. Sometimes she accompanies him when he's touring with the group, but not often. Not now. He has met only one woman who lights him nearly as much. A Shanghai slicko, wife of some Louisville-bound headknocker. Mamelon Kluver, her name. The other girls of the urbmon are just so many slots, Dillon often thinks, but Mamelon connects. He has never told Electra about her. Jealousy sterilizes.

He plays the vibrastar in a cosmos group. That makes him valuable personnel. "I'm unique, like a flow-sculpture," he sometimes boasts. Actually there's another vibrastar man in the building, but to be one out of merely two is still a decent accomplishment. There are only two cosmos groups in Urbmon 116: the building can't really afford much redundancy in its entertainers. Dillon doesn't think highly of the rival group, though his opinion is based more on prejudice than familiarity—he's heard them three times, is all. There's been talk of getting both groups together for an all-out headblaster of a joint concert, perhaps in Louisville, but no one takes such teasers seriously. Meanwhile they go their separately programed ways, moving up and down through the urbmon as the spiritual weather dictates. The usual gig is five nights in a city. That allows everybody in, say, Bombay, who stones on cosmos groups to see them the same week, thereby providing conversation fodder for the general sharing. Then they move along, and, counting nights off, they theoretically can make the circuit of the whole building every six months. But sometimes gigs are extended. Do the lower levels need excesses of bread and circuses? The group may be handed fourteen nights running in Warsaw, then. Do the upper levels need psychic deconstipation in a big way? A twelve-night run in Chicago, maybe. Or the group itself may go sour and have to get its filters reamed, necessitating a layoff of two weeks or more. Allowing for all of these factors, there have to be two groups roaming the urbmon if every city is going to get a crack at a cosmos show at least once a year. Right now, Dillon thinks, the other operation is playing Boston for the third week. Some kind of problem with sexual turnoffs there, of all wildnesses!

He wakes at noon. Electra loyally beside him; the littles long gone to school, except for the baby, gurgling in its maintenance slot. Artists and performers keep their own hours. Her lips touch his. A torrent of fiery hair across his face. Her hand at his loins, wandering, grasping. Fingertips playfully rimming him. "Love me?" she sings. "Love me not? Love me? Love me not?"

"You medieval witch."

"You look so pretty when you sleep, Dill. The long hair. The sweet skin. Like a girl, even. You bring out the sappho in me."

"Do I?" he laughs and crams his genitals out of sight between his lean thighs. Clamps his legs. "Then do me!" He gouges his palms against his chest, trying to push up ersatz breasts. "Come on," he says hoarsely. "Here's your chance. Get on board. Flick that tongue."

"Silly. Stop that!"

"I think I'd be very pretty as a girl."

"Your hips are all wrong," she says, and pulls his locked feet apart. Up pops penis, half-erect. She whangs it with the backs of two fingertips, gently. Further stiffening. But there will be no sex between them now. He rarely indulges at this time of day, with a performance coming up. And in any case the mood is wrong, too skittish, too brittle. She vaults off the sleeping platform and deflates it with a kick of the pedal while he is still on it. An airy whooshing. That sort of mood; presexual, childish. He watches her waltz to the cleanser. What a fine butt she has, he thinks. So pale. So full. The splendid deep cleft. The elegant dimples. He creeps toward her and stoops to nip a hinder cheek, carefully, not wanting to leave a blemish. They share the cleanser. The baby begins to yowl. Dillon glances over his shoulder. "God bless, god bless, god bless!" he sings, beginning basso, ending falsetto. What a good life, he thinks. How neat existence can be. Electra, pulling on her clothes, says, "Can I get you some fumes?" A transparent band over her breasts. Rosy nipples like little blind eyes. He is pleased that she has stopped nursing; biology is tremendously moving, yes, but the dribbles of bluish-white milk over everything annoyed him. Doubtless a failing to eradicate. Why be so fastidious? Electra enjoyed nursing. She still lets the little suck, saying it's for the child's pleasure, but there can hardly be much kick in a dry tit, so Dillon knows the locus of the joy in that particular transaction. He hunts for his clothing.

"Will you paint today?" he asks.

"Tonight. While you're performing."

"You haven't worked much lately."

"I haven't felt the strings pulling."

It is her special idiom. To practice her art she must feel rooted to the earth. Strings rising from the planet's core, entering her body, snaking into her slot, slipping through the openings of her nipples. And then tugging. As the world turns, the imagery is wrenched from her blazing distended body. Or so she says; Dillon never questions the claims of a fellow artist, especially when she is his wife. He admires her accomplishments. It would have been madness to marry another cosmos-grouper, although when he was eleven he had just such a thing in mind. To share his destinies with the comet-harp girl. He'd be a widower now if he had. Down the chute, down the chute! What a flippy filther that one had been. And had wrecked a perfectly wonderful incantator, too, Peregrun Connelly. Could have been me. Could have been me. Marry outside your art, boys; avoid unblessworthy invidiousness.

"*No fumar?*" Electra asks. She has been studying ancient languages lately. "*Por qué?*"

"Working tonight. It spills the galactic juices if I indulge this early."

"Mind if I?"

"Suit yourself."

She takes a fume, nipping the cap neatly with a daggered forefingernail. Quickly her face flushes, her eyes dilate. A lovable quality about her: She is such an easy turnon. She puffs vapors at the baby, who chortles, while the maintenance slot's field buzzes in a solemn attempt to purify the child's atmosphere. "*Grazie mille, mama!*" Electra says, mimicking ventriloquy. "*È molto bello! È delicioso! Was für schönes Wetter! Quella gioia!*" She dances around the room, chanting fragments of exclamations in strange tongues, and tumbles, laughing, into the deflated sleeping platform. Her frilly frock blows up; he sees an auburn pubic glow and is tempted to top her despite his resolutions, but he regains his austerity and merely blows her a kiss. As if perceiving the phases of his mental processes, she piously closes her thighs and covers herself. He switches on the screen, selecting the abstract channel, and patterns blaze on the wall. "I love you," he tells her. "Can I have something to eat?"

She breakfasts him. Afterward she goes out, saying that she is scheduled to visit the blessman this afternoon. He is privately glad to see her go, for just now her vitality is too much for him. He must slide into the mood of the concert, which requires some spartan denials from him. Once she has gone, he programs the terminal for a reverberant oscillation and, as the resonant tones march across his skull, he slips lightly into the proper frame of mind. The baby, meanwhile, remains in its slot, enjoying the best of care. He thinks nothing of leaving it alone when, at 1600 hours, he must go off to Rome to set up for the evening's performance.

The liftshaft shoots him 160 levels heavenward. When he gets off, he is in Rome. Crowded halls, tight faces. The people here are mostly minor bureaucrats, a middle echelon of failed functionaries, those who would never get to Louisville except to deliver a report. They are not smart enough to hope for Chicago or Shanghai or Edinburgh. Here they will stay in this good gray city, frozen in hallowed stasis, doing dehumanized jobs that any computer could handle forty times as well. Dillon feels a cosmic pity for everyone who is not an artist, but he pities the people of Rome most of all, sometimes. Because they are nothing. Because they can use neither their brains nor their muscles. Crippled souls; walking zeros; better off down the chute. A Roman slams right into him as he stands outside the liftshaft bank, considering these things. Male, maybe forty, all the spirit drained from his eyes. The walking dead. The running dead. "Sorry," the man mumbles, and speeds on. "Truth!" Dillon cries after him. "Love! Loosen up! Fuck a lot!" He laughs. But what good does it do; the Roman will not laugh with him. Others of his kind come rushing down the corridor, their leaden bodies absorbing the last vibrations of Dillon's exclamations. *"Truth! Love!"* Blurred sounds, fading, graying, going. Gone. I will entertain you tonight, he tells them silently. I will drive you out of your wretched minds and you will love me for it. If I could only burn your brains! If I could only singe your souls!

He thinks of Orpheus. They would tear me apart, he realizes, if I ever really reached them.

He saunters toward the sonic center.

Pausing by the elbow bend of the corridor, still halfway around the building from the auditorium, Dillon feels a sudden ecstatic awareness of the splendor of the urbmon. A frenzied epiphany: he sees it as a spike suspended between heaven and earth. And he is almost at the midway point right now, with a little more than five hundred floors over his head, a little less than five hundred floors under his feet. People moving around, copulating, eating, giving birth, doing a million blessworthy things, each one out of 800-how-many-thousand traveling on his own orbit. Dillon loves the building. Right now he feels he could almost soar on its multiplicity the way others might soar on a drug. To be at the equator, to drink the divine equilibrium—oh, yes, yes! But of course there is a way to experience the whole complexity of the urbmon in one wild rush of information. He has never tried it; he is not really heavy on groovers, and has stayed away from the more elaborate drugs, the ones that open your mind so wide that anything can wander in. Nevertheless, here in the middle of the urbmon, he knows that this is the night to try the multiplexer. After the performance. To pop the pill that will allow him to drop the mental barriers, to let the full immensity of Urban Monad 116 interpenetrate his consciousness. Yes. He will go to the 500th floor to do it. If the performance goes well. Nightwalking in Bombay. He really should turn on in the city where tonight's concert will be held, but Rome goes no father down than the 521st floor, and he must go to the 500th. For the mystic symmetry of the thing. Even though it is still inexact. Where is the true midpoint in a building of a thousand floors? Somewhere between 499 and 500, no? But the 500th floor will have to do. We learn to live with approximations.

He enters the sonic center.

A fine new auditorium, three stories high, with a toadstool of a stage in the center and audience webs strung concentrically around it. Lightglow drifts in the air. The mouths of speakers, set into the domed rich-textured ceilings, pucker and gape. A warm room, a good room, placed here by the divine mercy of Louisville to bring a little joy into the lives of these bleak juiceless Romans. There is no better hall for a cosmos group in the entire urbmon. The other members of the group are here already, tuning in. The comet-harp, the incantator, the orbital diver, the gravity-drinker, the doppler-inverter, the spectrum-rider. Already the room trembles with shimmering plinks of sound and jolly blurts of color, and a shaft of pure no-referent texture, abstract and immanent, is rising from the doppler-inverter's central cone. Everyone waves to him. "Late, man," they say, and "Where you been?" and "We thought you were skimming out," and he says, "I've been in the halls, peddling love to the Romans," which shatters them into strands of screeching laughter. He clambers onto the stage. His instrument sits untended near the perimeter, its lattices dangling, its lovely gaudy skin unilluminated. A lifting machine stands by, waiting to help him put it in its proper place. The machine brought the vibrastar to the auditorium; it would also tune it in for him, if he asked it to, but of course he will not do that. Musicians have a mystique about tuning in their own instruments. Even though it will take him at least two hours to do it, and the machine could do it in ten minutes. Maintenance workers and other humbles of the grubbo class have the same mystique. Not strange: one must battle constantly against one's own obsolescence if one is going to go on thinking of oneself as having a purpose in life.

"Over here," Dillon tells the machine.

Delicately it brings his vibrastar to the output node and makes the connection. Dillon could not possibly have moved the immense instrument. He does not mind letting machines do the things humans were never meant to do, like lifting three-ton loads. Dillon puts his hands on the manipulatrix and feels the power thrumming through the keyboard. Good. "Go," he tells the machine, and silently it slides away. He kneads and squeezes the projectrons of the manipulatrix. As if milking them. Sensual pleasure in making contact with the machine. A little orgasm with every crescendo. Yeah. Yeah. Yeah.

"Tuning in!" he warns the other musicians.

They make feedback adjustments in their own instruments; otherwise the sudden surge of his entrance might damage both instruments and players. One by one they nod their readiness to him, with the gravity-drinker lad chiming in last, and finally Dillon can let out the clutch. Yeah! The hall fills with light. Stars stream from the walls. He coats the ceiling with dripping nebulae. He is the basic instrument of the group, the all-important continuo, providing the foundation against which the others will do their things. With a practiced eye he checks the focus. Everything sharp. Nat the spectrum-rider says, "Mars is a little off-color, Dill." Dillon hunts for Mars. Yes. Yes. He feeds it an extra jolt of orange. And Jupiter? A shining globe of white fire. Venus. Saturn. And all the stars. He is satisfied with the visuals.

"Bringing up the sound, now," he says.

The heels of his hands hit the control panel. From the gaping speakers comes a tender blade of white noise. The music of the spheres. He colors it now, bringing up the gain on the galactic side, letting the stellar drift impart plangent hues to the tone. Then, with a quick downward stab on the projectrons, he kicks in the planetary sounds. Saturn whirls like a belt of knives. Jupiter booms, "Are you getting it?" he calls out. "How's the clarity?" Sophro the orbital diver says, "Fat up the asteroids, Dill," and he does it, and Sophro nods, happy, his chins trembling in pleasure.

After half an hour of preliminary maneuvers Dillon has his primary tuning finished. So far, though, he has done only the solo work. Now to coordinate with the others. Slow, delicate work: to reach reciprocity with them one by one, building a web of interrelationship, a seven-way union. Plagued all the way by heisenberging effects, so that a whole new cluster of adjustments has to be made each time another instrument is added to the set. Change one factor, you change everything; you can't just hold your own while keying in more and more and more output. He takes on the spectrum-rider first. Easy. Dillon gives forth a shower of comets and Nat modulates them pleasantly into suns. Then they add the incantator. A slight stridency at first, quickly corrected. Good going. Then the gravity-drinker. No problem. The comet-harp, now. Rasp! Rasp! The receptors go bleary and the entire thing falls apart. He and the incantator have to retune separately, rejoin, bring the comet-harp into the net again. This time all right. Great plumey curves of tone go lalloping through the hall. Then the orbital diver. Fifteen sweaty minutes; the balances keep souring. Dillon expects a system collapse any second, but no, they hang on and finally get the levels even. And now the really tough one, the doppler-inverter, which threatens always to clash with his own instrument because both rely as much on visuals as audio, and both are generators, not just modulators of someone else's playing. He almost gets it. But they lose the comet-harp. It makes a thin edgy whining sound and drops out. So they go back two steps and try again. Precarious balance, constantly falling off. Up till five years ago, there had been only five instruments in cosmos groups; it was simply too difficult to hold more than that together. Like adding a fourth actor in Greek tragedy; an impossible technical feat, or so it must have seemed to Aeschylus. Now they were able to coordinate six instruments reasonably well, and a seventh with some effort, by sending the circuit bouncing up to a computer nexus in Edinburgh, but it is still a filther to put them all in synch. Dillon gestures madly with his left shoulder, encouraging the doppler-inverter to get with it. "Come on, come on, come on, come *on*!" and this time they make it. The time is 1840. Everything sticks together.

"Lets's run it through, now," Nat sings out. "Give us an A for tuning, maestro."

Dillon hunches forward and clutches the projectrons. Feeds power. Gets a sensory shift; the knobs abruptly feel like the cheeks of Electra's buttocks in his hands. Smiles at the sensation. Firm, bouncy, cool. Up we go! And gives them the universe in one sizzling blare of light and sound. The hall swims with images. The stars leap and cross and mate. The incantator man picks up his sonics and does his trick, enhancing, multiplying, intensifying, until the whole urbmon shakes. The comet-harp makes bleeping blurting loops of dizzying counterpoint and starts to rearrange Dillon's constellations. The orbital diver, hanging back, makes a sudden plunge at an unexpected moment, and dials spin on everybody's control panel, but it is such a devastating entry that Dillon inwardly applauds it. The gravity-drinker smoothly sucks tone. Now the doppler-inverter goes at it, shooting up its own shaft of light, which sizzles and steams for perhaps thirty seconds before the spectrum-rider grabs it and runs with it, and now all seven of them are jamming madly, each trying to put the others on, shooting forth such a welter of signals that the sight must surely be visible from Boshwash to Sansan.

"Hold it! Hold it! Hold it!" Nat screams. "Don't waste it! Man, *don't waste it!*"

And they cut out of phase and go down, and sit there idling, sweaty, nerves twinkling. Withdrawal pains; it hurts to step away from such beauty. But Nat is right: they mustn't use themselves up before the audience gets here.

Dinner break, right on stage. No one eats much. They leave the instruments tuned and running, of course. Lunacy to disrupt the synch after working so hard to get it right. Now and then one of the idling instruments flares past its threshold and emits a blob of light or a squeak of sound. They'd play themselves if we'd only let them, Dillon thinks. It might just be a wild soar to turn everything on and sit back, doing nothing, while the instruments themselves give the concert, self-programed. You'd get some strange percepts then. The mind of the machine. On the other hand it might be a hell of a dropper to find out you were superfluous. How frail is our prestige. Celebrated artists today, but let the secret sneak out and we'll all be pushing junk-buckets in Reykjavik tomorrow.

The audience begins to show up at 1945. An older crowd; since this is the first night of the Rome run, the rules of seniority have governed the distribution of tickets and the undertwenties have been left out. Dillon, mid-stage, does not trouble to hide his scorn for the gray, baggy people settling into the audience webs all around him. Will the music reach them? Can anything reach them? Or will they sit passively, not even going halfway out to the performance? Dreaming of making more littles. Ignoring the sweating artists; taking up a good seat and getting nothing from the fireworks about them. We throw you the whole universe, and you don't catch. Is it because you're old? How much can a plumpish many-mother, thirty-three years old, pull from a cosmos show? No, it isn't age. In the more sophisticated cities there's no problem of audience response, young or old. No, it's a matter of your basic attitude toward the world of art. At the bottom of the building, the grubbos respond with their eyes, their guts, their balls. Either they're fascinated by the colored lights and the wild sounds, or else they're baffled and hostile, but they aren't indifferent. In the top levels, where the use of the mind is not only permitted but desired, they reach out for the show, knowing that the more they bring to it the more they get from it. And isn't that what life is all about, to wring all the sensory percepts you can out of the outputs drifting past your head? What else is there? But here, here in the middle levels, all the responses are dulled. The walking dead. The important thing is *being present in the auditorium*, grabbing that ticket away from someone else, showing off. The performance itself doesn't matter. That's just noise and light, some crazy kids from San Francisco having a workout. So there they sit, these Romans, disconnected from skull to crotch. What a joke. Romans? The real Rome wasn't like that, you bet. Calling their city Rome is a crime against history. Dillon glares at them. Then, overfocusing his eyes, he deliberately blurs them out; he does not want to see their flabby gray faces, for fear the sight of them will color his performance. He is here to give. If they aren't capable of taking, tough.

"Let's go up now," Nat murmurs. "Ready, Dill?"

He is ready. He brings his hands up for a virtuoso pounce and slams them down on the projectrons. The old headblaster! Moon and sun and planets and stars come roaring out of his instrument. The whole glittering universe erupts in the hall. He doesn't dare look at the audience. Did he rock them? Are they gasping and tugging at their droopy lower lips? Come on, come on, come on! The others, as if sensing that he's into something special, let him take an introductory solo. Furies fly through his brain. He jabs the manipulatrix. Pluto! Saturn! Betelgeuse! Deneb! Here sit people who spend their whole lives locked inside a single building; give them the stars in one skullblowing rush. Who says you can't start with your climax? The power drain must be immense; lights must be dimming all the way to Chicago. What of it? Did Beethoven give a fart about the power drain? There. There. There. Throw stars around. Make them shimmer and shake. An eclipse of the sun—why not? Let the corona crackle and fry. Make the moon dance. And bring up the sound, too, a great heaving pedal-point that sneaks up the webbing at them, a spear of fifty-cycle vibration nailing them in their assholes. Help them digest their dinner. Shake up all the old shit

64

clogging the colon. Dillon laughs. He wishes he could see his face now; something demonic, maybe. How long is the solo going to last? Why don't they pick up on him, now? He's going to burn out. He doesn't mind, throwing himself into the machine like that, except for the faint paranoid feeling that the others are deliberately allowing him to strain past his limits so he'll injure himself. The rest of his life sitting like a slug, going booble-booble-booble. Not me! He pulls out all the stops. Fantastic! He's never done things like this before. It must be his rage at these dull Romans that is inspiring him. And all of it wasted on them. Slot that, though: what counts is what's happening inside him, his own artistic fulfillment. If he can blow their skulls, that's a bonus. But this is ecstasy. The whole universe is vibrating around him. A gigantic solo. God himself must have felt this way when he got to work on the first day. Needles of sound descending from the speakers. A mighty crescendo of light and tone. He feels the power surging through him; he is so happy with what he is doing that he grows hard below, and tips himself back in his seat to make it ram more visibly against his clothes. Has anyone ever done something like this before, this improvised symphony for solo vibrastar? Hello, Bach! Hello, Mick! Hello, Wagner! Shoot your skulls! Let it all fly! He is past the crest, starting to come down now, no longer relying on raw energy but dabbling in subtler things, splashing Jupiter with golden splotches, turning the stars into icy white points, bringing up little noodling ostinatos. He makes Saturn trill: a signal to the others. Who ever heard of opening a concert with a cadenza? But they pick up on it.

Ah, now. Here they come. Gently the doppler-inverter noodles in with a theme of its own, catching something of the descending fervor of Dillon's stellar patterns. At once the comet-harp over-lays this with a more sensational series of twanging tones that immediately transmute themselves into looping blares of green light. These are seized by the spectrum-rider, who climbs up on top of them and, grinning broadly, skis off toward the ultraviolet in a shower of hissing crispness. Old Sophro now does his orbital dives, a swoop and a pickup followed by a swoop and a pickup again, playing against the spectrum-rider in the kind of cunning way that only someone right inside the meshing group can appreciate. Then the incantator enters, portentous, booming, sending reverberations shivering through the walls, heightening the significance of the tonal and astronomical patterns until the convergences become almost unbearably beautiful. It is the cue for the gravity-drinker, who disrupts everybody's stability with wonderful, wild liberating bursts of force. By this time Dillon has retreated to his proper place as the coordinator and unifier of the group, tossing a skein of melody to this one, a loop of light to that one, embellishing everything that passes near him. He fades into the undertones. His manic excitement passes; playing in a purely mechanical way, he is as much listener as performer, quietly appreciating the variations and divagations his partners are producing. He does not need to draw attention now. He can simply go *oomp oomp oomp* the rest of the night. Not that he will; the construct will tumble if he doesn't feed new data every ten or fifteen minutes. But this is his time to coast.

Each of the others takes a solo in turn. Dillon can no longer see the audience. He rocks, he pivots, he sweats, he sobs; he caresses the projectrons furiously; he seals

himself in a cocoon of blazing light; he juggles alterna-
tions of light and darkness. The rod in his pants has
softened. He is calm at the eye of the storm, fully professional, quietly doing his work. That moment of ecstasy
seems to belong to some other day, even to some other
man. How long had the solo lasted, anyway? He has lost
track of the time. But the performance is going well, and
he leaves it to methodical Nat to keep watch of the hour.

After its frenzied opening the concert has settled into
routine. The center of the action has shifted to the doppler-inverter man, who is spinning off a series of formula
flashes. Quite nice, but stale stuff, over-rehearsed,
unspontaneous. His offhandedness infects the others and
the whole group vamps for perhaps twenty minutes,
going through a set of changes that numb the ganglia
and abort the soul, until finally Nat spectacularly shrieks
through the whole spectrum from someplace south of
infrared into what, as far as anyone can tell, may be the
X-ray frequencies, and this wild takeoff not only stimu-
lates a rebirth of inventiveness but also signals the end
of the show. Everybody picks up on him and they blast
free, swirling and floating and coming together, forming
one entity with seven heads as they bombard the flaccid
data-stoned audience with mountains of overload. Yes
yes yes yes yes. Wow wow wow wow wow. Flash flash
flash flash flash. Oh oh oh oh oh. Come come come come
come. Dillon is at the heart of it, tossing off bright purple
sparks, pulling down suns and chewing them up, and he
feels even more plugged in than during his big solo, for
this is a joint thing, a blending, a merging, and he knows
that what he is feeling now explains everything: this is
the purpose of life, this is the reason for it all. To tune
in on beauty, to plunge right to the hot source of cre-

ation, to open your soul and let it all in and let it all out again, to give to give to give to give

to give

to give

and it ends. Pull the plug. They let him have the final chord and he cuts off with a skullblower, a five-way planetary conjunction and a triple fugue, the whole showoff burst lasting no more than ten seconds. Then down with the hands and off with the switch and a wall of silence rises ninety kilometers high. This time he's done it. He's emptied everybody's skull. He sits there shivering, biting his lip, dazed by the house lights, wanting to cry. He dares not look at the others in the group. How much time is passing? Five minutes, five months, five centuries, five megayears? And at last the reaction. A stampede of applause. All of Rome on its feet, yelling slapping cheeks—the ultimate tribute, 4,000 people struggling out of their comfortable webs to pound their palms against their faces—and Dillon laughs, throwing back his head, getting up himself, bowing, holding his hands out to Nat, to Sophro, to all six of them. Somehow it was better tonight. Even these Romans know it. What did they do to deserve it? By being such lumps, Dillon tells himself, they drew forth the best we had in us. To turn them on. And we did. We knocked them out of their miserable soggy skulls.

The cheering continues.

Fine. Fine. We are great artists. Now I've got to get out of here, before I come down from it all.

He never socializes with the rest of the group after a performance. They have all discovered that the less they see of each other in leisure hours, the more intimate their professional collaboration will be; there is no intragroup

friendship, not even intragroup sex. They all feel that
would be death, any kind of coupling, hetero, homo,
triple-up—save that for outsiders. They have their music
to unite them. So he goes off by himself. The audience
starts to flow toward the exits, and, without saying good
night to anybody, Dillon steps into the artists' trap door
and makes his escape one level down. His clothes are
stiff and wet with perspiration, clammy, uncomfortable.
He must do something about that quickly. Prowling along
the 529th floor for a dropshaft, he opens the first apartment door he comes to and finds a couple, sixteen, seventeen years old, squatting before the screen. He naked,
she wearing only breastcoils, both of them plainly soaring
on one of the harder ones, but not so high that they can't
recognize him. "Dillon Chrimes!" the girl gasps, her
squeal waking two or three littles.

"Hey, hello," he says. "I just have to use the cleanser,
okay? Don't let me disturb you. I don't even want to talk,
you know? I'm still way up." He strips off his sodden
clothes and gets under the cleanser. It hums and rumbles
and peels his grime from him. He lets it work on his
clothes next. The girl is creeping toward him. She has
the breastcoils off; the white imprints of the metal on
her pink dangling flesh are turning rapidly red. Kneeling
before him. Hand goes to his thighs. Her lips heading for
his loins. "No," he says. "Don't."

"No?"

"I can't do it here."

"But why?"

"Just wanted to use the cleanser. Couldn't stand my
own stink. I've got to do my nightwalking on 500
tonight." Her fingers sliding between his legs. Gently he

pries them. Back into his clothing; the girl looks on, astonished, as he covers himself.

"You aren't going to?" she asks.

"Not here. Not here." She continues to blink at him as he goes out. Her look of shock saddens him. Tonight he must go to the middle of the building, but tomorrow, for sure, he will come to her, and he'll explain everything then. He makes a note of the room number. 52908. Nightwalking is supposed to be random, but to hell with that; he owes her a thrill. Tomorrow.

In the hall he finds a groover dispenser and requisitions his pill, tapping his metabolic coefficient out on the console. The machine performs the necessary calculations and delivers a five-hour dose, timed to go off in twelve minutes. He swallows it and steps into the dropshaft.

Floor 500.

As close to halfway as he can get. A metaphysical fancy, but why not? He has not lost the capacity to play games. We artists remain happy because we remain as children. Eleven minutes to his high. He goes down the corridor, opening doors. In the first room he finds a man, a woman, another man. "Sorry," he calls. In the second room three girls. Momentarily tempting, but only momentarily. Anyway, they look fully busied with each other. "Sorry, sorry, sorry." In the third room a middle-aged couple; they give him a hopeful stare, but he backs out.

Fourth time lucky. A dark-haired girl, alone, pouting a little. Obviously her husband is out nightwalking and no one has come to her, a statistical fluke that distresses her. Early twenties, Dillon guesses, with fine tapering nose, glossy eyes, elegant breasts, olive skin. The flesh

70

over her eyelids is puffy, which may become a flaw of appearance ten years from now but which gives her a sultry, sensual look at the moment. She has been brooding for hours, he guesses, because her sullenness does not evaporate until he has actually been in the room fifteen seconds or so; she is slow to realize that she is being nightwalked with. "Hello," he says. "Smile? Won't you smile a little?"

"I know you. The cosmos group?"

"Dillon Chrimes, yes. On the vibrastar. We're playing Rome tonight."

"Playing Rome and nightwalking Bombay?"

"What the hell. I have philosophical reasons. To be in the middle of the building, you know? Or as close as I can come. Don't ask me to explain." He looks around the room. Six littles. One of them, awake, is at least nine years old, a skinny girl with her mother's olive skin. Mother isn't as young as she looks, then. At least twenty-five, maybe. Dillon doesn't mind. In a little while he'll be groping the whole urbmon, anyway, all the ages, sexes, shapes. He says, "I have to tell you about my trip. I'm on a multiplexer. It'll hit me in six minutes."

She puts her hand to her lips. "We don't have much time, then. You ought to be inside me before you go up."

"Is that the way they work?"

"Don't you know?"

"I've never gone that way before," he confesses. "Never got around to it."

"Neither have I. I didn't think anybody actually did take multiplexers, really. But I've heard of what you're supposed to do." She is disrobing as she talks. Heavy breasts, big dark circles around the nipples. Her legs strangely thin; when she stands straight the insides of her thighs are far apart. There is a folkmyth of some sort about girls built that way, but Dillon cannot remember it. He drops his clothes. The drug has started to get to him, several minutes ahead of schedule—the walls are shimmering, the lights look fuzzy. Odd. Unless the fact that he was already way up from performing should have been calculated into the dosage request. The metabolism turned to high, maybe, on nothing but sound and light. Well, no harm done. He moves toward the sleeping platform. "What's your name?" he asks.

"Alma Clune."

"I like the sound of that. Alma." She takes him into her arms. This will not be an extraordinary erotic experience for her, he fears. Once the multiplexer takes hold, he doubts that he can concentrate properly on her needs, and in any case the time element has made it necessary to skip all foreplay. But she seems to be understanding. She will not spoil his trip. "Get in," she says. "It's all right. I get wet fast there." He enters her. Her tongue against his; her sinewy thighs encircling him. He covers her body with his. "Are you grooving yet?" she asks.

He is silent a moment. In and out, in and out. "I feel it starting," he tells her. "It's like having two girls at once. I'm getting echoes." Tension. He doesn't want to wreck everything by coming before the effect hits him. On the other hand, if she's the quick-coming type, he'd be happy to let her have a spasm or two; the multiplexing must still be ninety seconds away. All these calculations chill him. And then they become pointless. "It's happening," he whispers. "Oh, god, here I go up!"

"Easy," Alma murmurs. "Don't rush anything.

Slow...slow....You're doing fine. You want this one to last. Don't worry about me. Just go on up."

In and out. In and out. And multiplexing now. His spirit is spreading out. The drug makes him psychosensitive; it breaks down his brain's chemical defenses against direct telepathic input, so that he can perceive the sensory intake of those around him. Reaching wider and wider, moment by moment. At the full high, they say, everyone's eyes and ears become your own; you pick up an infinity of responses, you are everywhere in the building at once. Is it true? Are other minds pouring their intake through his? It does seem so. He watches the fluttering fiery mantle of his soul engulf and absorb Alma, so that now he is face up as well as face down, and each time he thrusts deep into her hot cavern he can also feel the blunt sword sliding into his own vitals. That's just the beginning. He is spreading over Alma's littles now. The unfleeced nine-year-old. The gurgling baby. He is six children and their mother. How easy this is! He is the family next door. Eight littles, mother, nightwalker from the 495th floor. He extends his reach upward one level. And downward. And along the corridors. In dreamy multiplexication he is taking possession of the whole building. Layers of drifting images enshroud him: 500 floors above his head, 499 below, and he sees all 999 of them as a column of horizontal striations, tiny notches on a tall shaft. With ants. And he is all the ants at once. Why has he never done this before? To become an entire urbmon!

He must reach at least twenty floors in each direction now. And still spreading out. Tendrils of him going everywhere. Just the beginning. Intermingling his substance with the totality of the building.

With Alma rocking beneath him. Pelvis grinding against pelvis; he is dimly aware of her as she softly moans her pleasure. But only one atom of himself is occupied with her. The rest is roaming the halls of the cities that make up Urban Monad 116. Entering every room. Part of him up in Boston, part of him down in London, and all of him in Rome and Bombay as well. Hundreds of rooms. Thousands. The swarm of biped bees. He is fifty squalling littles crammed into three London rooms. He is two doddering Bostonians entering upon their 5,000th sexual congress. He is a hot-blooded thirteen-year-old nightwalker prowling the 483rd floor. He is six swapping couples in a London dorm. Now he is into a wider range, reaching down to San Francisco, up to Nairobi. The farther he goes, the easier it gets. The hive. The mighty hive. He embraces Tokyo. He embraces Chicago. He embraces Prague. He touches Shanghai. He touches Vienna. He touches Warsaw. He touches Toledo. Paris! Reykjavik! Louisville! *Louisville*! Top to bottom, top to bottom! Now he is all 881,000 people on all thousand floors. His soul is stretched to its fullest. His skull is snapping. The images come and go across the screen of his mind, drifting films of reality, oily wisps of smoke bearing faces, eyes, fingers, genitals, smiles, tongues, elbows, profiles, sounds, textures. Gently they mesh and lock and drift apart. He is everywhere and everyone at once. God bless! For the first time he understands the nature of the delicate organism that is society; he sees the checks and balances, the quiet conspiracies of compromise that paste it all together. And it is wondrously beautiful. Tuning this vast city of many cities is just like tuning the cosmos group: everything must relate, everything must belong to everything else.

The poet in San Francisco is part of the grubbo stoker in Reykjavik. The little snotty ambition-monger in Shanghai is part of the placid defeated Roman. How much of this, Dillon wonders, will stay with him when he comes down? His spirit whirls. He grooves on thousands of souls at once.

And the sexual thing. The hundred thousand copulatory transactions taking place behind his forehead. The spread thighs, the offered rumps, the parted lips. He loses his virginity; he takes a virginity; he surrenders to men, women, boys, girls; he is agressor and aggressed; he spurts ecstasy, he narrowly misses orgasm, he triumphantly impales, he shamefully suffers loss of erection, he enters, he is entered, he takes pleasure, he gives pleasure, he retreats from pleasure, he denies pleasure.

He rides the liftshafts of his mind. Going up! 501, 502, 503, 504, 505! 600! 700! 800! 900! He stands on the landing stage at the summit of the urbmon, staring out into the night. Towers all around him, the neighboring monads, 115, 117, 118, the whole crowd of them. Occasionally he has wondered what life is like in the other buildings that make up the Chipitts constellation. Now he does not care. There is wonder enough in 116. More than 800,000 intersecting lives. He has heard some of his friends say, in San Francisco, that it was an evil deed to change the world this way, to pile up thousands of people in a single colossal building, to create this beehive life. But how wrong those mutterers are! If they could only multiplex and get true perspective. Taste the rich complexity of our vertical existence. Going down! 480, 479, 476, 475! City upon city. Each floor holding a thousand puzzleboxes of pure delight. Hello, I'm Dillon Chrimes, can I be you for a while? And you? And you?

And you? Are you happy? Why not? Have you *seen* this gorgeous world you live in?

What? You'd like a bigger room? You want to travel? You don't like your littles? You're bored with your work? You're full of vague unfocused discontent? Idiot. Come up here with me, fly from floor to floor, *see*! And groove on it. And love it.

"Is it really good?" Alma asks. "Your eyes are shining!"

"I can't describe it," Dillon murmurs, soaring, threading himself down the service core to the levels below Reykjavik, then floating up to Louisville again, and simultaneously intersecting every point between root and tip. An ocean of broiling minds. A sizzle of snarled identities. He wonders what time it is. The trip is supposed to last five hours. His body is still joined to Alma's, which leads him to think he has not been up more than ten or fifteen minutes, but perhaps it is more than that. Things are becoming very tactile now. As he drifts through the building he touches walls, floors, screens, faces, fabrics. He suspects he may be coming down. But no, No. Still on his way up. The simultaneity increases. He is flooded with percepts. People moving, talking, sleeping, dancing, coupling, bending, reaching, eating, reading. I am all of you. You are all parts of me. He can focus sharply on individual identities. Here is Electra, here is Nat the spectrum-rider, here is Mamelon Kluver, here is a tight-souled sociocomputator named Charles Mattern, here is a Louisville administrator, here is a Warsaw grubbo, here is. Here is. Here are. Here am I. The whole blessing building.

Oh what a beautiful place. Oh how I love it here. Oh this is the real thing. Oh!

When he comes down, he sees the dark-haired woman

curled in a corner of the sleeping platform, asleep. He cannot remember her name. He touches her thigh and she awakes quickly, eyes fluttering. "Hello," she says. "Welcome back."

"What's your name?"

"Alma. Clune. Your eyes are all red."

He nods. He feels the weight of the whole building on him: 500 floors jamming down on his head, 499 floors pressing up against his feet. The meeting place of the two forces is somewhere close to his pancreas. If he does not leave here quickly, his internal organs must surely pop. Only shreds of his trip remain. Straggly streamers of debris clutter his mind. Vaguely he feels columns of ants trekking from level to level behind his eyes.

Alma reaches for him. To comfort him. He shakes her off and hunts for his clothing. A cone of silence surrounds him. He will go back to Electra, he thinks, and try to tell her where he has been and what has been happening to him, and then perhaps he will cry and feel better. He leaves without thanking Alma for her hospitality and looks for a dropshaft. Instead he finds a liftshaft, and somehow, pretending it is an accident, he gets off at 530. Heading for Rome's sonic center. Dark there. The instruments still on stage. Quietly he slips down in front of the vibrastar. Switches it on. His eyes are wet. He dredges up some phantom images of his trip. The faces, the thousand floors. The ecstasy. Oh what a beautiful place. Oh how I love it here. Oh this is the real thing. Oh! Certainly he felt that way. But no longer. A thin sediment of doubt is all that remains. Asking himself: Is this how it was meant to be? Is this how it has to be? Is this the best we can do? This building. This mighty hive. Dillon's hands caress the projectrons, which feel prickly and hot; he depresses them at random and sour colors drift out of the instrument. He cuts in the audio and gets sounds that remind him of the shifting of old bones within flabby flesh. What went wrong? He should have expected it. You go all the way up, then you come all the way down. But why does down have to be so far down? He cannot bear to play. After ten minutes he switches the vibrastar off and goes out. He will walk to San Francisco. 160 floors down. That's not too many levels; he'll be there before dawn.

4

Jason Quevedo lives in Shanghai, though just barely: his apartment is on the 761st floor, and if he lived only one level lower he would be in Chicago, which is no place for a scholar. His wife Micaela frequently tells him that their lowly status in Shanghai is a direct reflection of the quality of his work. Micaela is the sort of wife who often says things like that to her husband.

Jason spends most of his working time down in Pittsburgh, where the archives are. He is a historian and needs to consult the documents, the records of how it used to be. He does his research in a clammy little cubicle on the urbmon's 185th floor, almost in the middle of Pittsburgh. He does not really have to work down there, since anything in the archives can easily be piped up to the data terminal in his own apartment. But he feels it is a matter of professional pride to have an office where he can file and arrange and handle the source materials. He said as much when he was pulling strings to have the office assigned to him: "The task of recreating previous eras is a delicate and complex one, which must be performed under optimal circumstances, or—"

The truth is that if he didn't escape from Micaela and their five littles every day, he'd go flippo. That is, accumulated frustration and humiliation would cause him to commit nonsocial acts, perhaps violent ones. He is aware that there is no room for the nonsocial person in an urban monad. He knows that if he loses his temper and behaves in a seriously unblessworthy way they will simply throw him down the chute and turn his mass into energy. So he is careful.

He is a short, soft-spoken man with mild green eyes and thinning sandy hair. "Your meek exterior is deceptive," lovely Mamelon Kluver told him throatily at a party last summer. "Your type is like a sleeping volcano. You explode suddenly, astonishingly, passionately." He thinks she may be right. He fears the possibilities.

He has been desperately in love with Mamelon Kluver for perhaps the last three years, and certainly since the night of that party. He has never dared to touch her. Mamelon's husband is the celebrated Siegmund Kluver, who though not yet fifteen is universally recognized as one of the urbmon's future leaders. Jason is not afraid that Siegmund would object. In an urban monad, naturally, no man has a right to withhold his wife from anyone who desires her. Nor is Jason afraid of what Micaela would say. He knows his privileges. He is simply afraid of Mamelon. And perhaps of himself.

For ref. only. Urbmon sex mores.

Univ. sex. accessibility. Trace decline of proprietary marriage, end of adultery concept. Nightwalkers: when first socially acceptable? Limit of allowable frustration: how determined? Sex as panacea. Sex as compensation for lessened quality of life under urbmon conditions. Query: was quality of life really lessened by triumph of urbmon system? (Careful—beware the chute!) Separation of sex & procreation. Value of max. interchange of partners in high-density culture. Problem: what is still forbidden (any thing?). Examine taboo on extracity nightwalking. How powerful? How widely observed? Check effects of univ. permiss. on contemp. fiction. Loss of dramatic

tension? Erosion of raw material of narr. conflict? Query:
is urbmon moral struc. amoral, postmoral, per-, im-?

Jason dictates such memoranda whenever and
wherever some new structural hypothesis enters his mind.
These are thoughts that come to him during a nightwalking excursion on the 155th floor, in Tokyo. He is with a
thickset young brunette named Gretl when the sequence
of ideas arrives. He has been fondling her for some
minutes and she is panting, ready, her hips pumping, her
eyes narrowed to steamy slits.

"Excuse me," he says, and reaches across her heavy
quivering breasts for a stylus. "I have to write something
down." He activates the data terminal's input screen and
punches the button that will relay a printout of his
memorandum to his desk at his research cubicle in Pittsburgh. Then, quickly pursing his lips and scowling, he
begins to make his notations.

He frequently goes nightwalking, but never in his own
city of Shanghai. Jason's one audacity: boldly he flouts
the tradition that one should stay close to home during
one's nocturnal prowls. No one will punish him for his
unconventional behavior, since it is merely a violation
of accepted custom, not of urban law. No one will even
criticize him to his face for doing it. Yet his wanderings
give him the mild thrill of doing the forbidden. Jason
explains his habit to himself by saying that he prefers
the crosscultural enrichment that comes from sleeping
with women of other cities. Privately he suspects that he
is just uneasy about getting mixed up with women he
knows, such as Mamelon Kluver. Especially Mamelon
Kluver.

So on his nightwalking nights he takes the dropshafts
far into the depths of the building, to such cities as Pitt-

sburgh or Tokyo, even to squalid Prague or grubby Reykjavik. He pushes open strange doors, lockless by statute, and takes his place on the sleeping platforms of unknown women smelling of mysterious lower-class vegetables. By law they must embrace him willingly. "I am from Shanghai," he tells them, and they go "Ooooh!" in awe, and he mounts them tigerishly, contemptuously, swollen with status.

Breasty Gretl waits patiently while Jason records his latest notions. Then he turns toward her again. Her husband, bloated on whatever the local equivalent of tingle or mindblot may be, lies belly-up at the far side of the sleeping platform, ignoring them. Gretl's large dark eyes glow with admiration. "You Shanghai boys sure got brains," she says, as Jason pounces and takes her in a single fierce thrust.

Later he returns to the 761st floor. Wraiths flit through the dim corridors: other citizens of Shanghai, back from their own nightwalking rounds. He enters his apartment. Jason has forty-five square meters of floor space, not really enough for a man with a wife and five littles, but he does not complain. God bless, you take what you get: others have less. Micaela is asleep, or pretends to be. She is a long-legged, tawny-skinned woman of twenty-three, still quite attractive, though quirky lines are beginning to appear in her face. She frowns too much. She lies half uncovered, her long black glossy hair spread out wildly around her. Her breasts are small but perfect; Jason compares them favorably to the udders of Tokyo's Gretl. He and Micaela have been married nine years. Once he loved her a great deal, before he discovered the gritty residue of bitter shrewishness at the bottom of her soul.

She smiles an inward smile, stirs, still sleeping, brushes

her hair back from her eyes. She has the look of a woman who has just had a thoroughly satisfactory sexual experience. Jason has no way of knowing whether some nightwalker visited Micaela tonight while he was gone, and, of course, he cannot ask. (Search for evidence? Stains on the sleeping platform? Stickiness on her thighs? Don't be barbaric!) He suspects that even if no one had come to her tonight, she would try to make him think that someone had; and if someone had come and had given her only modest pleasure, she would nevertheless smile for her husband's benefit as though she had been embraced by Zeus. He knows his wife's style.

The children seem peaceful. They range in age from two to eight. Soon he and Micaela will have to think about having another. Five littles is a fair-sized family, but Jason understands his duty to serve life by creating life. When one ceases to grow, one begins to die; it is true of a human being and also of the population of an urban monad, of an urbmon constellation, of a continent, of a world. God is life and life is god.

He lies down beside his wife.

He sleeps.

He dreams that Micaela has been sentenced to the chute for countersocial behavior.

Down she goes! Mamelon Kluver makes a condolence call. "Poor Jason," she murmurs. Her pale skin is cool against him. The musky fragrance of her. The elegance of her features. The look of total mastery of self. Not even seventeen; how can she be so imperiously complete? "Help me dispose of Siegmund and we'll belong to each other," Mamelon says. Eyes bright, mischievous, goading him to be her creature. "Jason," she whispers. "Jason, Jason, Jason." Her tone a caress. Her hand on his manhood. He wakes, trembling, sweating, horrified, half an inch from messy ecstasy. He sits up and goes through one of the forgiveness modes for improper thoughts. God bless, he thinks, god bless, god bless, god bless. I did not mean such things. It was my mind. My monstrous mind free of shackles. He completes the spiritual exercise and lies down once more. He sleeps and dreams more harmless dreams.

In the morning the littles run madly off to school and Jason prepares to go to his office. Micaela says suddenly, "Isn't it interesting that you go 600 floors *down* when you go to work, and Siegmund Kluver goes up on top, to Louisville?"

"What the god bless do you mean by that?"

"I see symbolic meaning in it."

"Symbolic garbage. Siegmund's in urban administration; he goes up where the administrators are. I'm in history; I go down where the history is. So?"

"Wouldn't you like to live in Louisville someday?"

"No."

"Why don't you have any ambition?"

"Is your life so miserable here?" he asks, holding himself in check.

"Why has Siegmund made so much of himself at the age of fourteen or fifteen, and here you are at twenty-six and you're still just an input-pusher?"

"Seigmund is ambitious," Jason replies evenly, "and I'm merely a time-server. I don't deny it. Maybe it's genetic. Siegmund strives and gets away with it. Most men don't. Striving sterilizes, Micaela. Striving is primitive. God bless, what's wrong with my career? What's wrong with living in Shanghai?"

"One floor lower and we'd be living in—"

"—Chicago," he says. "I know. But we aren't. May I go to my office now?"

He leaves. He wonders whether he ought to send Micaela to the consoler's office for a reality adjustment. Her threshold of thwarting-acceptance has dipped alarmingly of late; her expectations-level has risen just as disturbingly. Jason is well aware that such things should be dealt with at once, before they become uncontrollable and lead to countersocial behavior and the chute. Probably Micaela needs the services of the moral engineers. But he puts aside the idea of calling the consoler. It is because I dislike the idea of having anyone tamper with my wife's mind, he tells himself piously, and a mocking inner voice tells him that he is taking no action because he secretly wishes to see Micaela become so countersocial that she must be thrown down the chute.

He enters the dropshaft and programs for the 185th floor. Down he goes to Pittsburgh. He sinks, inertia-free, through the cities that make up Urbmon 116. Down he goes through Chicago, through Edinburgh, through Nairobi, through Colombo.

He feels the comforting solidity of the building about him as he descends. The urbmon is his world. He has never been outside it. Why should he go out? His friends, his family, his whole life are here. His urbmon is adequately supplied with theaters, sports arenas, schools, hospitals, houses of worship. His data terminal gives him access to any work of art that is considered blessworthy for human consumption. No one he knows has ever left the building, except for the people who were chosen by lot to settle in the newly opened Urbmon 158 a few months ago, and they, of course, will never come back. There are rumors that urban administrators sometimes go from building to building on business, but Jason is not sure that this is true, and he does not see why such travel would be necessary or desirable. Are there not systems of instantaneous communication linking the urbmons, capable of transmitting all relevant data?

It is a splendid system. As a historian, privileged to explore the records of the pre-urbmon world, he knows more fully than most people how splendid it is. He understands the awful chaos of the past. The terrifying freedoms; the hideous necessity of making choices. The insecurity. The confusion. The lack of plan. The formlessness of contexts.

He reaches the 185th floor. He makes his way through the sleepy corridors of Pittsburgh to his office. A modest room, but he loves it. Glistening walls. A wet mural over his desk. The necessary terminals and screens.

Five small glistening cubes lie on his desk. Each holds the contents of several libraries. He has been working with these cubes for two years, now. His theme is *The Urban Monad as Social Evolution: Parameters of the Spirit Defined by Community Structure.* He is attempting to show that the transition to an urbmon society has brought about a fundamental transformation of the human soul. Of the soul of Western man, at any rate. An orientalization of the Occidentals, as formerly aggressive people accept the yoke of the new environment. A more pliant, more acquiescent mode of response to events, a turning away from the old expansionist-individualist philosophy, as marked by territorial ambition, the *conquistador* mentality, and the pioneering way, toward a kind of communal expansion centered in the orderly and unlimited growth of the human race. Definitely a psychic evolution of some sort, a shift toward graceful acceptance of hive-life. The malcontents bred out of the system generations ago. We who have not gone down the chute accept the inexorabilities. Yes. Yes. Jason believes that he has struck upon a significant subject. Micaela disparaged the theme when he announced it: "You mean you're going to write a book showing that people who live in different kinds of cities are different? That urbmon people have a different attitude than jungle people? Some scholar. I could prove your point in six sentences." Nor was there much enthusiasm for the subject when he proposed it at a staff meeting, although he did manage to get clearance for it. His technique so far has been to steep himself in the images of the past, to turn himself, so far as is possible, into a citizen of the pre-urbmon society. He hopes that that will give him the essential parallax, the perspective on his own society, that he will need when he begins to write his study. He expects to start writing in another two or three years.

He consults a memorandum, chooses a cube, plugs it into a playback slot. His screen brightens.

A kind of ecstasy comes over him as scenes out of the ancient world materialize. He leans close to his input speaker and begins to dictate. Frantically, frenziedly, Jason Quevedo sets down notes on the way it used to be.

Houses and streets. A horizontal world. Individual family shelter units: this is my house, this is my castle. Fantastic! Three people, taking up maybe a thousand square meters of surface. Roads. Concept of road hard for us to understand. Like a hallway going on and on. Private vehicles. Where are they all going? Why so fast? Why not stay home? Crash! Blood. Head goes through glass. Crash again! In the rear. Dark combustible fluid flows in street. Middle of day, springtime, major city. Street scene. Which city? Chicago, New York, Istanbul, Cairo. People walking about IN THE OPEN. Paved streets. This for walkers, this for drivers. Filth. Estimated grid reading: 10,000 pedestrians this sector alone, in strip eight meters wide and eighty meters long. Is that figure right? Check it. Elbow to elbow. And they'd think our world was overcrowded? At least we don't impinge on each other like that. We know how to keep our distances within the overall structure of urbmon life. Vehicles move down middle of street. The good old chaos. Chief activity: the purchase of goods. Private consumption. Cube 11Ab8 shows interior vector of a shop. Exchanging of money for merchandise. Not much different there except random nature of transaction. Do they need what they buy? Where do they PUT it all?

This cube holds nothing new for him. Jason has seen such city scenes many times before. Yet the fascination is ever fresh. He is tense, with sweat flowing freely, as he strains to comprehend a world in which people may live where they please, where they move about on foot or in vehicles in the open, where there is no planning, no order, no restraint. He must perform a double act of imagination: it is necessary for him to see that vanished world from within, as though he lived in it, and then he must try to see the urbmon society as it might seem to someone wafted forward from the twentieth century. The magnitude of the task dismays him. He knows roughly how an ancient would feel about Urbmon 116: it is a hellish place, the ancient would say, in which people live hideously cramped and brutal lives, in which every civilized philosophy is turned on its head, in which uncontrolled breeding is nightmarishly encouraged to serve some incredible concept of a deity eternally demanding more worshipers, in which dissent is ruthlessly stifled and dissenters are peremptorily destroyed. Jason knows the right phrases, the sort of words an intelligent liberal American of, say, 1958 would use. But the inner spirit is missing. He tries to see his own world as a species of hell, and fails. To him it is not hellish. He is a logical man; he knows why the vertical society had to evolve out of the old horizontal one, and why it then became obligatory to eliminate—preferably before they were old enough to reproduce—all those who would not adapt or could not be adapted to the fabric of society. How could troublemakers be allowed to remain in the tight, intimate, carefully balanced structure of an urbmon? He knows that the probable result of tossing flippos down the chute has been, over a couple of centuries, the creation of a new style of human being through selective breeding. Is there now a *Homo urbmonensis*, placid, adjusted, fully content? These are topics he means to explore intensively when he writes his book. But it is so hard, so absurdly hard, to grasp them from the viewpoint of ancient man!

Jason struggles to understand the uproar over overpopulation in the ancient world. He has drawn from the archives scores of tracts directed against indiscriminate human spawning—angry polemics composed at a time when less than 4,000,000,000 people inhabited the world. He is aware, of course, that humans can choke a whole planet quickly when they live spread out horizontally the way they did; but why were they so worried about the future? Surely they could have forseen the beauties of the vertical society!

No. No. That's just the point, he tells himself unhappily. They did *not* foresee any such thing. Instead they talked about limiting fertility, if necessary by imposing a governmental authority to hold population down. Jason shivers. "Don't you see," he asks his cubes, "that only a totalitarian regime could enforce such limits? You say that *we're* a repressive society. But what kind of society would you have built, if the urbmons hadn't developed?"

The voice of ancient man replies, "I'd rather take my chances on limiting births and allowing complete freedom otherwise. You've accepted the freedom to multiply, but it's cost you all the other freedoms. Don't you see—"

"You're the one who doesn't see," Jason blurts. "A society must sustain its momentum through the exploitation of god-given fertility. We've found a way to make room for everybody on Earth, to support a population ten or twenty times greater than what you imagined was the absolute maximum. You see it merely as suppression and authoritarianism. But what about the billions of lives that could never have come into being at all under your system? Isn't that the ultimate suppression—forbidding humans to exist in the first place?"

"But what good is letting them exist, if the best they can hope for is a box inside a box inside a box? What about the quality of life?"

"I see no defects in the quality of our life. We find fulfillment in the interplay of human relationships. Do I need to go to China or Africa for my pleasures, when I can find them within a single building? Isn't it a sign of inner dislocation to feel compelled to roam all over the world? In your day everybody traveled, I know, and in mine no one does. Which is a more stable society? Which is happier?"

"Which is more human? Which exploits man's potential more fully? Isn't it our nature to seek, to strive, to reach out—?"

"What about seeking within? Exploring the inner life?"

"But don't you see—?"

"But don't you see—?"

"If you only would listen—"

"If you only would listen—"

Jason does not see. Ancient man's spokesman does not see. Neither will listen. There is no communication. Jason wastes another dismal day wrestling with his intractable material. Only as he is about to leave does he remember last night's memorandum. He will study ancient sexual mores in a new attempt to gain insight into that vanished society. He punches out his requisition. The cubes will be on his desk when he returns to his office tomorrow.

He goes home to Shanghai, home to Micaela.

That evening the Quevedos have dinner guests: Michael, Micaela's twin brother, and his wife Stacion. Michael is a computer-primer; he and Stacion live in Edinburgh, on the 704th floor. Jason finds his company challenging and rewarding, although the physical resemblance between his brother-in-law and his wife, which he once found amusing, now alarms and disturbs him. Michael affects shoulder-length hair, and is barely a centimeter taller than his tall, slender sister. They are, of course, only fraternal twins, yet their facial features are virtually identical. They have even settled into the same pattern of tense, querulous smirks and scowls. From the rear Jason has difficulties in telling them apart unless he sees them side by side; they stand the same way, arms akimbo, heads tilted backward. Since Micaela is small-breasted, the possibility of confusion exists also in profile, and sometimes, looking at one of them in front view, Jason has momentarily wondered whether he beholds Michael or Micaela. If only Michael would grow a beard! But his cheeks are smooth.

Now and again Jason feels sexually drawn to his brother-in-law. It is a natural attraction, considering the physical pull Micaela has always exerted on him. Seeing her across the room, angled away from him, her smooth back bare, the little globe of one breast visible under her arms as she reaches toward the data terminal, he feels the urge to go to her and caress her. And if she were Michael? And if he slid his hand to her bosom and found it flat and hard? And if they tumbled down together in a passionate tangle? His hand going to Micaela's thighs and finding not the hot hidden slot but the dangling flesh of maleness? And turning her over. Him? Parting the pallid muscular buttocks. The sudden strange thrust. No, Jason flushes the fantasy from his mind. Once again. Not since the rough easy days of boyhood has he had any kind of sexual contact with his own sex. He will not permit it. There are no penalties for such things, naturally, in the society of the urbmon, where all adults are equally accessible. Many of them do it. For all he knows, Michael himself. If Jason wants Michael, he has only to ask. Refusal a sin. He does not ask. He fights the temptation. It is not fair, a man who looks so much like my wife. The devil's snare. Why do I resist, though? If I want him, why not take? But no. I don't really want. It's just a sneaky urge, a sidewise way of desiring Micaela. And yet the fantasy surges again. Himself and Michael, spoon-fashion, mouths gaping and stuffed. The image glows so brightly that Jason rises in a brusque tense motion, knocking over the flask of wine that Stacion has brought tonight, and, as Stacion dives for and rescues it, he crosses the room, aghast at the erection prodding his taut gold and green shorts. He goes to Micaela and cups one of her breasts. The nipple is soft. He snuggles against her, nibbles the nape of her neck. She tolerates these attentions in a remote way, not interrupting the programing of dinner. But when, still distraught, he slips his left hand into the open side of her sarong and runs it across her belly to her loins, she wriggles her hips in displeasure and whispers harshly, "*Stop* it! Not with *them* sitting there!"

Wildly he finds the fumes and offers them around. Stacion refuses; she is pregnant. A plump pleasant red-haired girl, complacent, easy. Out of place in this congregation of hypertense. Jason sucks the smoke deep and feels the knots loosen slightly inside. Now he can look at Michael and not fall prey to unnatural urges. Yet he still speculates. Does Michael suspect? Would he laugh if I told him? Take offense? Angry at me for wanting to? Angry at me for not trying to? Suppose he asked *me* to, what would I do? Jason takes a second fume and the swarm of buzzing questions leaves his mind. "When is the little due?" he asks, in counterfeit geniality.

"God bless, fourteen weeks," Michael says, "Number five. A girl, this time."

"We'll name her Celeste," Stacion puts in, patting her middle. Her maternity costume is a short yellow bolero and a loose brown waist sash. Leaving the bulging belly bare. The everted navel like the stem of the swollen fruit. Milky breasts swaying in and out of visibility under the open jacket. "We're talking about requesting twins for next year," she adds. "A boy and a girl. Michael's always telling me about the good times he and Micaela used to have together when they were young. Like a special world for twins."

Jason is caught unawares by the bringdown, and is plunged abruptly into feverish fantasy once more. He sees Micaela's spread legs sticking out from under Michael's lean pumping body, sees her childish ecstatic face looking up over his busy shoulder. The good times they used to have. Michael the first one into her. At nine, ten, maybe? Even younger? Their awkward experiments. Let me get on top of you this time, Michael. Oh, it's deeper this way. Do you think we're doing anything wrong? No, silly, didn't we sleep together for nine whole months? Put your hand here. And your mouth on me again. Yes. You're hurting my breasts, Michael. Oh. Oh, that's nice. But wait, just another few seconds. The good times they used to have. "Is something the matter, Jason?" Michael's voice. "You look so tight," Jason forces himself to pull out of it. Hands trembling. Another fume. He rarely takes three before dinner.

Stacion has gone to help Micaela unload the food from the delivery slot. Michael says to Jason, "I hear you've started a new research project. What's the basic theme?"

Kind of him. Senses that I'm ill at ease. Draw me out of my morbid brooding. All these sick thoughts.

Jason replies, "I'm investigating the notion that urbmon life is breeding a new kind of human being. A type that adapts readily to relatively little living space and a low privacy quotient."

"You mean a genetic mutation?" Michael asks, frowning. "Literally, an inherited social characteristic?"

"So I believe."

"Are such things possible, though? Can you call it a

genetic trait, really, if people voluntarily decide to band together in a society like ours and—"

"Voluntarily?"

"Isn't it?"

Jason smiles. "I doubt that it ever was. In the beginning, you know, it was a matter of necessity. Because of the chaos in the world. Seal yourself up in your building or be exposed to the food bandits. I'm talking about the famine years, now. And since then, since everything stabilized, has it been so voluntary? Do we have any choice about where we live?"

"I suppose we could go outside if we really wanted to," Michael says, "and live in whatever they've got out there."

"But we don't. Because we recognize that that's a hopeless fantasy. We stay here, whether we like it or not. And those who don't like it, those who eventually can't take it—well, you know what happens to them."

"But—"

"Wait. Two centuries of selective breeding, Michael. Down the chute for the flippos. And no doubt some population loss through leaving the buildings, at least at the beginning. Those who remain adapt to circumstances. They *like* the urbmon way. It seems altogether natural to them."

"Is this really genetic, though? Couldn't you simply call it psychological conditioning? I mean, in the Asian countries, didn't people always live jammed together the way we do, only much worse, no sanitation, no regulation—and didn't they accept it as the natural order of things?"

"Of course," Jason says. "Because rebellion against the natural order of things had been bred out of them thousands of years ago. The ones who stayed, the ones who reproduced, were the ones who accepted things as they were. The same here."

Doubtfully Michael says, "How can you draw the line between psychological conditioning and long-term selective breeding? How do you know what to attribute to which?"

"I haven't faced that problem yet," Jason admits.

"Shouldn't you be working with a geneticist?"

"Perhaps later I will. After I've established my parameters of inquiry. You know, I'm not ready to *defend* this thesis, yet. I'm just collecting data to discover if it can be defended. The scientific method. We don't make a priori assumptions and look around for supporting evidence; we examine the evidence first and—"

"Yes, yes, I know. Just between us, though, you do think it's really happening, don't you? An urbmon species."

"I do. Yes. Two centuries of selective breeding, pretty ruthlessly enforced. And all of us so well adapted now to this kind of life."

"Ah. Yes. All of us so well adapted."

"With some exceptions," Jason says, retreating a bit. He and Michael exchange wary glances. Jason wonders what thoughts lie behind his brother-in-law's cool eyes. "General acceptance, though. Where has the old Western expansionist philosophy gone? Bred out of the race, I say. The urge to power? The love of conquest? The hunger for land and property? Gone. Gone. Gone. I don't think that's just a conditioning process. I suspect it's a matter of stripping the race of certain genes that lead to—"

"Dinner, professor," Micaela calls.

A costly meal. Proteoid steaks, root salad, bubble pudding, relishes, fish soup. Nothing reconstituted and hardly anything synthetic. For the next two weeks he and Micaela will have to go on short rations until they've made up the deficit in their luxury allotment. He conceals his annoyance. Michael always eats lavishly when he comes here; Jason wonders why, since Micaela is not nearly so solicitous of her seven other brothers and sisters. Scarcely ever invites two or three of them. But Michael here at least five times a year, always getting a feast. Jason's suspicions reawaken. Something ugly going on between those two? The childhood passions still smoldering? Perhaps it is cute for twelve-year-old twins to couple, but should they still be at it when twenty-three and married? Michael a nightwalker in my sleeping platform? Jason is annoyed at himself. Not bad enough that he has to fret over his idiotic homosexual fixation on Michael; now he has to torment himself with fears of an incestuous affair behind his back. Poisoning his hours of relaxation. What if they are? Nothing socially objectionable in it. Seek pleasure where you will. In your sister's slot if you be so moved. Shall all the men of Urban Monad 116 have access to Micaela Quevedo, save only the unfortunate Michael? Must his status as her wombmate deny her to him? Be realistic, Jason tells himself. Incest taboos make sense only where breeding is involved. Anyway, they probably aren't doing it, probably never have. He wonders why so much nastiness has sprouted in his soul lately. The frictions of living with Micaela, he decides. Her coldness is driving me into all kinds of unblessworthy attitudes, the bitch. If she doesn't stop goading me I'll—

—I'll what? Seduce Michael away from her? He laughs at the intricacy of his own edifice of schemes.

"Something funny?" Micaela asks. "Share it with us, Jason."

He looks up, helpless. What shall he say? "A silly thought," he improvises. "About you and Michael, how much you look like each other. I was thinking, perhaps some night you and he could switch rooms, and then a nightwalker would come here, looking for you, but when he actually got under the covers with you he'd discover that he was in bed with a man, and—and—" Jason is smitten with the overwhelming fatuity of what he is saying and descends into a feeble silence.

"What a peculiar thing to imagine," Micaela says.

"Besides, so what?" Stacion asks. "The nightwalker might be a little surprised for a minute, maybe, but then he'd just go ahead and make it with Michael, wouldn't he? Rather than make a big scene or bother to go someplace else. So I don't see what's funny."

"Forget it," Jason growls. "I told you it was silly. Micaela insisted on knowing what was crossing my mind, and I told you, but I'm not responsible if it doesn't make any sense, am I? Am I?" He grabs the flask of wine and pours most of what remains into his cup. "This is good stuff," he mutters.

After dinner they share an expander, all but Stacion. They groove in silence for a couple of hours. Shortly before midnight, Michael and Stacion leave. Jason does not watch as his wife and her brother make their farewell embraces. As soon as the guests are gone, Micaela strips away her sarong and gives him a bright, fierce stare, almost defying him to have her tonight. But though he knows it is unkind to ignore her wordless invitation, he is so depressed by his own inner performance this evening that he feels he must flee. "Sorry," he says. "I'm restless." Her expression changes: desire fades and is replaced by bewilderment, and then by rage. He does not wait. Hastily he goes out, rushing to the dropshaft and plummeting to the 59th floor. Warsaw. He enters an apartment and finds a woman of about thirty, with fuzzy blond hair and a soft fleshy body, asleep alone on an unkempt sleeping platform. At least eight littles stacked up on cots in the corners. He wakes her. "Jason Quevedo," he says. "I'm from Shanghai."

She blinks. Having trouble focusing her eyes. "Shanghai? But are you supposed to be here?"

"Who says I can't?"

She ponders that. "Nobody says. But Shanghai never comes here. Really, Shanghai? You?"

"Do I have to show you my identiplate?" he asks harshly.

His educated inflections destroy her resistance. She begins to primp, arranging her hair, reaching for some kind of cosmetic spray for her face, while he drops his clothing. He mounts the platform. She draws her knees up almost to her breasts, presenting herself. Crudely, impatiently, he takes her. Michael, he thinks, Micaela. Michael. Micaela. Grunting, he floods her with his fluid.

In the morning, at his office, he begins his newest line of inquiry, summoning up data on the sexual mores of ancient times. As usual, he concentrates on the twentieth century, which he regards as the climax of the ancient era, and therefore most significant, revealing as it does the entire cluster of attitudes and responses that had accumulated in the pre-urbmon industrial era. The twenty-first century is less useful for his purposes, being, like all transitional periods, essentially chaotic and unschematic, and the twenty-second century brings him into modern times with the beginning of the urbmon age. So the twentieth is his favorite area of study. Seeds of the collapse, portents of doom running through it like bad-trip threads in a psychedelic tapestry.

Jason is careful not to fall victim to the historian's fallacy of diminished perspective. Though the twentieth century, seen from this distance, seems to be a single seamless entity, he knows that this is an error of evaluation caused by overfacile abstracting; there may be certain apparent patterns that ride one unbroken curve across the ten decades, but he realizes that he must allow for certain qualitative changes in society that have created major historical discontinuities between decade and decade. The unleashing of atomic energy created one such discontinuity. The development of swift intercontinental transportation formed another. In the moral sphere, the availability of simple and reliable contraception caused a fundamental change in sexual attitudes, a revolution not to be ascribed to mere rebelliousness. The arrival of the psychedelic age, with its special problems and joys, marked one more great gulf, setting off part of the century from all that went before. So 1910 and 1930 and 1950 and 1970 and 1990 occupy individual summits in Jason's jagged image of the century, and in any sampling of its mentality that he takes, he draws evidence from each of its discrete subepochs.

Plenty of evidence is available to him. Despite the dislocations caused by the collapse, an enormous weight of data on the eras of pre-urbmon time exists, stored in some subterranean vault, Jason knows not where. Certainly the central data bank (if there is indeed only one, and not a redundant series of them scattered through the world) is not anywhere in Urbmon 116, and he doubts that it is even in the Chipitts constellation. It does not matter. He can draw from that vast deposit any information that he requires, and it will come instantaneously. The trick lies in knowing what to ask for.

He is familiar enough with the sources to be able to make intelligent data requisitions. He thumbs the keys and the new cubes arrive. Novels, Films, Television programs, Leaflets, Handbills. He knows that for more than half the century popular attitudes toward sexual matters were recorded both in licit and illicit channels: the ordinary novels and motion pictures of the day, and an underground stream of clandestine, "forbidden" erotic works. Jason draws from both groups. He must weigh the distortions of the erotica against the distortions of the legitimate material: only out of this Newtonian interplay of forces can the objective truth be mined. Then, too, he surveys the legal codes, making the appropriate allowances for laws observed only in the breach. What is this in the laws of New York: "A person who willfully and lewdly exposes his person or the private parts thereof, in any public place, or in any place where others are present, or procures another to so expose himself shall be guilty of..."? In the state of Georgia, he reads, any sleeping car passenger who remains in a compartment other than the one to which he is assigned is guilty of a misdemeanor and is subject to a maximum fine of $1000 or twelve months' imprisonment. The laws of the state of Michigan tell him: "Any person who shall undertake to medically treat any female person, and while so treating her shall represent to such female that it is, or will be necessary, or beneficial to her health that she shall have sexual intercourse with a man, and any man, not being the husband of such female, who shall have sexual intercourse with her by reason of such representation, shall be guilty of a felony, and be punished by a maximum term of ten years." Strange. Stranger still: "Every person who shall carnally know, or shall have sexual intercourse in any manner with any animal or bird, is guilty of sodomy...." No wonder everything's extinct! And this? "Whoever shall carnally know any male or female by the anus (rectum) or with the mouth or tongue, or who shall attempt intercourse with a dead body...$2000 and/or five years' imprisonment...." Most chilling of all: in Connecticut the use of contraceptive articles is forbidden, under penalty of a minimum fine of $50 or sixty days to one year in prison, and in Massachusetts "whoever sells, lends, gives, exhibits (or offers to) any instrument or drug, or medicine, or any article whatever for the prevention of conception, shall be subject to a maximum term of five years in prison or a maximum fine of $1000." What? What? Send a man to prison for decades for cunnilingualizing his wife, and impose so trifling a sentence on the spreaders of contraception? Where was Connecticut, anyway? Where was Massachusetts? Historian that he is, he is not sure. God bless, he thinks, but the doom that came upon them was well merited. A bizarre folk to deal so lightly with those who would limit births!

He skims a few novels and dips into several films. Even though it is only the first day of his research, he perceives patterns, a fitful loosening of taboos throughout the century, accelerating greatly between 1920 and 1930 and again after 1960. Timid experiments in revealing the ankle lead, shortly, to bared breasts. The curious custom of prostitution erodes as liberties become more commonly obtained. The disappearance of taboos on the popular sexual vocabulary. He can barely believe some of what he learns. So compressed were their souls! So thwarted were their urges! And why? And why? Of course, they did grow looser. Yet terrible restraints prevail throughout that dark century, except toward the end, when the collapse was near and all limits burst. But even then there was something askew in their liberation. He sees a forced, self-conscious mode of amorality coming into being. The shy nudists. The guilt-wracked orgiasts. The apologetic adulterers. Strange, strange, strange. He is endlessly fascinated by the twentieth century's sexual concepts. The wife as husband's property. The premium on virginity: well, they seemed to get rid of *that*! Attempts by the state to dictate positions of sexual intercourse and to forbid certain supplementary acts. The restrictions even on words! A phrase leaps out of a supposedly serious twentieth-century work of social criticism: "Among the most significant developments of the decade was the attainment of the freedom, at last, for the responsible writer to use such words as *fuck* and *cunt* where necessary in his work." Can that have been so? Such importance placed on mere words? Jason pronounces the odd monosyllables aloud in his research cubicle. "Fuck. Cunt. Fuck. Cunt. Fuck." They sound merely antiquated. Harmless, certainly. He tries the modern equivalents. "Top. Slot. Top. Slot. Top." No impact. How can words ever have held such inflammatory content that an apparently penetrating scholar would feel it worthwhile to celebrate their free public use? Jason is aware of his limitations as a historian when he runs into such things. He simply cannot comprehend the twentieth century's obsession with words. To insist on giving God a capital letter, as though He might be displeased to be called a god! To suppress books for printing words like c–t and f–k and s–t!

By the close of his day's work he is more convinced than ever of the validity of his thesis. There has been a monumental change in sexual morality in the past three hundred years, and it cannot be explained only on cultural grounds. We are different, he tells himself. We have changed, and it is a cellular change, a transformation of the body as well as the soul. They could not have permitted, let alone encouraged, our total-accessibility society. Our nightwalking, our nudity, our freedom from taboos, our lack of irrational jealousies, all of this would have been wholly alien to them, distasteful, abominable. Even those who lived in a way approaching ours, and there were a few, did so for the wrong reasons. They were responding not to a positive societal need but to an existing system of repression. We are different. We are fundamentally different.

Weary, satisfied with what he has found, he leaves his office an hour ahead of time. When he returns to his apartment, Micaela is not there.

This puzzles him. Always here at this hour. The littles left alone, playing with their toys. Of course it is a bit early, not much. Just stepped out for a chat? I don't understand. She hasn't left a message. He says to his eldest son, "Where's Mommo?"

"Went out."

"Where?"

A shrug. "Visiting."

"How long ago?"

"An hour. Maybe two."

Some help. Fidgety, perturbed, Jason calls a couple of women on the floor, Micaela's friends. They haven't seen her. The boy looks up and says brightly, "She was going to visit a man." Jason stares sharply at him. "A man? Is that what she said? What man?" But the boy has exhausted his information. Fearful that she has gone off for a rendezvous with Michael, he debates phoning Edinburgh. Just to see if she's there. A lengthy inner debate. Furious images racing in his skull. Micaela and Michael entangled, indistinguishable, united, inflamed. Locked together in incestuous passion. As perhaps every afternoon. How long has this been going on? And she comes to me at dinnertime every evening hot and wet from *him*. He calls Edinburgh and gets Stacion on the screen. Calm, bulgy. "Micaela? No, of course she isn't here. Is she supposed to be?"

"I thought maybe—dropping in—"

"I haven't heard from her since we were at your place."

He hesitates. Just as she moves to break the connection he blurts, "Do you happen to know where Michael is right now?"

"Michael? He's at work. Interface Crew Nine."

"Are you sure?"

Stacion looks at him in obvious surprise. "Of course I'm sure. Where else would he be? His crew doesn't break till 1730." Laughs. "You aren't suggesting that Michael— that Micaela—"

"Of course not. What kind of fool do you think I am? I just wondered—that perhaps—if—" He is adrift. "Forget it, Stacion. Give him my love when he comes home." Jason cuts the contact. Head bowed, eyes full of unwanted visions. Michael's long fingers encircling his sister's breasts. Rosy nipples poking through. Mirror-image faces nose to nose. Tonguetips touching. No. Where is she, then? He is tempted to try to reach him in Interface Crew Nine. Find out if he really is on duty. Or maybe off in some dark cubbyhole topping his sister. Jason throws himself face down on the sleeping platform to consider his position. He tells himself that it is not important that Micaela is letting her brother top her. Not at all. He will not let himself be trapped into primeval twentieth-century attitudes of morality. On the other hand, it is a considerable violation of custom for Micaela to go off in midafternoon to be topped. If she wants Michael, Jason thinks, let him come here decently after midnight, as a nightwalker. Instead of this skulking and sneaking. Does she think I'd be shocked to know who her lover is? Does she have to hide it from me this way? It's a hundred times as bad to steal away like this. It introduces a note of deceit. Old-fashioned adultery; the secret rendezvous. How ugly! I'd like to tell her—

The door opens and Micaela comes in. She is naked under a translucent flutter-robe and has a flushed, rumpled look. She smirks at Jason. He perceives the loathing behind the smirk.

"Well?" he says.

"Well?"

"I was surprised not to find you here when I got home."

Coolly Micaela disrobes. She gets under the cleanser. From the way she scrubs herself there can be no doubt that she has just been topped. After a moment she says, "I got back a little late, didn't I? Sorry."

"Got back from where?"

"Siegmund Kluver's."

He is astounded and relieved all at once. What is this?

Daywalking? And a woman taking the sexual initiative? But at least it wasn't Michael. At least it wasn't Michael. If he can believe her. "Siegmund?" he says. "What do you mean, Siegmund?"

"I visited him. Didn't the littles tell you? He had some free time today and I went up to his place. Quite blessworthy, I must say. An expert slotman. Not my first time with him, of course, but by far the best."

She steps out from the cleanser, seizes two of the littles, strips them, thrusts them under for their afternoon bath. Paying almost no attention to Jason. He contemplates her lithe bare body in dismay. A lecture on urbmon sexual ethics almost spills from him, but he dams his lips, baffled and agog. Having laboriously adjusted himself to accept the unacceptable notion of her incestuous love, he cannot easily come to terms with this other business of Siegmund. Chasing after him? Daywalking. *Daywalking.* Has she no shame? Why has she done this? Purely for spite, he tells himself. To mock me. To anger me. To show me how little she cares for me. Using sex as a weapon against me. Flaunting her illicit hour with Siegmund. But Siegmund should have had more sense. A man with his ambitions, violating custom? Perhaps Micaela overwhelmed him. She can do that. Even to Siegmund. The bitch! The bitch! He sees her looking at him now, eyes sparkling, mouth quirked in a hostile smile. Daring him to start a fight. Begging him to try to make trouble. No, Micaela, I won't play your game. As she bathes the littles he says quite serenely, "What are you programing for dinner tonight?"

At work the next day he decubes a motion picture of 1969—ostensibly a comedy, he imagines, about two California couples who decide to exchange mates for a night, then find themselves without the courage to go through with it. Jason is wholly drawn into the film, enthralled not only by the scenes of private houses and open countryside but by the sheer alienness of the characters' psychology—their transparent bravado, their intense anguish over a matter as trivial as who will poke what into whom, their ultimate cowardice. It is easier for him to understand the nervous hilarity with which they experiment with what he takes to be cannabis, since the film, after all, dates from the dawn of the psychedelic era. But their sexual attitudes are wondrously grotesque. He watches the film twice, taking copious notes. Why are these people so timid? Do they fear an unwanted pregnancy? A social disease? No, the time of the film is after the venereal era, he believes. Is it pleasure itself that they fear? Tribal punishment for violation of the monopolistic concept of twentieth-century marriage? Even if the violation is conducted with absolute secrecy? That must be it, Jason concludes. They dread the laws against extramarital intercourse. The rack and the thumbscrew, the stocks and the ducking stool, so to speak. Hidden eyes watching. The shameful truth destined to out. So they draw back; so they remain locked in the cells of their individual marriages.

Watching their antics, he suddenly sees Micaela in the context of twentieth-century bourgeois morality. Not a timid fool like the four people in the film, of course. Brazen, defiant—bragging about her visit to Siegmund, using sex as a way of diminishing her husband. A very twentieth-century attitude, far removed from the easy acceptance characteristic of the urbmon world. Only someone whose view of sex is tied to its nature as a commodity could have done what Micaela has done. She has reinvented adultery in a society where the concept has no meaning! His anger rises. Out of 800,000 people in Urban Monad 116, why must he be married to the one sick one? Flirting with her brother because she knows it annoys me, not because she's really interested in topping him. Going to Siegmund instead of waiting for Siegmund to come to her. The slotty barbarian! I'll show her, though. I know how to play her silly sadistic game!

At midday he leaves his cubicle, having done less than five hours' work. The liftshaft takes him to the 787th floor. Outside the apartment of Siegmund and Mamelon Kluver he succumbs to sudden terrible vertigo and nearly falls. He recovers his balance; but his fear is still great, and he is tempted to leave. He argues with himself, trying to purge his timidity. Thinking of the people in the motion picture. Why is he afraid? Mamelon's just another slot. He's had a hundred as attractive as she. But she's clever. Might cut me down with a couple of quick quips. Still, I want her. Denied myself all these years. While Micaela blithely marches off to Siegmund in the afternoon. The bitch. The bitch. Why should I suffer? We aren't supposed to have to feel frustration in the urbmon environment. I want Mamelon, therefore. He pushes open the door.

The Kluver apartment is empty. A baby in the maintenance slot, no other sign of life.

"Mamelon?" he asks. Voice almost cracking.

The screen glows and Mamelon's pre-programed image appears. How beautiful, he thinks. How radiant she is. Smiling. She says, "Hello. I have gone to my afternoon polyrhythm class and will be home at 1500 hours. Urgent messages may be relayed to me in Shanghai Somatic

Fulfillment Hall, or to my husband Siegmund at Louisville Access Nexus. Thank you." The image fades.

1500 hours. Nearly a two-hour wait. Shall he go?

He craves another glimpse of her loveliness. "Mamelon?" he says.

She reappears on screen. He studies her. The aristocratic features, the dark mysterious eyes. A self-contained woman, undriven by demons. A personality in her own right, not, like Micaela, a frayed neurotic whipped by the psychic winds. "Hello. I have gone to my afternoon polyrhythm class and will be home at 1500 hours. Urgent messages may be relayed—"

He waits.

The apartment, which he has seen before, impresses him anew with its elegance. Rich textures of hangings and draperies, sleek objects of art. Marks of status; soon Siegmund will move up to Louisville, no doubt, and these private possessions are harbingers of his coming elevation to the ruling caste. To ease his impatience Jason toys with the wall panels, inspects the furniture, programs all the scent apertures. He peers at the baby, cooing in its maintenance slot. He paces. The other Kluver child must be two years old by now. Will it come home from the creche soon? He is not eager to entertain a little all afternoon while waiting tautly for Mamelon.

He tunes the screen and watches one of the afternoon abstractions. The flow of forms and colors carries him through another impatient hour. Mamelon will be here soon.

1450. She comes in, holding her little's hand. Jason rises, athrob, dry-throated. She is dressed simply and unglamorously in a cascading blue tunic, knee-length, and gives an unusually disheveled impression. Why not?

She has spent the afternoon in physical exercise; he cannot expect her to be the impeccable, glistening Mamelon of the evenings.

"Jason? Is something wrong? Why—"

"Just a visit," he says, barely able to recognize his own voice.

"You look half flippo, Jason! Are you ill? Can I get you anything?" She discards her tunic and tosses it, crumpled, under the cleanser. Now she wears only a filmy wrap; he averts his eyes from her blazing nudity. And stares out of the corners as she drops the wrap also, washes, and dons a light housecoat. Turning to him again, she says, "You're acting very strangely."

Out with it in a rush.

"Let me top you, Mamelon!"

A surprised laugh from her. "Now? Middle of the afternoon?"

"Is that so wicked?"

"It's unusual," she says. "Especially coming from a man who hasn't ever been to me as a nightwalker. But I suppose there's no harm in it. All right; come on."

As simple as that. She takes off the housecoat and inflates the sleeping platform. Of course; she will not frustrate him, for that would be unblessworthy. The hour is strange, but Mamelon understands the code by which they live, and does not hold him strictly to the rules. She is his. The white skin, the high full breasts. Deep-set navel. Black matted thatch curling lavishly onto her thighs. She beckons to him from the platform, smiles, rubs her knees together to ready herself. He removes his clothing, carefully folding everything. He lies down beside her, takes one of her breasts nervously in his hand, lightly nips her earlobe. He wants desperately to tell her

111

that he loves her. But that would be a breach of custom far more serious than any he has committed thus far. In a sense, not the twentieth-century sense, she belongs to Siegmund, and he has no right to intrude his emotions between them, only his rigid organ. With a quick tense leap he climbs her. As usual, panic makes him hurry. He goes into her and they begin to move. I'm topping Mamelon Kluver. Actually. At last. He gains control of himself and slows it down. He dares to open his eyes and is gratified to find that hers are closed. The nostrils flared, the lips drawn back. Such perfect white teeth. She seems to be purring. He moves a little faster. Clasping her in his arms; the mounds of her breasts flattening against him. Abruptly, amazingly, something extraordinary is kindled within her, and she shrieks and pumps her hips and makes hoarse animal noises as she claws at him. He is so astonished by the fury of her coming that he forgets to notice his own. So it ends. Exhausted, he clings to her a little while after, and she strokes his sweaty shoulders. Analyzing it in the afterward coolness, he realizes that it was not so very different from what he has experienced elsewhere. One wilder-than-usual moment, perhaps. But otherwise only the familiar process. Even with Mamelon Kluver, the object of his incandescent imaginings for three years, it was only the old two-backed beast: I thrust and she thrusts and up we go. So much for romanticism. In the dark all cats are gray: old twentieth-century proverb. So now I've topped her. He withdraws and they go to the cleanser together.

She says, "Better, now?"

"I think so."

"You were terribly tight when I came in."

"I'm sorry," he says.

"Can I get you anything?"

"No."

"Would you like to talk about it?"

"No. No." He is averting his eyes from her body again. He searches for his clothing. She does not bother to dress. "I guess I'll go," he says.

"Come back some time. Perhaps during regular night-walking hours. I don't mean that I really mind your coming in the afternoon, Jason, but it might be more relaxed at night. Do you follow what I'm saying?"

She is frighteningly casual. Does she realize that this is the first time he has topped a woman of his own city? What if he told her that all his other adventures had been in Warsaw and Reykjavik and Prague and the other grubbo levels? He wonders now what he had feared. He will come back to her, he is sure. He makes his exit amid a flurry of grins, nods, half winks, and furtive direct glances. Mamelon blows him a kiss.

In the corridor. Still early afternoon. The whole point of this excursion will be lost if he comes home on time. He takes the dropshaft to his office and consumes two futile hours there. Even so, too early. Returning to Shanghai a little past 1800, he enters the Somatic Fulfillment Hall and dumps himself into an imagebath; the warm undulating currents are soothing, but he responds badly to the psychedelic vibrations from below and his mind fills with visions of shattered, blackened urbmons, all girders and skewed concrete. When he comes up it is 1920 and the screen in the dressing room, picking up his emanations, says, "Jason Quevedo, your wife is trying to trace you." Fine. Late for dinner. Let her squirm. He nods to the screen and goes out. After walking the halls for close to an hour, beginning at the 770th floor and snaking his way up to 792, he drops to his own level and heads for home. A screen in the hall outside the shaft tells him again that tracers are out for him. "I'm coming, I'm coming," he mutters, irritated.

Micaela looks rewardingly worried. "Where have you been?" she asks the instant he appears.

"Oh, around. Around."

"You weren't working late. I called you there. I had tracers on you."

"As if I were a lost boy."

"It wasn't like you. You don't just disappear in the middle of the afternoon."

"Have you had dinner yet?"

"I've been waiting," she says sourly.

"Let's eat, then, I'm starved."

"You won't explain?"

"Later." Working hard at an air of mystery.

He scarcely notices his food. Afterward, he spends the usual time with the littles. They go off to sleep. He rehearses what he will say to Micaela, arranging the words in various patterns. He tries inwardly to practice a self-satisfied smirk. For once he will be the aggressor. For once he will hurt *her*.

She has become absorbed in the screen transmission. Her earlier anxiety about his disapperance seems to have vanished. Finally he is forced to say, "Do you want to discuss what I did today?"

She looks up. "What you did? Oh, you mean this afternoon?" She no longer cares, it appears. "Well?"

"I went to Mamelon Kluver."

"Daywalking? You?"

"Me."

"Was she good?"

"She was superb," he says, puzzled by Micaela's air of unconcern. "She was everything I imagined she'd be."

Micaela laughs.

"Is it funny?" he asks.

"It isn't. *You* are."

"Tell me what you mean by that."

"All these years you deny yourself nightwalking in Shanghai, and go off to the grubbos. Now, for the stupidest possible reason, you finally allow yourself Mamelon—"

"You knew I never nightwalked here?"

"Of course I knew," she says. "Women talk. I ask my friends. You never topped any of them. So I started to wonder. I had some checking done on you. Warsaw. Prague. Why did you have to go down *there*, Jason?"

"That doesn't matter now."

"What does?"

"That I spent the afternoon on Mamelon's sleeping platform."

"You idiot."

"Bitch."

"Failure."

"Sterilizer!"

"Grubbo!"

"Wait," he says. "Wait. Why did you go to Siegmund?"

"To annoy you," she admits. "Because he's a runggrabber, and you aren't. I wanted to get you excited. To make you move."

"So you violated all custom and aggressively daywalked with the man of your choice. Not pretty, Micaela. Not at all feminine, I might add."

"That keeps things even, then. A female husband and a mannish wife."

"You're quick with the insults, aren't you?"

"Why did you go to Mamelon?"

"To get you angry. To pay you back for Siegmund. Not that I give a damn about your letting him top you. We can take that stuff for granted, I think. But your *motives*. Using sex as a weapon. Deliberately playing the wrong role. Trying to stir me up. It was ugly, Micaela."

"And *your* motives? Sex as revenge? Nightwalking is supposed to reduce tensions, not create them. Regardless of the time of day you do it. You want Mamelon, fine; she's a lovely girl. But to come here and *brag* about it, as if you think I care whose slot you plow—"

"Don't be a filther, Micaela."

"Listen to him! Listen to him! Puritan! Moralist!"

The littles begin to cry. They have never heard shouting before. Micaela makes a hushing gesture at them behind her back.

"At least I *have* morals," he says. "What about you and your brother Michael?"

"What about us?"

"Do you deny you've let him top you?"

"When we were kids, yes, a couple of times," she says, flushing. "So? You never put it up your sisters, I suppose?"

"Not only when you were kids. You're still making it with him."

"I think you're insane, Jason."

"You deny it?"

"Michael hasn't touched me in ten years. Not that I see anything wrong with his doing it, except that it hasn't happened. Oh, Jason, Jason, Jason! You've spent so much time mucking around in your archives that you've turned yourself into a twentieth-century man. You're jealous,

Jason. Worried about incest, no less. And whether I obey the rules about female initiative. What about you and your Warsaw nightwalking? Don't we have a propinquity custom? Are you imposing a double standard, Jason? You do what you like, and I observe custom? And upset about Siegmund. Michael. You're jealous, Jason. *Jealous.* We abolished jealousy a hundred fifty years ago!"

"And you're a social climber. A would-be slicko. You aren't satisfied with Shanghai, you want Louisville. Well, ambition is obsolete too, Micaela. Besides, you were the one who started this whole business of using sex to score debating points. By going to Siegmund and making sure I knew it. You think *I'm* a puritan? You're a throwback, Micaela. You're full of pre-urbmon morality."

"If I am, I got that way from you," she cries.

"No. I got that way from you. You carry the poison around in you! When you—"

The door opens. A man looks in. Charles Mattern, from 799. The sleek, fast-talking sociocomputator; Jason has worked with him on several research projects. Evidently he has overheard the unblessworthy furor going on in here, for he is frowning in embarrassment. "God bless," he says softly, "I'm just out nightwalking, and I thought I'd—"

"No," Micaela screams. "Not now! Go away!"

Mattern shows his shock. He starts to say something, then shakes his head and ducks out of the room, muttering an apology for his intrusion.

Jason is appalled. To turn away a legitimate nightwalker? To order him out of the room?

"Savage!" he cries, and slaps her across the face. "How could you have done that?"

She recoils, rubbing her cheek. "Savage? Me? And you hitting? I could have you thrown down the chute for—"

"I could have *you* thrown down the chute for—"

He stops. They both are silent.

"You shouldn't have sent Mattern away," he says quietly, a little later.

"You shouldn't have hit me."

"I was worked up. Some rules just mustn't be broken. If he reports you—"

"He won't. He could see we were having an argument. That I wasn't exactly available to him right then."

"Even having an argument," he says. "Screaming like that. Both of us. At the very least it could get us sent to the moral engineers."

"I'll fix things with Mattern, Jason. Leave it to me. I'll get him back here and explain, and I'll give him the topping of his life." She laughs gently. "You dumb flippo." There is affection in her voice. "We probably sterilized half the floor with our screeching. What was the sense, Jason?"

"I was trying to make you understand something about yourself. Your essentially archaic psychological makeup, Micaela. If you could only see yourself objectively, the pettiness of a lot of your motivations lately—I don't want to start another fight, I'm just trying to explain things now—"

"And your motivations, Jason? You're just as archaic as I am. We're both throwbacks. Our heads are both full of primitive moralistic reflexes. Isn't that so? Can't you see it?"

He walks away from her. Standing with his back to her, he fingers the rubbing-node set into the wall near the cleanser, and lets some of the tensions flow from him into it. "Yes," he says after a long while. "Yes, I see it. We have a veneer of urbmonism. But underneath—jealousy, envy, possessiveness—"

"Yes. Yes."

"And you see what discovering this does to my work, of course?" He manages a chuckle. "My thesis that selective breeding has produced a new species of human in the urbmons? Maybe so, but *I* don't belong to the species. *You* don't belong. Maybe *they* do, some of them. But how many? How many, really?"

She comes up behind him and leans close. He feels her nipples against his back. Hard, tickling him. "Most of them, perhaps," she says. "Your thesis may still be right. But we're wrong. We're out of place."

"Yes."

"Throwbacks to an uglier age."

"Yes."

"So we've got to stop torturing each other, Jason. We have to wear better camouflage. Do you see?"

"Yes. Otherwise we'll end up going down the chute. We're unblessworthy, Micaela."

"Both of us."

"Both of us."

He turns. His arms surround her. He winks. She winks.

"Vengeful barbarian," she says tenderly.

"Spiteful savage," he whispers, kissing her earlobe.

They slip together onto the sleeping platform. The nightwalkers will simply have to wait.

He has never loved her as much as he does this minute.

5

In Louisville, Siegmund Kluver still feels like a very small boy. He cannot persuade himself that he has any rightful business up there. A prowling stranger. An illicit intruder. When he goes up to the city of the urbmon's masters a strange boyish shyness settles over him that he must consciously strive to hide. He finds himself forever wanting to peer nervously over his shoulder. Looking for the patrols that he fears will intercept him. The stern brawny figure blocking the wide corridor. What are you doing here, son? You shouldn't be wandering around on these floors. Louisville is for the administrators, don't you know that? And Siegmund will babble excuses, his face blazing. And rush for the dropshaft.

He tries to keep this silly sense of embarrassment a secret. He knows it doesn't fit with the image of himself that everyone else sees. Siegmund the cool customer. Siegmund the man of destiny. Siegmund who was obviously Louisville-bound from childhood. Siegmund the swaggering cocksman, plowing his way lustily through the finest womanhood Urban Monad 116 has to offer.

If they only knew. Underneath it all a vulnerable boy. Underneath it a shy, insecure Siegmund. Worried that he's climbing too fast. Apologizing to himself for his success. Siegmund the humble, Siegmund the uncertain.

Or is that just an image too? Sometimes he thinks that this hidden Siegmund, this private Siegmund, is merely a façade that he has erected so that he can go on liking himself, and that beneath this subterranean veneer of shyness, somewhere beyond the range of his insight, lies the real Siegmund, every bit as ruthless and cocky and rung-grabbing as the Siegmund that the outer world sees.

He goes up to Louisville nearly every morning, now. They requisition him as a consultant. Some of the top men there have made a pet of him—Lewis Holston, Nissim Shawke, Kipling Freehouse, men at the very highest levels of authority. He knows they are exploiting him, dumping on him all the dreary, tedious jobs they don't feel like handling themselves. Taking advantage of his ambitions. Siegmund, prepare a report on working-class mobility patterns. Siegmund, run a tabulation of adrenal balances in the middle cities. Siegmund, what's the waste-recycling ratio this month? Siegmund. Siegmund. Siegmund. But he exploits them too. He is rapidly making himself indispensable, as they slide into the habit of using him to do their thinking. In another year or two, beyond much doubt, they will have to ask him to move up in the building. Perhaps they'll jump him from Shanghai to Toledo or Paris; more likely they'll take him right into Louisville at the next vacancy. Louisville before he's twenty! Has anyone ever done that before?

By that time, maybe, he'll feel comfortable among the members of the ruling class.

He can see them laughing at him behind their eyes. They made it to the top so long ago that they've forgotten that others still have to strive. To them, Siegmund knows, he must seem comical—an earnest, pushy little rung-grabber, his gut afire with the upward urge. They tolerate him because he's capable—more capable, maybe, than most of them. But they don't respect him. They think he's a fool for wanting so badly something that they've had time to grow bored with.

Nissim Shawke, for instance. Possibly one of the two or three most important men of the urbmon. (Who is the *most* important? Not even Siegmund knows. At the top level, power becomes a blurry abstraction; in one sense everybody in Louisville has absolute authority over the entire building, and in another sense no one has.) Shawke is about sixty, Siegmund supposes. Looks much younger. A lean, athletic, olive-skinned man, cool-eyed, physically powerful. Alert, wary, a man of great tensile strength. He gives the illusion of being enormously dynamic. A teeming reservoir of potential. Yet so far as Seigmund can see, Shawke does nothing at all. He refers all governmental matters to his subordinates; he glides through his offices at the crest of the urbmon as though the building's problems are mere phantoms. Why should Shawke strive? He's at the summit. He has everybody fooled, everyone but Siegmund, perhaps. Shawke need not *do* but only *be*. Now he marks time and enjoys the comforts of his position. Sitting there like a Renaissance prince. One word from Nissim Shawke could send almost anybody down the chute. A single memorandum from him might be able to reverse some of the urbmon's most deeply cherished policies. Yet he originates no programs, he vetoes no proposals, he ducks all challenges. To have such power, and to refuse to exercise it, strikes Siegmund as making a joke out of the whole idea of power. Shawke's passivity carries implied contempt for Siegmund's values. His sardonic smile mocks all ambition. It denies that there is merit in serving society. I am here, Shawke says with every gesture, and that is sufficient for me; let the urbmon look after itself; anyone

who voluntarily assumes its burdens is an idiot.
Siegmund, who yearns to govern, finds that Shawke
blights his soul with doubt. What if Shawke is right?
What if I get to his place fifteen years from now and
discover that it's all meaningless? But no. Shawke is sick,
that's all. His soul is empty. Life *does* have a purpose,
and service to the community fulfills that purpose. I am
well qualified to govern my fellow man; therefore I
betray mankind and myself as well if I refuse to do my
duty. Nissim Shawke is wrong. I pity him.

But why do I shrivel when I look into his eyes?

Then there is Shawke's daughter, Rhea. She lives in
Toledo, on the 900th floor, and is married to Kipling
Freehouse's son Paolo. There is a great deal of intermar-
riage among the families of Louisville. The children of
the administrators do not generally get to live in Louisville themselves; Louisville is reserved for those who
actually govern. Their children, unless they happen to
find places of their own in the ranks of the administrators, live mostly in Paris and Toledo, the cities immediately below Louisville. They form a privileged enclave
there, the offspring of the great. Siegmund does much
of his nightwalking in Paris and Toledo. And Rhea
Shawke Freehouse is one of his favorites.

She is ten years older than Siegmund. She has her
father's wiry, supple form: a lean, somewhat masculine
body, with small breasts and flat buttocks and long solid
muscles. Dark complexion; eyes that glitter with private
amusement; a sharp elegant nose. She has only three
littles. Siegmund does not know why her family is so
small. She is quick-witted, knowing, well-informed. She
is more nearly bisexual than anyone Siegmund knows;
he finds her tigerishly passionate, but she has told him

also of the joy she takes in loving other women. Among her conquests has been Siegmund's wife Mamelon, who, he thinks, is in many ways a younger version of Rhea. Perhaps that's why he finds Rhea so attractive: she combines all that he finds most interesting about Mamelon and Nissim Shawke.

Siegmund was sexually precocious. He made his first erotic experiments in his seventh year, two years ahead of the urbmon norm. By the time he was nine he was familiar with the mechanics of intercourse, and consistently drew the highest marks in his physical relations class, doing so well that he was allowed to enroll with the eleven-year-olds. Puberty began for him at ten; at twelve he married Mamelon, who was more than a year his senior; shortly he had her pregnant and the Kluvers were on their way out of the Chicago newlywed dorm and off to an apartment of their own in Shanghai. Sex always has seemed agreeable to him for its own sake, but lately he has come to realize its value in building character.

He nightwalks assiduously. Young women bore him; he prefers those who are past twenty, like Principessa Mattern and Micaela Quevedo of Shanghai. Or Rhea Freehouse. Women of their experience tend to be better in bed than most adolescents, of course. Not that that is his prime concern. One slot isn't ever that much better than another, and the pursuit of slot for its own sake is no longer very important to him; Mamelon can give him all the physical pleasure he needs. But he feels that these older women teach him a great deal about the world, sharing their experience with him in an implicit way. From them he draws subtle insights into the dynamics of adult life, the crises, conflicts, rewards, depths of character. He loves to learn. His own maturity, he is convinced, stems from his extensive sexual encounters with women of the older generation.

Mamelon tells him that he is generally believed to nightwalk even in Louisville. This is in fact not so. He had never dared. There are women up there who tempt him, women in their thirties and forties, even some younger ones, such as Nissim Shawke's second wife, who is hardly older than Rhea. But the self-confidence that makes him seem so awesome to his peers vanishes at the thought of topping the wives of the administrators. It is bold enough for him to venture out of Shanghai to use women of Toledo or Paris. But Louisville? To slip into bed with Shawke's wife, and then have Shawke himself arrive, smiling coldly, saluting, offering him a bowl of tingle—hello, Siegmund, are you having a good time? No. Maybe five years from now, when he's living in Louisville himself. Not yet. But he does have Rhea Shawke Freehouse and some others of her stature. Not bad for a start.

In Nissim Shawke's lavishly furnished office. There's space to waste in Louisville. Shawke has no desk; he conducts his business, such that it is, from a gravity-web slung hammock-fashion near the broad gleaming window. It is midmorning. The sun is high. From here one has a stunning view of the neighboring urbmons. Siegmund enters, having received a summons from Shawke five minutes before. Uneasily he meets Shawke's cold gaze. Trying not to look too humble, too obsequious, too defensive, too hostile. "Closer," Shawke orders. Playing his usual game. Siegmund crosses the immense room. He must stand virtually nose-to-nose with Shawke. A mockery of intimacy; instead of forcing Siegmund to remain at a distance, as one usually requires of subordinates, he brings him so close that it is impossible for Siegmund to keep his eyes locked on both of Shawke's. The image wanders; the strain is painful. Sharp focus is lost and the features of the older man seem distorted. In a casual, barely audible voice, Shawke says, "Will you take care of this?" and flips a message cube to Siegmund. It is, Shawke explains, a petition from the civic council of Chicago requesting a liberalization of the urbmon's sex-ratio restrictions. "They want more freedom to pick the sex of their children," Shawke says. "Claiming that the present rules unnecessarily violate individual liberties and are generally unblessworthy. You can play it later for the details. What do you think, Siegmund?"

Siegmund examines his mind for whatever theoretical information it may contain on sex-ratio questions. Not much there. Work intuitively. What kind of advice does Shawke want? He usually wants to be told to leave things just as they are. All right. How, now, to justify the sex-ratio rules without seeming intellectually lazy? Siegmund improvises swiftly. His gift is an easy penetration into the logic of administration.

He says, "My impulse is to tell you to refuse the request."

"Good. Why?"

"The basic dynamic thrust of an urban monad has to be toward stability and predictability, and away from randomness. The urbmon can't expand physically, and our facilities for offloading surplus population aren't all that flexible. So we need to program orderly growth, above all else."

Shawke squints at him chillingly and says, "If you

don't mind the obscenity, let me tell you that you sound exactly like a propagandist for limiting births."

"No!" Siegmund blurts. "God bless, no! Of *course* there's got to be universal fertility!" Shawke is silently laughing at him again. Goading, baiting. A streak of sadism his main diversion in life. "What I was getting at," Siegmund continues doggedly, "is that within the framework of a society that encourages unlimited reproduction, we've got to impose certain checks and balances to prevent disruptive destabilizing processes. If we allow people to pick the sex of their children themselves, we could very possibly get a generation that's 65 percent male and 35 percent female. Or vice versa, depending on whims and fads of the moment. If that happened, how would we deal with the uncoupled surplus? Where would the extras go? Say, 15,000 males of the same age, all with no available mates. Not only would we have extraordinarily unblessworthy social tensions—imagine an epidemic of rape!—but those bachelors would be lost to the genetic pool. An unhealthy competitive aspect would establish itself. And such ancient customs as prostitution might have to be revived to meet the sexual needs of the unmated. The obvious consequences of an unbalanced sex ratio among a newborn generation are so serious that—"

"Obviously," Shawke drawls, not hiding his boredom.

But Siegmund, wound up in an exposition of theory, cannot easily stop. "Freedom to choose your child's sex would therefore be worse than having no sex-determination processes at all. In medieval times the ratios were governed by random biological events, and naturally tended to gravitate toward a 50-50 split, not taking into account such special factors as war or emigration, which of course would not concern us. But since we *are* able to control our society's sex ratio, we must be careful not to allow the citizens to bring about an arbitrarily gross imbalance. We cannot afford the risk that in a given year an entire city may opt for female children, let's say—and stranger phenomena of mass fancy than that have been known. On compassionate grounds we may allow a particular couple to request and receive permission for, say, a daughter as their next little, but such requests must be compensated for elsewhere in the city in order to ensure the desired overall 50-50 division, even if this causes some distress or inconvenience to certain citizens. Therefore I would recommend a continuation of our present policy of loose control over sex ratios, maintaining the established parameters for free choice but always working within an understood assumption that the good of the urbmon as a whole must be—"

"God bless, Siegmund, that's enough."

"Sir?"

"You've made your point. Over and over. I wasn't asking for a dissertation, just an opinion."

Siegmund feels mashed. He steps back, unable to face Shawke's stony, contemptuous eyes at such close range. "Yes, sir," he murmurs. "What shall I do about this cube, then?"

"Prepare a reply to go out in my name. Covering basically what you've told me, only embellishing it a little, dragging in some scholarly authority. Talk to a sociocomputator and get him to give you a dozen impressive-sounding reasons why free choice of sex would probably lead to an imbalance. Get hold of some historian and ask for figures on what actually happened to society the last time sex-ratio freedom was allowed.

Wrap it all up with an appeal to their loyalty to the larger community. Clear?"

"Yes, sir."

"And tell them, without quite putting it in those words, that the request is refused."

"I'll say we're referring it to the high council for further study."

"Exactly," Shawke says. "How much time will you need for all this?"

"I could have it done by tomorrow afternoon."

"Take three days. Don't hurry it." Shawke makes a gesture of dismissal. As Siegmund leaves, Shawke winks cruelly and says, "Rhea sends her love."

"I don't understand why he has to treat me that way," Siegmund says, fighting to keep the whine out of his voice. "Is he like that with everyone?"

He lies beside Rhea Freehouse. Both of them naked; they have not yet made love tonight. Above them a pattern of lights twines and shifts. Rhea's new sculpture, purchased during the day from one of the San Francisco artists. Siegmund's hand on her left breast. Hard little lump of flesh, all pectoral muscle and mammary tissue, practically no fat in it. His thumb to her nipple.

She says, "Father has a very high regard for you."

"He shows it in a strange way. Toying with me, almost sneering at me. He finds me very funny."

"You're imagining it, Siegmund."

"No. Not really. Well, I suppose I can't blame him. I must seem ridiculous to him. Taking the problems of urbmon life so seriously. Spouting long theoretical lectures. Those things don't matter to him any more, and I can't expect a man to remain as committed to his career at the age of sixty as he was at thirty, but he makes me feel like such an idiot for being committed myself. As if there's something inherently stupid about anyone who's involved with administrative challenges."

"I never realized you thought so little of him," Rhea says.

"Only because he falls so far short of realizing his abilities. He could be such a great leader. And instead he sits up there and laughs at everything."

Rhea turns toward him. Her expression is grave. "You're misjudging him, Siegmund. He's as committed to the community welfare as you are. You're so put off by his manner that you don't see what a dedicated administrator he is."

"Can you give me one example of—"

"Very often," she continues, "we project onto other people our own secret, repressed attitudes. If *we* think, down deep, that something is trivial or worthless, we indignantly accuse other people of thinking so. If we wonder privately if we're as conscientious and devoted to duty as we say we are, we complain that others are slackers. It might just happen that your passionate involvement with administrative affairs, Siegmund, represents more of a desire for mere rung-grabbing than it does a strong humanitarian concern, and you feel so guilty about your intense ambitions that you believe others are thinking about you in the same terms that yourself—"

"Wait! I absolutely deny—"

"Stop it, Siegmund. I'm not trying to pull you down. I'm just offering some possible explanations of your troubles in Louisville. If you'd rather I kept quiet—"

"Go on."

"I'll say just one more thing, and you can hate me

afterward, if you like. You're terribly young, Siegmund, to be where you are. Everybody knows you have tremendous ability, that you *deserve* to be on the brink of going to Louisville, but you're uneasy yourself over how fast you've risen. You try to hide it, but you can't hide it from me. You're afraid that people resent your climb—even some people who are still above you may resent you, you sometimes think. So you're self-conscious. You're extra-sensitive. You read all sorts of terrible things into people's innocent expressions. If I were you, Siegmund, I'd relax and try to enjoy myself more. Don't worry about what people think, or seem to think, about you. Don't fret about grabbing rungs—you're headed for the top, you can't miss, you can afford to slack off and not always worry about the theory of urban administration. Try to be cooler. Less businesslike, less obviously dedicated to your career. Cultivate friendships among people your own age—value people for their own sake, not for where they can help you get. Soak up human nature, work at being more human yourself. Go around the building; do some nightwalking in Warsaw or Prague, maybe. It's irregular, but not illegal, and it'll knock some of the tightness out of you. See how simpler people live. Does any of this make sense to you?"

Siegmund is silent.

"Some," he says finally. "More than some."

"Good."

"It's sinking in. Nobody's ever spoken to me like that before."

"Are you angry with me?"

"No. Of course not."

Rhea runs her fingertips lightly along the line of his jaw. "Do you mind topping me now, then? I'd rather not have to be a moral engineer when I have company on my platform."

His mind is full of her words. He is humiliated but not offended, for much of what she has said rings true. Lost in self-analysis, he turns mechanically to her, caressing her breasts, taking his place between her thighs. His belly against hers. Trying to do combat with a limp sword; he is so preoccupied with the intricacies of her entry into his character that he scarcely notices that he is unable to enter her. She finally makes him aware of the failure of his virility. Playfully dangling him. "Not interested tonight?" she asks.

"Tired," he lies. "All slot and no sleep makes Siegmund a feeble topper."

Rhea laughs. She puts her lips to him and he rises; it was lack of attention, not fatigue, that held him down, and the stimulus of her warm wet mouth returns him to the proper business of the moment. He is ready. Her lithe legs encircle him. With a quick eager thrust he plugs her slot. The only coin with which he can repay her for her wisdom. Now she ceases to be the perceptive, mature arbiter of personality; she is just another writhing woman. She snorts. She bucks. She quivers. Siegmund gives value for value, pumping her full of ecstasy. While he waits for her he thinks about how he must reshape his public image. Not to look ridiculous before the men of Louisville. Much he must do. She trembles now at the abyss of completion, and he pushes her over and follows her, and subsides, sweaty, depressed, when the climax has swept by.

Home again, not long after midnight. Two heads on his sleeping platform. Mamelon is entertaining a nightwalker. Nothing unusual about that; Siegmund knows that his wife is one of the most desired women in the urbmon. For good reason. Standing by the door, he idly watches the humping bodies under the sheet. Mamelon is making sounds of passion, but to Siegmund they sound false and forced, as though she is courteously flattering an incompetent partner. The man grunts hoarsely in his final frenzies. Siegmund feels vague resentment. If you're going to have my wife, man, at least give her a decent time. He strips and cleanses himself, and when he steps out from under the ultrasonic field the pair on the platform lie still, finished. The man gasping. Mamelon barely breathing hard, confirming Siegmund's suspicion that she was pretending. Politely Siegmund coughs. Mamelon's visitor looks up, blinking, red-faced, alarmed. He's Jason Quevedo, the innocuous little historian, Micaela's man. Mamelon is rather fond of him, though Siegmund can't see why. Nor does Siegmund understand how Quevedo manages to cope with that tempestuous woman Micaela. Mine not to reason why. The sight of Quevedo reminds him that he must visit Micaela again soon. Also that he has work for Jason. "Hello, Siegmund," Jason says, not meeting his eyes. Getting off the platform, looking for his scattered clothes. Mamelon winks at her husband. Siegmund blows her a kiss.

He says, "Before you go, Jason. I was going to call you tomorrow, but this'll do. A project. Historical research."

Quevedo looks eager to get out of the Kluver apartment.

Siegmund continues, "Nissim Shawke is preparing a response to a petition from Chicago concerning possible abandonment of sex-ratio regulations. He wants me to get together some background on how it was in the early days of ratio determination, when people were picking their children's sexes without regard to what anyone else was doing. Since your specialty is the twentieth century, I wondered if you could—"

"Yes, certainly. Tomorrow, first thing. Call me." Quevedo edging doorwards. Eager to flee.

Siegmund says, "What I need is some fairly detailed documentation covering first the medieval period of random births, what the sex distribution was, you see, and then going into the early period of control. While you're getting that, I'll talk to Mattern, I guess, get some sociocomputation on the political implications of—"

"It's so late, Siegmund!" Mamelon complains. "Jason said you can talk to him about it in the morning." Quevedo nods. Afraid to walk out while Siegmund is speaking, yet obviously unwilling to stay. Siegmund realizes he is being too diligent again. Change the image, change the image; business can wait. "All right," he says. "God bless, Jason, I'll call you tomorrow." Grateful, Quevedo escapes, and Siegmund lies down beside his wife. She says, "Couldn't you see he wanted to run? He's so hideously shy."

"Poor Jason," Siegmund says. Stroking Mamelon's sleek flank.

"Where did you go tonight?"

"Rhea."

"Interesting?"

"Very. In unexpected ways. She was telling me that I'm too earnest, that I have to try to be more relaxed."

"She's wise," Mamelon says. "Do you agree with her?"

"I suppose so." He dims the lights. "Meet frivolity with frivolity, that's the secret. Take my work casually. I'll try. I'll try. But I can't help getting involved in what I do. This petition from Chicago, for example. Of *course* we can't allow free choice of children's sexes! The consequences would be—"

"Siegmund." She takes his hand and slides it to the base of her belly. "I'd rather not hear all that now. I need you. Rhea didn't use you all up, did she? Because Jason certainly wasn't much good tonight."

"The vigor of youth remains. I hope." Yes. He can manage it. He kisses Mamelon and slips into her. "I love you," he whispers. My wife. My only true. I must remember to talk to Mattern in the morning. And Quevedo. Get the report on Shawke's desk by the afternoon, anyway. If only Shawke *had* a desk. Statistics, quotations, footnotes. Siegmund visualizes every detail of it. Simultaneously he moves atop Mamelon, carrying her to her quick explosive coming.

Siegmund ascends to the 975th floor. Most of the key administrators have their offices here—Shawke, Freehouse, Holston, Donnelly, Stevis. Siegmund carries the Chicago cube and his draft of Shawke's reply, loaded with quotes and data supplied by Charles Mattern and Jason Quevedo. He pauses in the hallway. So peaceful here, so opulent; no littles barging past you, no crowds of working folk. Someday mine. He sees a vision of a sumptuous suite on one of Louisville's residential levels, three or even four rooms, Mamelon reigning like a queen over it all; Kipling Freehouse and Monroe Stevis dropping by with their wives for dinner; an occasional awed visitor coming up from Chicago or Shanghai, an old friend; power and comfort, responsibility and luxury. Yes.

"Siegmund?" A voice from an overhead speaker. "In here, We're in Kipling's place." Shawke's voice. They have picked him up on the scanners. Instantly he rearranges his face, knowing that it must have worn a vacuous, dreaming look. All business now. Angry with himself for forgetting that they might have been watching. He turns left and presents himself outside the office of Kipling Freehouse. The door slides back.

A grand, curving room lined with windows. The glittering face of Urbmon 117 revealed outside, tapering stunningly to its landing-stage summit. Siegmund is startled by the number of top-rank people gathered here. Their potent faces dazzle him. Kipling Freehouse, the head of the data-projection secretariat, a big plump-cheeked man with shaggy eyebrows. Nissim Shawke. The suave, frosty Lewis Holston, dressed as always in incandescently elegant costume. Wry little Monroe Stevis. Donnelly. Kinsella. Vaughan. A sea of greatness. Everyone who counts is here, except only a few; a flippo with a psych-bomb, loose in this room, could cripple the urbmon's government. What terrible crisis has brought them together like this? Frozen in awe, Siegmund can barely manage to step forward. A cherub among the archangels. Stumbling into the making of history. Perhaps they want him here, as if unwilling to take whatever step it is that they're considering without a representative of the coming generation of leaders to give his approval. Siegmund is dizzingly flattered by his own interpretation. I will be part of it. Whatever it is. His self-importance expands and the glare of their aura diminishes, and he moves in something close to a swagger as he approaches them. Then he realizes that there are some others present who might not be thought to belong at any high-powered policy session. Rhea Freehouse? Paolo, her indolent husband? And these girls, no more than fifteen or sixteen, in gossamerwebs or even less: mistresses of the great ones, handmaidens. Everyone knows that Louisville administrators keep extra girls. But here? Now? Giggling on the brink of history? Nissim Shawke salutes Siegmund without rising and says, "Join the party. You name the groover, we've probably got some. Tingle, mindblot, millispans, multiplexers, anything."

Party? Party?

"I've got the sex-ratio report here. Historical data—the socio-computator—"

"Crot that, Siegmund. Don't spoil the fun."

Fun?

Rhea comes toward him. Lurching, blurred, obviously grooving. Yet her keen intelligence showing through the haze of druggedness. "You forgot what I told you. Loosen up, Siegmund." Whispering. Kisses the tip of his nose. Takes his report from him, puts it on Freehouse's desk. Draws her hands across his cheeks; fingers wet. Wouldn't be surprised if she's leaving stains on me. Wine. Blood. Anything. Rhea says, "Happy Somatic Fulfillment Day. We're celebrating. You can have me, if you like, or one of the girls, or Paolo, or anybody else you want." She giggles. "My father, too. Have you ever dreamed of topping Nissim Shawke? Just don't be a spoiler."

"I came up here because I had to give an important document to your father and—"

"Oh, shove it up the access nexus," Rhea says, and turns away from him, her disgust unhidden.

Somatic Fulfillment Day. He had forgotten. The festival will start in a few hours; he should be with Mamelon. But he is here. Shall he leave? They are looking at him. A place to hide. Sink into the undulating psychosensitive carpet. Don't spoil the fun. His mind is still full of the business of the morning. *Whereas the random, or purely biological, determination of the sex of unborn infants normally results by expectable statistical distribution in a relatively symmetrical division of. Removal of the element of chance introduces the danger that. It was the experience of the former city of Tokyo, between 1987 and 1996, that the incidence of birth of female offspring declined by a factor of almost. Risks are not counterbalanced by. Therefore it is recommended that.* The party, he sees, looking more closely, is essentially an orgy. He has been to orgies before, but not with people of this level. Fumes rising. The nakedness of Monroe Stevis. A huddled heap of fleshy girls. "Come on," Kipling Freehouse bellows, "enjoy yourself, Siegmund! Pick a girl, any girl!" Laughter. A wanton child pushes a capsule into his hand. He is trembling, and it drops. Seized and gobbled by one of the other girls. People are still coming in. Dignified, elegant Lewis Holston has a girl on each knee. And one kneeling before him. "Nothing, Siegmund?" Nissim Shawke asks. "You won't have a *thing*? Poor Siegmund. If you're going to live in Louisville, you've got to know how to play as well as work."

Judging him. Testing his compatibility: will he fit in with the elite, or must he be relegated to the ranks of the drudges, the middle-level bureaucracy? Siegmund sees himself demoted to Rome. His ambitions take over. If knowing how to play is the criterion for admission, he'll play. Grins. "I'd like some tingle," he says. Stick to what you know you can handle.

"Tingle, coming up!"

He makes the effort. A golden-hair nymph offers him the tingle bowl; he gulps, pinches her, gulps again. The sparkling fluid popping in his throat. A third gulp. Swill it down; you aren't paying! They cheer him. Rhea nods approval. Clothes are coming off around the room. The amusements of the masters. There must be fifty people in here now. A clap on the back. Kipling Freehouse. Shouting, deafeningly hearty: "You're all right, boy! Worried about you, you know! So serious, so dedicated! Not bad virtues to have, eh, but there's got to be more, you follow? A playful spirit. Eh? Eh?"

"Yes, sir. I know what you mean, sir."

Siegmund dives into the heap. Breasts, thighs, buttocks, tongues. Musky womansmells. A fountain of sensation. Someone pops something into his mouth. He swallows, and moments later feels the back of his skull lift. Laughter. He is being kissed. Forced down against the carpet by his assailant. Gropes and feels small hard breasts. Rhea? Yes. And her husband Paolo closing in on the other side of him. Music blaring from above. In the tangle he discovers himself sharing a girl with Nissim Shawke. A cold wink from him; an icy grin. Shawke testing his capacity for pleasure. Everyone watching him, seeing if he's decadent enough to deserve promotion to their midst. Let yourself go! Let everything go!

Urgently he compels himself to revel. Much depends on this. Below him 974 wondrous floors of urbmon and if he wants to stay up here he must know how to play. Disillusioned that the administrators are like this. So common, so vulgar, the cheap hedonism of a ruling class. They could be Florentine dukes, Parisian grandees, Borgias, drunken boyars. Unable to accept this image of them, Siegmund constructs a fantasy; they have staged this revel solely to test his character, to determine whether he is indeed merely a dreary drudge or if he has the breadth of spirit a Louisville man needs. Folly to think they spend their priceless time swilling and topping like this; but they are flexible, they can enjoy life, they turn from work to play with equal gusto. And if he wants to live among them he must demonstrate equal many-sidedness. He will. He will.

His furry brain swirls with conflicting chemical messages.

"Let's sing!" he yells desperately. "Everybody sing!" Bellowing:

> *"If you come to me by the dark of night*
> *With your blessman all aglow*
> *And you slip down beside me*
> *And try to get inside me—"*

They sing with him. He cannot hear his own voice. Dark eyes peer into his. "God bless," a long rippling lass murmurs. "You're cute. The famous Siegmund Kluver." She belches tingle-bubbles.

"We've met before, haven't we?"

"Once, I think, in Nissim's office. Scylla Shawke."

The great man's wife. Startling in her beauty. Young. Young. No more than twenty-five. He had heard a rumor that the first Mrs. Shawke, Rhea's mother, went down the chute, flippo. Someday he must check on the truth of that. Scylla Shawke wriggles close to him. Her soft black hair dangling in his face. He is almost paralyzed with fear. The consequences; can this be going too far? Recklessly he grabs her and plunges his hand into her tunic. She cooperates. Full warm breasts. Soft moist lips. Can he fail this test by an excess of shamelessness? Never mind. Never mind. Happy Somatic Fulfillment Day! Her body grinds against his, and he realizes, in shock, that it would be no problem to top her right now, here, in this heaving mass of high-level humanity on the floor of Kipling Freehouse's sprawling office. Too far, too fast. He slides free of her grasp. Catching the single flicker of disappointment and reproach in her eyes at his withdrawal. Rolls over: Rhea. "Why didn't you?" she whispers. And Siegmund says, "I couldn't," just before another girl, straddling him, kneels and pours something sweet and sticky into his mouth. He whirls within his skull. "It was a mistake," Rhea tells him. "She was being set up for you." Her words fracture and the pieces rebound, soaring high and drifting about the room. Something strange has happened to the lights; everything has become prismatic, and from all plane surfaces an eerie radiance is streaming. Siegmund crawls through the tumult, searching for Scylla Shawke. Instead he finds Nissim.

"I'd like to discuss the business of the Chicago sex-ratio petition with you now," the administrator tells him.

When Siegmund returns to his apartment hours later, he finds Mamelon pacing grimly about. "Where have you been?" she demands. "Somatic Fulfillment Day's almost over. I've called the access nexus, I've had tracers all over the building, I've—"

"I was in Louisville," Siegmund says. "Kipling Free-house had a party." Stumbles past her. Drops face-down on the sleeping platform. First come the dry sobs, then the tears, and by the time they stop flowing Somatic Fulfillment Day might just as well be over.

6

Interface Crew Nine works in a flat, high strip of gloomy space stretching along the outside of the service core of Urban Monad 116 from the 700th to the 730th floors. Though the work area is lofty, it is scarcely more than five meters deep, a skimpy envelope through which dust motes dance toward sucking filters. Standing within it, the ten men of Interface Crew Nine are sandwiched between the urbmon's outlayer of residential and commercial sectors and its hidden heart, the service core, in which the computers are housed.

The crewmen rarely enter the core itself. They function on its periphery, keeping watch over the looming wall that bears the access nodes of the building's master computer nexus. Soft green and yellow lights gleam on the nodes, constantly relaying information about the health of the unseen mechanisms. The men of Interface Crew Nine serve as the ultimate backup for the platoons of self-regulating devices that monitor the workings of the computers. Whenever heavy load causes some facet of the control system to sag, the crewmen quickly prime it so that it can go on bearing its burden. It is not difficult work, but it is vital to the life of the entire gigantic building.

Each day at 1230, when their shift-time begins, Michael Statler and his nine crewmates crawl through the Edinburgh irishatch on 700 and make their way into the perpetual dusk of the interface to take up their primer

143

stations. Pushchairs carry them to their assigned levels—Michael starts by monitoring the nodes spanning floors 709 to 712—and as the day progresses they slide up and down the interface to the changing zones of trouble.

Michael is twenty-three years old. He has been a computer-primer in this interface crew for eleven years. By now the work is purely automatic for him; he has become simply an extension of the machinery. Drifting along the interface, he boosts or drains, shunts or couples, blends or splits, meeting every need of the computer he serves, and does it all in cool mindless efficiency, operating on reflex alone. There is nothing reprehensible about this. It is not desirable for a primer to think, merely to act correctly; even here in the fifth century of computer technology the human brain is still given a high rating for its information-handling capacity per cubic centimeter, and a properly trained interface crew is in effect a group of ten of these excellent little organically grown computers jacked into the main unit. So Michael follows the shifting patterns of lights, making all necessary adjustments, and the cerebral centers of his mind are left free for other things.

He dreams a great deal as he works.

He dreams of all the strange places outside Urban Monad 116, places that he has seen on the screen. He and his wife Stacion are devoted screen-viewers, and they rarely miss one of the travelog shows. The portrayals of the old pre-urbmon world, of the relicts, the dusty remnants. Jerusalem, Istanbul, Rome. The Taj Mahal. The stumps of New York. The tips of London's buildings above the waves. All the bizarre, romantic, alien places beyond the urbmon's skin. Mount Vesuvius. The geysers

144

of Yellowstone. The African plains. The isles of the South Pacific. The Sahara. The North Pole, Vienna. Copenhagen, Moscow. Angkor Wat. The Great Pyramid and the Sphinx. The Grand Canyon. Chichén Itzá. The Amazon jungle. The Great Wall of China.

Do any of these places still exist?

Michael has no idea. A lot of what they show on the screen is a hundred years old or older. He knows that the spread of urbmon civilization has required the demolition of much that is ancient. The wiping away of the cultured past. Everything carefully recorded in three dimensions first, of course. But gone. A puff of white smoke; the smell of pulverized stone, dry on the nostrils, bitter. Gone. Doubtless they've saved the famous monuments. No need to chew up the Pyramids just to make room for more urbmons. But the big sprawls must have been cleaned away. The former cities. After all, here we are in the Chipitts constellation, and he has heard his brother-in-law Jason Quevedo, the historian, say that once there were two cities called Chicago and Pittsburgh that marked the polar ends of the constellation, with a continuous strip of urban settlement between them. Where are Chicago and Pittsburgh now? Not a trace left, Michael knows; the fifty-one towers of the Chipitts constellation rise along that strip. Everything neat and well-organized. We eat our past and excrete urbmons. Poor Jason; he must miss the ancient world. As do I. As do I.

Michael dreams of adventure outside Urban Monad 116.

Why not go outside? Must he spend all his remaining years hanging here in a pushchair on the interface, tickling access nodes? To go out. To breathe the strange unfiltered air with the smell of green plants on it. To see a river. To fly, somehow, around this barbered planet, looking for the shaggy places. Climb the Great Pyramid! Swim in an ocean, any ocean! *Salt water. How curious.* Stand under the naked sky, exposing his skin to the dread solar blaze, letting the chilly moonlight bathe him. The orange glow of Mars. At dawn to blink at Venus.

"Look, I could do it," he tells his wife. Placid bulgy Stacion. Carrying their fifth little, a girl, coming a few months hence. "It wouldn't be any trouble at all to reprime a node so it would give me an egress pass. And down the shaft and out the building before anybody's the wiser. Running in the grass. Traveling cross-country. I'd go east, I'd go to New York, right by the edge of the sea. They didn't tear New York down, Jason says so. They just went right around it. A monument to the troubles."

"How would you get food?" Stacion asks. A practical girl.

"I'd live off the land. Wild seeds and nuts, like the Indians did. Hunt! The herds of bison. Big, slow brown things; I'd come up behind one and jump on its back, right up there on the smelly greasy hump, and my hands into its throat, *yank*! It wouldn't understand. No one hunts any more. Fall down dead, and I'd have meat for weeks. Even eat it raw."

"There aren't any bison, Michael. There aren't any wild animals at all. You know that."

"Wasn't serious. Do you think I'd really kill? *Kill*? God bless, I may be peculiar, but I'm not crazy! No. Listen, I'd raid the communes. Sneak in at night, grab off vegetables, a load of proteoid steak, anything that's loose. Those places aren't guarded. They don't *expect* urbmon folk to come sneaking around. I'd eat. And I'd see New York, Stacion, I'd see New York! Maybe even find a whole society of wild men there. With boats, planes, something to take me across the ocean. To Jerusalem! To London! To Africa!"

Stacion laughs. "I love you when you start going flippo like this," she says, and pulls him down next to her. Rests his throbbing head on the smooth taut curve of her gravidity. "Do you hear the little yet?" Stacion asks. "Is she singing in there? God bless, Michael, how I love you."

She doesn't take him seriously. Who would? But he'll go. Hanging there on the interface, flipping switches and palming shunt-plates, he envisions himself as a world traveler. A project: to visit all the real cities for which the cities of Urbmon 116 were named. As many as are left. Warsaw, Reykjavik, Louisville, Colombo, Boston, Rome, Tokyo, Toledo, Paris, Shanghai, Edinburgh, Nairobi, London, Madrid, San Francisco, Birmingham, Leningrad. Vienna, Seattle, Bombay, Prague. Even Chicago and Pittsburgh, unless they really are gone. And the others. Did I name them all? He tries to count up. Warsaw, Reykjavik, Vienna, Colombo. He loses track. But anyway, I'll go out. Even if I can't cover the world. Maybe it's bigger than I imagine it is. But I'll see something. I'll feel rain on my face. Listen to the surf. My toes wriggling in cold wet sand. And the sun! The sun, the sun! Tanning my skin!

Supposedly, scholars still travel around, visiting the ancient places, but Michael doesn't know of anyone who has. Jason, though he specializes in the twentieth century, certainly hasn't gone. He could visit the ruins of New York, couldn't he? Get a more vivid feel of what it was like. Of course, Jason is Jason, he wouldn't go even if he could. But he ought to. I'd go in his place. Were we meant to spend all our lives inside a single building? He has seen some of Jason's cubes of the old days, the open streets, the moving cars, the little buildings housing only a single family, three or four people. Incredibly strange. Irresistibly fascinating. Of course, it didn't work; the whole scrambled society fell apart. We have to have something that's better organized. But Michael understands the pull of that kind of life. He feels the centrifugal yank toward freedom, and wants to taste a bit of it. We don't have to live the way they did, but we don't have to live this way, either. Not all the time. To go out. To experience horizontality. Instead of up and down. Our thousand floors, our Somatic Fulfillment Halls, our sonic centers, our blessmen, our moral engineers, our consolers, our everything. There must be more. A short visit outside: the supreme sensation of my life. I'll do it. Hanging on the interface, serenely nudging his nodes downspectrum as the priming impulses impinge on his reflexes, he promises himself that he won't die with his dream unfulfilled. He'll go out. Someday.

His brother-in-law Jason has unknowingly fed the fires of Michael's secret yearning. His theories about a special race of urbmon people, expressed one night when Michael and Stacion were visiting the Quevedos. What had Jason said? *I'm investigating the notion that urbmon life is breeding a new kind of human being. A type that adapts readily to relatively little living space and a low privacy quotient.* Michael had had his doubts about that. It didn't seem like so much of a genetic thing to him, that people were cooping themselves up in urban monads. More like psychological conditioning. Or even voluntary acceptance of the situation in general. But the more Jason spoke, the more sense his ideas made. Explaining why we don't go outside the urbmons, even though there's no real reason why we can't. *Because we recognize that that's a hopeless fantasy. We stay here, whether we like it or not. And those who don't like it, those who eventually can't take it—well, you know what happens to them.* Michael knows. *Down the chute for the flippos. Those who remain adapt to circumstances. Two centuries of selective breeding, pretty ruthlessly enforced. And all of us so well adapted now to this kind of life.*

And Michael saying, *Ah. Yes. All of us so well adapted.* Not believing it was true about all of us.

With some exceptions. Jason's mild concession.

Michael thinks about that, hanging on the interface. No doubt selective breeding accounts for a lot of it. The universal acceptance of urbmon life. Almost universal. Everybody takes it for granted that this is what life is like, 885,000 people under the same roof, a thousand floors, have lots of littles, cuddle up close. Everybody accepts. With some exceptions. A few of us who look through the windows, out at the naked world, and rage and sweat inside our guts. Wanting to get out there. Are we missing the gene for acceptance?

If Jason is right, if the urbmon population's been bred to enjoy the life it has to lead, then there must be a few recessives in the stack. Laws of genetics. You can't eradicate a gene. You just bury it somewhere, but it pops up to haunt you eight generations along the track. Me. In me. I carry the filthy thing. And so I suffer.

Michael decides to confer with his sister about these matters.

He goes to her one morning, 1100 hours, when he's fairly sure of finding her at home. She is, busy with the littles. His luscious twin, only looking a bit harried just now. Her dark hair askew. Her only garment a dirty towel slung over her shoulder. A smudge on her cheek. Looking around, suspicious, as he enters. "Oh. You." She smiles at him. How lovely she looks, all lean and flat like that. Stacion's breasts are full of milk; they swing and joggle, big juicy bags. He prefers supple women. "Just visiting," he tells Micaela. "Mind if I stay awhile?"

"God bless, whatever you like. Don't mind me. The littles are running me up the wall."

"Can I help you?" But she shakes him no. He sits cross-legged, watching her run around the room. Pop this one under the cleanser, that one into the maintenance slot. The others off at school, thank god. Her legs long and lean, her buttocks tight, unpuckered by excess flesh. He is half tempted to top her, right now, only she's too tense from her morning chores. Somehow he hasn't ever done it, at least not in years and years. Not since they were children. He put it into her then, sure, everybody topped his sister. Especially that they were twins; it was natural to get together. A very special closeness, like having an extra self, only female. Asking each other things. She touching him, when they were maybe nine. "What does it feel like, having all that growing between your legs? Dangling. Don't they get in your way when you walk?" And he trying to explain. Later, when she grew her breasts, he asked her the same sort of question. Actually she developed ahead of him. Hair on hers long before he had any on his. And she was bleeding early. That was a kind of gulf between them for a while, she adult, he still a child, and them womb-fellows despite it all. Michael smiles. "If I ask you some things," he says, "will you promise not to tell anyone? Even Jason?"

"Have I ever been a blabber?"

"All right. Just making sure."

She finishes with the littles and sinks down, exhausted, facing him. Lets the towel drape itself on her thighs. Chastely. He wonders what she would think if he asked her to. Oh, yes, she'd do it, she'd have to, but would she want to? Or be uncomfortable about opening it for her brother. She wasn't, once. But that was long ago.

He says, "Have you ever wanted to leave the urbmon, Micaela?"

"To go to another one, you mean?"

"Just to go out. To the Grand Canyon. The Pyramids. Outside. Do you ever feel restless inside the building?"

Her dark eyes glitter. "God bless, yes! Restless. I never thought much about the Pyramids, but there are days when I feel the walls on me like a bunch of hands. Pressing in."

"You too, then!"

"What are you talking about, Michael?"

"Jason's theory. People who've been bred generation after generation to tolerate urbmon existence. And I was thinking, some of us aren't like that. We're recessives. The wrong genes."

"Throwbacks."

"Throwbacks, yes! Like we're out of place in time. We shouldn't have been born now. But when people were free to move around. I know I feel that way. Micaela, I want to leave the building. Just roam around outside."

"You aren't serious."

"I think I am. Not that I'll necessarily do it. But I want to. And that means I'm a, well, a throwback. I don't fit into Jason's peaceful population. The way Stacion does. She loves it here. An ideal world. But not me. And if it's a genetic thing, if I'm really not fit for this civilization, you ought to be the same way. You having all my genes and me all yours. So I thought I'd check. To understand myself better. Finding out how well adjusted *you* are."

"I'm not."

"I knew it!"

"Not that I want to leave the building," Micaela says. "But other things. Emotional attitudes. Jealousy, ambition. I have a lot of unblessworthy stuff in my head, Michael. So does Jason. We had a fight over it only last week." She chuckles. "And we decided that we *were* throwbacks, the two of us. Like savages out of ancient times. I don't want to go into all the details, but yes, yes, basically I think you're right, you and I aren't really urbmon people inside. It's just a veneer. We pretend."

"Exactly! A veneer!" Michael slaps his hands together. "All right. It's what I wanted to know."

"You won't go out of the building, will you?"

"If I do, it'll just be a short while. To see what it's like. But forget I said it." He detects distress in her eyes. Going to her, pulling her up into his arms, he says, "Don't mess me up, Micaela. If I do it, it'll be because I *have* to. You know me. You understand that. So keep quiet until I'm back. If I go."

He has no doubts at all now, except about some of the peripheral problems, like saying good-bye. Shall he slip out without saying a word to Stacion? He'd better; she'd never understand, and she might cause complications. And Micaela. He is tempted to visit her just before he goes. A special farewell. There's no one he's closer to in the entire building, and he might just not return from his outbuilding jaunt. He thinks he'd like to top her, and he suspects she wants him. A loving farewell, just in case. But can he risk it? He mustn't place too much faith in this genetic thing; if she finds out that he's actually planning to leave the urbmon, she might just have him picked up and sent to the moral engineers. For his own sake. No doubt she considers his project a flippo idea. Weighing everything, Michael decides not to say anything to her. He will top her in his mind. Her lips to his, her tongue busy, his hands stroking her springy firmness. The thrust. Their bodies moving in perfect coordination. We are only the sundered halves of a single entity, now joined once more. For this brief moment. It becomes so vivid in his imagination that he nearly abandons his resolution. Nearly.

But in the end he goes without telling anyone.

Done rather easily. He knows how to make the great machine serve his needs. On his regular shift that day he stays a little wider awake than usual, dreams a little less. Monitoring his nodes, riding again on all the fugitive impulses floating through the giant building's mighty ganglia: food requisitions, birth and death statistics, atmospheric reports, a sonic center's amplification level, the replenishment of groovers in the mechanical dispensers, the urine-recycling figures, communications links, et cetera cetera cetera. And as he makes his adjustments he casually fingers a node and obtains a plug-in to the data reservoir. Now he is in direct contact with the central brain, the big machine. It flashes him a string of brassy spurts of golden light: telling him that it is ready to accept repriming. Very well. He instructs it to issue one egress pass for Michael Statler of apartment 70411, obtainable by the said Statler on demand at any terminal and valid until used. Seeing the possibilities for cowardice in that, he amends the order immediately: valid only for twelve hours after issuance. Plus ingress privileges whenever requested. The node flashes him an acceptance symbol. Good. Now he records two messages, noting them down for delivery fifteen hours after the issuance of the egress pass. To Mrs. Micaela Quevedo, apartment 76124. Dear Sister, I did it, wish me luck. I'll bring you some sand from the seashore. And the other message to Mrs. Stacion Statler, apartment 70411. Explaining briefly where he has gone and why. Telling her he'll be back soon, not to worry, this is something he has to do. So much for farewells.

He finishes his shift. Now it is 1730. It makes no sense to leave the building with night coming on. He returns to Stacion; they have dinner, he plays with the littles, they watch the screen awhile, they make love. Maybe the last time. She says, "You seem very withdrawn tonight, Michael."

"Tired. A lot of shunting on the wall today."

She dozes. He cuddles her in his arms. Soft and warm and big, getting bigger every second. The cells dividing in her belly, the magical mitosis. God bless! He is almost unable to bear the idea of going away from her. But then the screen blazes with images of lands afar. The isle of Capri at sunset, gray sky, gray sea, horizon meeting the zenith, roads winding along a cliff overgrown with lush greenery. Here the villa of the Emperor Tiberius. Farmers and shepherds here, living as they did ten thousand years ago, untouched by the changes in the mainland world. No urbmons here. Lovers rolling in the grass, if they want. Pull up her skirt. Laughter; the thorns of berry-laden vines scratching the pink acreage of her buttocks as she pumps beneath you, but she doesn't mind. Hearty hot-slotted peasant wench. An example of obsolete barbarism. You and she get dirty together, soil between your toes and ground into the skin of your knees. And look here, these men in ragged grimy clothes, they're passing a flask of golden wine around, right in the fields where the grapes are grown. How dark their skins are! Like leather, if that's what leather really looked like—how can you be sure? Brown, tough. Tanned by the authentic sun. Far below, the waves roll gently in. Grottoes and fantastic sculptured rocks by the edge of the sea. The sun is gone behind the clouds, and the grayness of sky and shore deepens. A fine mist of rain comes. Night. Birds singing their hymns to the coming of darkness. Goats settling down. He walks the leafy paths, avoiding the hot shining turds, pausing to touch the rough bark of this tree, to taste the sweetness of this swollen berry. He can almost smell the salt spray from below. Sees himself running along the beach at dawn with Micaela, both of them naked, the nightfog lifting, the first crimson light splashing their pale skins. The water all golden. They leap in, swim, float, the salty water giving them buoyancy. They dive and paddle underwater, eyes open, studying each other. Her hair streaming out behind her. A trail of bubbles pursuing her kicking feet. He catches up with her and they embrace far from shore. Friendly dolphins watching them. They engender an incestuous little while coupling in the famous Mediterranean. Where Apollo nailed his sister, didn't he? Or was that another god. Classical echoes all around. Textures, tastes, the chilly bite of the dawn breeze as they drag themselves up on shore, the sand sticking to their wet skins, a bit of seaweed tangled in her hair. A boy with a baby goat coming toward them. *Vino? Vino?* Holding out a flask. Smiling. Micaela petting the goat. The boy admiring her slender naked body. *Si*, you say, *vino*, but of course you have no money, and you try to explain, but the boy doesn't care about that. He gives you the flask. You drink deep. Cold wine, alive, tingling. The boy looks at Micaela. *Un bacio?* Why not, you think. No harm in it. *Si, si, un bacio*, you say, and the boy goes to Micaela, puts his lips shyly to hers, reaches up as though to touch her breasts, then does not dare to, and just kisses. And pulls away, grinning, and goes to you and kisses you too, quickly, and then runs, he and his goat, madly down the beach, leaving you with the flask of wine. You pass it to Micaela. The wine dribbling past her chin, leaving bright beads in the brightening sunlight. When the wine is gone you hurl the flask far out to sea. A gift for the mermaids. You take Micaela's hand. Up the cliff, through the brambles, pebbles turning beneath your bare feet. Textures, changes of temperature, scents, sounds. Birds. Laughter. The glorious isle of Capri. The boy with the goat is just ahead, waving to you from beyond a ravine, telling you to hurry, hurry, come and see. The screen goes dark. You are lying on the sleeping platform beside your drowsy pregnant wife on the 704th floor of Urban Monad 116.

He must leave. He *must* leave.

He gets up. Stacion stirs. "Shhh," he says. "Sleep."

"Going nightwalking?"

"I think so," he says. Strips, stands under the cleanser. Then puts on a fresh tunic, sandals, his most durable clothes. What else shall he take? He has nothing. He will go like this.

Kisses Stacion. *Un bacio. Ancora un bacio.* The last one, perhaps. Hand resting lightly on her belly a moment. She'll get his message in the morning. Good-bye, good-bye. To the sleeping littles. He goes out. Looks upward as if seeing through the intervening fifty-odd floors.

Good-bye, Micaela. Love. It is 0230 hours. Still long before dawn. He will move slowly. Pausing, he studies the walls about him, the metallic-looking dark plastic with the warmth of burnished bronze. A sturdy building, well-designed. Rivers of unseen cables snaking through the service core. And that huge watchful man-made mind in the middle of everything. So easily deceived. Michael finds a terminal in the corridor and identifies himself. Michael Statler, 70411. One egress pass, please. Of course, sir. Here you are. From the slot a gleaming blue circlet for his wrist. Slips it on. Takes the dropshaft down. Gets off at 580 for no particular reason. Boston. Well, he has time to kill. Like a visitor from Venus he wanders the hall, occasionally meeting a sleepy nightwalker on his way home. As is his privilege, he opens a few doors, peers in at the people within, some awake, most not. A girl invites him to share her platform. He shakes his head. "Just passing through," he says, and goes to the drop-shaft. Down to 375. San Francisco. The artists live here. He can hear music. Michael has always envied the San Franciscans. They have purpose in life. They have their art. He opens doors here too.

"Come on," he wants to say, "I have an egress pass, I'm going outside! Come with me, all of you!" Sculptors, poets, musicians, dramatists. He will be the pied piper. But he is not sure his pass will get more than one out of the building, and he says nothing. Down, instead. Birmingham. Pittsburgh, where Jason toils to rescue the past, which is beyond rescue. Tokyo, Prague. Warsaw. Reykjavik. The whole vast building is sitting on his back now. A thousand floors, 885,000 people. A dozen littles are being born as he stands here. A dozen more are being conceived. Maybe someone is dying. And one man is escaping. Shall he say good-bye to the computer? Its tubes and coils, its liquid-filled guts, its tons of skeleton. A million eyes everywhere in the city. Eyes watching him, but it's all right, he has a pass.

First floor. All out.

This is so easy. But where is the exit? *This?* Just a tiny hatch. But he was expecting a grand lobby, onyx floors, alabaster pillars, bright lights, polished brass, a shining swinging glass door. Of course no one important ever uses this exit. High dignitaries travel by quickboat, arriving and departing at the landing stage on the thousandth floor. And the courier pods of farm produce from the communes enter the urbmon far below-ground. Perhaps years at a time go by between each traversal of the first-floor opening. Yet he will. How shall he do it? Holds his egress pass up, hoping there are scanners nearby. Yes. A red light blazes above the hatch. And it opens. And it opens. He goes forward, finding himself in a long, cool tunnel, poorly lit. The hatch door closing behind him. Yes, well, preventing contamination by outside air, he supposes. He waits, and a second door opens in front of him, creaking a little. Michael sees nothing beyond, only darkness, but he goes through the door, and feels steps, seven or eight of them, and descends them, coming unexpectedly to the last. Bump. And then the ground. Strangely spongy, strangely yielding. Earth. Soil. Dirt. He is outside.

He is outside.

He feels somewhat like the first man to walk on the moon. A faltering step, not knowing what to expect. So many unfamiliar sensations to absorb at once. The hatch closing behind him. On his own, then. But unafraid. I must concentrate on one thing at a time. The air, first.

He pulls it deep into his throat. Yes, it has a different taste, sweeter, more alive, a natural taste; the air seems to expand as he breathes it, seeking out the folds and byways of his lungs. In a minute, though, he can no longer isolate the factors of novelty in it. It is simply air, neutral, familiar. As if he has breathed it all his life. Will it fill him with deadly bacteria? He comes from an aseptic, sealed environment, after all. Lying puffed and discolored on the ground in final agonies an hour from now, maybe. Or strange pollen borne by the breeze, sprouting in his nostrils. Choked by massing fungi. Forget the air. He looks up.

Dawn is still more than an hour away. The sky is blue-black; there are stars everywhere, and a crescent moon is high. From the windows of the urbmon he has seen the heavens, but never like this. Head back, legs flung wide, arms outstretched. Embracing the starlight. A billion icy lances striking his body. He is tempted to strip and lie naked in the night until he is starburned, moon-burned. Smiling, he takes another ten steps away from the urbmon. Glancing back then. A pillar of salt. Three kilometers high. It hangs in the air like a toppling mass, terrifying him; he begins to count the floors, but the effort dizzies him and he gives up before the fiftieth. At this angle most of the building is invisible to him, rising so steeply over his head, yet what he sees is enough. Its bulk threatens to crush him. He moves away, into the gardened plaza. The frightening mass of a nearby ur-bmon looms in front of him, at a distance sufficient to give him a truer picture of its size. Jabbing the stars, almost. So much, so much! All those windows. And behind them 850,000 people, or more, whom he has never met. Littles, nightwalkers, computer-primers, consolers, wives, mothers, a whole world up there. Dead. Dead. He looks to his left. Another urbmon, shrouded in the mists of coming day. To his right. Another. He brings his gaze down, closer to earth. The garden. Formal pathways. This is grass. Kneels, breaks off a blade, feels instant remorse as he cradles the green shaft in his cupped hands. *Killer.* He puts the grass in his mouth; not much taste. He had thought it might be sweet. This is soil. Digs his fingertips in. Blackness under his nails. Draws a grooved row through a flower bed. Sniffs a yellow globe of petals. Looks up at a tree. Hand against the bark.

A robot gardener is moving through the plaza, pruning things, fertilizing things. It swings around on its heavy black base and peers at him. Interrogative. Michael holds up his wrist and lets the gardener scan his egress pass. It loses interest in him.

Now he is far from Urbmon 116. Again he turns and studies it, seeing its full height at last. Indistinguishable from 117 and 115. He shrugs and follows a path that takes him out of the line in which the row of urbmons is set. A pool: he crouches beside it, dipping his hand in. Then puts his face to its surface and drinks. Splashes the water gaily. Dawn has begun to stain the sky. The stars are gone, the moon is going. Hastily he strips. Slowly into the pool, hissing when the water reaches his loins. Swims carefully, putting his feet down now and then to feel the cold muddy floor, at last coming to a place where he no longer can touch bottom. Birds singing. This is the first morning of the world. Pale light slides across the silent sky. After a while he comes out of the water and stands dripping and naked by the edge of the pool, shivering a little, listening to the birds, watching the red disk of the sun climbing out of the east. Gradually he becomes aware that he is crying. The beauty of it. The solitude. He is alone at time's first dawn. To be naked is right; I am Adam. He touches his genitals. Looking off afar, he sees three urbmons glowing with pearly light, and wonders which is 116. Stacion in there, and Micaela. If only she was with me now. Both of us naked by this pool. And turning to her, and sinking myself into her. While the snake watches from the tree. He laughs. God bless! He is alone, and not frightened at all by it, no one within sight and he loves it, though he misses Micaela, Stacion, both, each. Trembling. Hard with desire. Dropping to the moist black earth beside the pool. Still crying a little, hot teardrops trickling down his face occasionally, and he watches the sky turn blue, and puts his hand on himself, and bites his lip, and summons his vision of the beach at Capri, the wine, the boy, the goat, the kisses, Micaela, the two of them bare at dawn, and he gasps as his seed spurts. Fertilizing the naked earth. Two hundred million unborn littles in that sticky puddle. He swims again; then he begins to walk once more, carrying his clothes over his arm, and after perhaps an hour he puts them on, fearing the kiss of the soaring sun on his tender indoor hide.

By noon, plazas and pools and formal gardens are far behind, and he has entered the outlying territory of one of the agricultural communes. The world is wide and flat here, and the distant urbmons are glossy brown spikes on the horizon, receding to east and west. There are no trees. No unruly wild vegetation at all, in fact, none of the chaotic tumble of greenery that was so appealing in that tour of Capri. Michael sees long aisles of low plants, separated by strips of bare dark soil, and here and there an entire tremendous field totally empty, as if awaiting seed. These must be the vegetable fields. He inspects the plants: thousands of something spherical and coiled, clutching itself to itself, and thousands of something vertical and grassy, with dangling tassels, and thousands of another kind, and another, and another. As he walks along the crops keep changing. Is this corn? Beans? Squash? Carrots? Wheat? He has no way of matching the product to its source. His childhood geography lessons have faded and run; all he can do is guess, and probably to guess badly. He breaks leaves from this and this and this. He tastes shoots and pods. Sandals in hand, he walks barefoot through the voluptuous turned-up clods of earth.

He thinks he is heading east. Going toward the place where the sun came from. But now that the sun is high overhead it is hard to determine directions. The dwindling row of urbmons is no help. How far is it to the sea? At the thought of a beach his eyes grow damp again. The heaving surf. The taste of salt. A thousand kilometers? How far is that? He works out an analogy. Lay an urbmon on end, then put another one at its tip, and another one beyond that. It will take 333 urbmons, end to end, to reach from here to the sea, if I am a thousand kilometers from the sea now. His heart sinks. And he has no real idea of distances. It might be ten thousand kilometers. He imagines what it would be like to walk from Reykjavik to Louisville 333 times, even horizontally. But with patience he can do it. If only he can find something to eat. These leaves, these stalks, these pods do him no good. Which part of the plant is edible, anyway? Must he cook it? How? This journey will be more complex than he imagined. But his alternative is to scurry back to the urbmon, and he will not do that. It would be like dying, never having lived. He goes on.

Tiring. A little lightheaded from hunger, since he's been on the trek six or seven hours now. Physical fatigue, too. This horizontal walking must use different muscles. Going up and down stairs is easy; riding dropshafts and liftshafts is easier still; and the short horizontal walks along the corridors have not prepared him for this. The ache in the backs of the thighs. The rawness in the ankles, as of bone grating against bone. The shoulders struggling to keep the head held high. Scrambling over this irregular earthy surface multiplies the problem. He rests awhile. Soon afterward he comes to a stream, a sort of ditch, cutting across the fields; he drinks, then strips and bathes. The cool water refreshes him. He goes on, stopping three times to sample the unripened crops. Suppose you get too far from the urbmon to get back, if you begin starving? Struggling through these fields as strength leaves you, trying to drag yourself across the kilometers toward the far-off tower. Dying of hunger amidst all this green plenty. No. He'll manage.

Being alone starts to upset him, too. Something of a surprise, that. In the urbmon he frequently was irritated by the sheer surging multiplicitous masses. Littles underfoot everywhere, clots of women in the halls, that kind of thing. Relishing, in a distinctly unblessworthy way, the daily hours on the interface, in the dimness, no one around him except his nine crewmates and they far away, minding their own nodes. For years cherishing this vision of escaping into privacy, his cruel retrogressive fantasy of solitude. Now he has it, and at the beginning he wept for sheer joy of it, but by afternoon it does not seem so charming. He finds himself darting little hopeful glances to the periphery of his sight, as if he might pick up the aura of a passing human being. Perhaps if Micaela had come with him it would be better. Adam, Eve. But of course she wouldn't have. Only his fraternal twin; not precisely the same genes; she's restless but she'd never have done anything as wild as this. He pictures her trudging beside him. Yes. Stopping now and then to top her in the green crops. But the aloneness is getting him.

He shouts. Calls his name, Micaela's, Stacion's. Cries out the names of his littles. "I am a citizen of Edinburgh!" he bellows. "Urban Monad 116! The 704th floor!" The sounds float away toward the fleecy clouds. How lovely the sky is now, blue and gold and white.

A sudden droning sound out of the—north?—growing louder moment by moment. Harsh, throbbing, raucous. Has he brought some monster upon himself by his noise? Shading his eyes. There it is: a long black tube soaring slowly toward him at a height of, oh, maybe a hundred meters at most. Throws himself to the ground, huddles between the rows of cabbages or turnips or whatever. The black thing has a dozen stubby nozzles protruding along its sides, and from each nozzle spurts a cloudy green mist. Michael understands. Spraying the crops, probably. A poison to kill insects and other pests. What will it do to me? He coils, knees to his chest, hands to his face, eyes closed, mouth buried in palm. That terrible roaring overhead; kill me with decibels if not with your filthy spray. The intensity of the sound diminishes. The thing is past him. The pesticide drifting down, he supposes, trying not to breathe. Lips clamped. Fiery petals dropping from heaven. Flowers of death. There it is, now, a faint dampness on his cheeks, a clinging moist veil.

How soon will it kill him? He counts the passing minutes. Still alive. The flying thing no longer in earshot. Cautiously, he opens his eyes and stands up. Perhaps no danger, then; but he runs through the fields toward the glittering ribbon of a nearby creek, and plunges in, peeling in panic, to scrub himself. And only coming out realizes the creek must have been sprayed too. Well, not dead yet, anyway.

How far is it to the nearest commune?

Somehow, in their infinite wisdom, the planners of this farm have allowed one low hill to survive. Mounting it in midafternoon, Michael takes stock. There are the urbmons, curiously dwindled. There are the cultivated fields. He sees machines, now, moving in some of the rows, things with many arms, possibly pulling up weeds. No sign of a settlement, though. He descends the hill and shortly encounters one of the agricultural machines. The first company he's had all day. "Hello, Michael Statler, from Urbmon 116. What's your name, machine? What kind of work do you do?"

Baleful yellow eyes study him and turn away. The machine is loosening the soil at the base of each plant in the row. Squirting something milky over the roots. Unfriendly filther, aren't you? Or just not programed to talk. "I don't mind," he says. "Silence is golden. If you could just tell me where I could get a little to eat, though. Or find some people."

Droning sound again. Crot! Another stinking cropsprayer! He gets down, ready to curl up again, but no, this flying thing is not spraying, nor does it go past. Hovering overhead, it swings into a tight circle, making an infernal holocaust of noise, and a hatch opens in its belly. Out drops a double strand of fine golden fiber, reaching to the ground. Down it, riding a clip-pod, slides a human being, a woman, followed by a man. They land deftly and come toward him. Grim faces. Beady eyes. Weapons at their waists. Their only garments are glossy red wraps covering them from thigh to belly. Their skins are tanned; their bodies are lean. The man has a stiff, bushy black beard: incredible, grotesque facial hair! The woman's breasts are small and hard. Both of them drawing their weapons now. "Hello!" Michael calls hoarsely. "I'm from an urbmon! Just visiting your country. Friend! Friend! Friend!"

The woman says something unintelligible.

He shrugs. "Sorry, I don't under–"

The weapon poking in his ribs. How cold her face is! The eyes like icy buttons. Will they kill him? Now the man speaks. Slowly and clearly, very loud, as one would speak to a three-year-old. Every syllable an alien one. Accusing him of trespassing in the fields, probably. One of the farming machines must have reported him to the commune. Michael points; the urbmons can still be seen from here. Indicates them, taps his chest. For whatever good that will do. They must know where he's from. His captors nod, unsmiling. A frosty pair. Arrested. Intruder menacing the sanctity of the fields. Woman takes him by the elbow. Well, at least they aren't going to kill him outright. The devilish noisy flying thing still racketing overhead in its narrow orbit. They guide him toward the dangling fiber strands. The woman is in the clip-pod, now. Goes up. Then the man tells Michael something which he suspects means "Now you." Michael smiles. Cooperation his only hope. Figures out how to get into the clip-pod; the man makes the adjustments, locking him in, and up he goes. The woman, waiting above, depods him and pushes him into a webwork cradle. Keeps her weapon ready. A moment later the man is aboard too; the hatch closes and the flying machine goes roaring off. During the flight both of them interrogate him, hurling little jabbing bursts of words at him, but he can only reply apologetically, "I don't speak your language. How can I tell you what you want to know?"

Minutes later the machine lands. They jostle him out onto a bare reddish-brown field. Along its rim he sees low flat-roofed brick buildings, curious snub-fronted gray vehicles, several many-armed farming machines, and dozens of men and women wearing the glossy red loincloths. Not many children; perhaps they're at school, although it's getting late in the day. Everyone pointing at him. Speaking rapidly. Harsh unintelligible comments. Some laughter. He is frightened somewhat, not by the possibility that he is in peril so much as by the strangeness of everything. He knows this must be an agricultural commune. All this day's walking was prelude; he now has truly passed over from one world to another.

The man and woman who captured him push him across the bare field and through the crowd of farming folk into one of the buildings nearby. As he passes, the farmers finger his clothing, touch his bare arms and face, murmur softly. Wonderstruck. Like a man from Mars in their midst. The building is poorly lit, roughly constructed, with crooked walls, low ceilings, warped floors of some pale pocked plastic material. Dumped into a bare, dismal room. A sour smell pervading it: vomit? Before she leaves him, the woman points out the facilities with a few brusque gestures. From this he can get water; it is a basin of some white artificial substance with the texture of smooth stone, yellowing and cracked in places. There is no sleeping platform, but probably he is meant to use the heap of rumpled blankets against one wall. No sign of a cleanser. For excretion he has a single unit, nothing more than a kind of plastic funnel going into the floor, with a button to push when he wishes to clear it. Evidently it is for urine and feces both. An odd arrangement; but then he realizes they wouldn't need to recycle wastes here. The room has no source of artificial light. Through its one window there streams the last feeble sun of the afternoon. The window faces the plaza where the farmers still are gathered, discussing him; he sees them pointing, nodding, nudging each other. There are metal bars on the window, set too close together to permit a man to slip through. A prison cell, then. He checks the door. Locked. How friendly of them. He'll never reach the seacoast this way.

"Listen," he calls to those in the plaza, "I don't mean any harm! You don't need to lock me up!"

They laugh. Two young men stroll over and stare solemnly at him. One of them puts his hand to his mouth and painstakingly covers his entire palm with saliva; when this is done he offers the palm to his companion, who presses his hand against it, and both break into wild laughter. Michael watches, mystified. He has heard about the barbaric customs in the communes. Primitive, incomprehensible. The young men say something contemptuous-sounding to him and walk away. A girl takes their place by his window. Fifteen, sixteen years old, he guesses. Her breasts are large and deeply tanned, and between them hangs an explicit phallic amulet. She fondles it in what strikes him as lascivious invitation. "I'd love to," he says. "If you can only get me out of here." He puts his hands through the bars as if to caress

her. She leaps back, wild-eyed, and makes a fierce gesture, jabbing her left hand at him with the thumb
clenched under and the other four fingers aimed at his
face. Clearly an obscenity. As she goes, some older people
come to stare. A woman taps her chin in slow, steady,
apparently meaningful rhythm; a withered man soberly
presses his left palm to his right elbow three times;
another man stoops, puts his hands on the ground, and
rises, lifting them far above his head, perhaps pantomim-
ing the growth of a lofty plant, perhaps the construction
of an urban monad. Whatever, he breaks into shrill
laughter and stumbles off. Night is coming, now. Through
the dusk Michael sees a succession of cropspraying
machines landing in the plaza like birds returning to the
nest at sundown, and dozens of many-legged mobile
farming units come striding out of the fields. The
onlookers vanish; he watches them going into the other
buildings around the plaza. Despite the uncertainties of
being a prisoner, he is captivated by the alien nature of
this place. To live so close to the ground, to walk about
all day long under the naked sun, to know nothing of
an urbmon's crowded richness—

An armed girl brings him dinner, popping his door
open, setting down a tray, leaving without a word.
Stewed vegetables, a clear broth, some unfamiliar red
fruits, and a capsule of cold wine: the fruits are bruised
and, to his taste, overripe, but everything else is excellent.
He eats greedily, cleaning the tray. Then he goes to the
window. The center of the plaza is still empty, although
at the far side eight or ten men, evidently a maintenance
crew, have gone to work on the farming machines by
the light of three floating luminous globes. His cell now
is in complete darkness. Since there is nothing else to

do, he removes his clothes and sprawls out on the blankets. Though he is exhausted by his long day's trek, sleep will not come at first: his mind ticks furiously, contemplating options. Doubtless they will interrogate him tomorrow. Someone around here must know the language of the urbmons. With luck he can demonstrate that he means no harm. Smile a lot, act friendly, an air of innocence. Perhaps even get them to escort him out of their territory. Fly him eastward, dump him in some other commune's land, let him make his way to the sea. Will he be arrested at commune after commune? A dreary prospect. Maybe he can find a route that bypasses the agricultural zone—through the ruins of some former cities, possibly. Unless there are wild men living there. At least the farmers are civilized, in their fashion. He envisions himself cooked by cannibals in some blasted rubbleheap, the former Pittsburgh, say. Or just eaten raw. Why are the farmers so suspicious? What can one lone wanderer do to them? The natural xenophobia of an isolated culture, he decides. Just as we wouldn't want a farmer loose in an urbmon. But of course urbmons are closed systems. Everybody numbered, inoculated, assigned to a proper place. These folk have a less rigid system, don't they? They don't need to fear strangers. Try convincing them of that.

He drifts into an uneasy sleep.

He is awakened, not more than an hour or two later, by discordant music, raw and disturbing. Sits up: red shadows flickering on the wall of his cell. Some kind of visual projections? Or a fire outside? Rushes to the window. Yes. An immense mound of dried stems, branches, vegetable debris of all sorts, is ablaze in the middle of the plaza. He has never seen fire before, except sometimes on the screen, and the sight of it terrifies and delights him. Those wavering bursts of redness rising and vanishing—where do they go? And he can feel the surging heat even from where he stands. The constant flux, the shifting shape of the dancing flames—how incredibly beautiful! And menacing. Aren't they afraid, letting fire loose like this? But of course there's that zone of bare dirt around it. Fire can't cross that. The earth doesn't burn.

He forces his eyes away from the hypnotic frenzy of the fire. A dozen musicians sit close together to the left of the blaze. The instruments weirdly medieval; everything operated by blowing or pounding or scraping or pressing keys, and the sounds are uneven and imprecise, flickering around the proper pitches but missing by a fraction of a tone. The human element; Michael, whose sense of pitch is unusually good, cringes at these tiny but perceptible variations from the absolute. Yet the farmers don't seem to mind. Unspoiled by the mechanical perfection of modern scientific music. Hundreds of them, perhaps the entire population of the village, sit in ragged rows along the perimeter of the plaza, nodding in time to the wailing, screeching melodies, pounding their heels against the ground, rhythmically clapping their hands to their elbows. The light of the fire transforms them into an assemblage of demons; the red glow ripples eerily over their half-nude bodies. He sees children among them, but still not very many. Two here, three there, many adult couples with one or none. Stunned by the realization: *they limit births here.* His skin crawls. He is amused by his own involuntary reaction of horror; it tells him that no matter what configuration his genes may have, he is by conditioning a man of the urbmons.

The music grows even wilder. The fire soars. The

farmers begin to dance. Michael expects the dancing to be amorphous and frantic, a helter-skelter flinging-out of arms and legs, but no: surprisingly, it is tight and disciplined, a controlled and formal series of movements. Men in this row, women in that; forward, back, interchange partners, elbows high, head thrown back, knees pumping, now hop, turn around, form lines again, link hands. The pace constantly accelerating, but the rhythms always distinct and coherent. A ritualized progression of patterns. Eyes glazed, lips tight. This is no revel, he is suddenly aware; it is a religious festival. The rites of the commune people. What are they building toward? Is he the sacrificial lamb? Providence has sent them an urbmon man, eh? Panicky, he looks about for signs of a caldron, a spit, a stake, anything on which they might cook him. Tales of the communes circulate gaudily in the urbmon; he has always dismissed them as ignorant myths. But possibly not.

When they come for him, he decides, he will lunge and attack them. Better to be shot down quickly than to die on the village altar.

Yet half an hour passes, and no one has even looked in the direction of his cell. The dancing has continued without a break. Oiled with sweat, the farmers seem like dream figures, glittering, grotesque. Bare breasts bobbling; nostrils distended, eyes aglow. New boughs on the fire. The musicians goading one another into fresh frenzies. And now, what's this? Masked figures parading solemnly into the plaza: three men, three women. Faces hidden by intricate spherical constructions, nightmarish, bestial, garish. The women carry oval baskets in which can be seen products of the commune: seeds, dried ears of corn, ground meal. The men encircle a seventh person, a woman, two of them tugging at her arms and one pushing her from behind. She is pregnant, well along, into her sixth or even seventh month. She wears no mask, and her face is tense and rigid, the lips clamped, the eyes wide and frightened. They fling her down before the fire, and stand flanking her. She kneels, head drooping, long hair almost touching the ground, swollen breasts swaying with each ragged intake of breath. One of the masked men—it is impossible not to think of them as priests—intones a resonant invocation. One of the masked women places an ear of corn in each hand of the pregnant one. Another sprinkles her back with meal; it sticks to her sweaty skin. The third scatters seeds in her hair. The other two men join the chant. Michael, gripping the bars of his cell, feels as though he has been hurled thousands of years back in time, to some Neolithic festival; it is almost impossible for him to believe that one day's march from here there rises the thousand-story bulk of Urban Monad 116.

They have finished anointing the pregnant woman with produce. Now two of the priests lift her, shaking, to a standing position, and one of the priestesses rips away her single garment. A howl from the villagers. They spin her around. Displaying her nakedness to all. The heavy protruding belly, drum-tight, glistening in the firelight. The broad hips and solid thighs, the meaty buttocks. Sensing something sinister just ahead, Michael presses his face against the bars, fighting off terror. Is she and not he the sacrificial victim? A flashing knife, the unborn fetus ripped from the womb, a devilish propitiation of the harvest gods? Please, no. Maybe he is to be the chosen executioner. His feverish imagination, unbidden, supplies the scenario: he sees himself taken from the cell, thrust into the plaza, a sickle pushed into his hand, the woman lying spread-eagled near the fire, belly upturned, the priests chanting, the priestesses leaping, and in pantomime they tell him what he must do, they indicate the taut curve of her body, draw their fingers across the preferred place of incision, while the music climbs toward insanity and the fire flares ever higher, and. No. No. He turns away, flinging one arm over his eyes. Shivering, nauseated. When he can bring himself to look again, he sees that the villagers are getting up and dancing toward the fire, toward the pregnant woman. She stands flatfooted, bewildered, clutching the ears of corn, pressing her thighs together, wriggling her shoulders in a way that somehow indicates she is shamed by her nudity. And they caper around her. Shouting raucous abuse. Making the four-fingered jab of contempt. Pointing, mocking, accusing. A condemned witch? An adulteress? The woman shrinks into herself. Suddenly the mob closes in on her. He sees them slapping her, pushing her, spitting at her. God bless, no! "Let her alone!" he screams. "You filthy grubbos, get your hands off her!" His wails are drowned by the music. A dozen or so farmers now ring the woman and they are shoving her back and forth. A double-handed push; she staggers, barely managing to stay upright, and stumbles across the ring, only to be seized by her breasts and slammed back the other way. She is panting, wild with terror, searching for escape, but the ring is tight, and they fling her around. when at last she drops, they tug her upright and toss her some more, grabbing her arms and whirling her from hand to hand around the ring. Then the circle opens. Other villagers sweep toward her. More abuse. The blows all are open-handed ones, and no one seems

to hit her belly, yet they are delivered with great force;
a trickle of blood stains her chin and throat, and one
knee and one buttock are scraped raw from when she
has been knocked to the ground. She is limping, too; she
must have turned an ankle. Vulnerable as she is in her
nakedness, she makes no attempt to defend herself or
even to protect her pregnancy. Clutching the ears of corn,
she simply accepts her torment, letting herself be hurled
about, allowing the vindictive hands to poke and pinch
and slap her. The mob surges about her, everyone having
a turn. How much more can she take? Is the idea to beat
her to death? To make her drop her baby while they
watch? He has never imagined anything so chilling. He
feels the blows as if they are landing on his own body.
If he could, he would strike these people dead with
thunderbolts. Where is their respect for life? That woman
should be sacred, and instead they torture her.

She vanishes under a horde of screaming attackers.

When they clear away, a minute or two later, she is
kneeling, half-conscious, close to collapse. Her lips writhe
in hysterical choking sobs. Her entire body is trembling.
Her head hangs forward. Someone's clawed hand has
left a series of parallel bloody tracks across the globe of
her right breast. She is smudged everywhere with dirt.

The music grows oddly soft, as if some climax is
approaching and momentum must be gained. Now they
come for me, Michael thinks. Now I'm supposed to kill
her, or top her, or kick her in the belly, or god knows
what. But no one even looks toward the building in
which he is jailed. The three priests are chanting in uni-
son; the music gains gradually in intensity; the villagers
fall back, clustering along the perimeter of the plaza.
And the woman rises, shakily, uncertainly. Looks down

at her bloodied and battered self. Face wholly blank; she is beyond pain, beyond shame, beyond terror. Slowly walks toward the fire. Stumbles once. Recovers, stays upright. Now she stands by the edge of the fire, almost within reach of the licking tongues of flame. Her back to him. Plump heavy rump, deeply dimpled. Scratches on her back. Wide pelvis, the bone's spreading out as the little's time approaches. The music is deafening now. The priests silent, frozen. Obviously the great moment. Does she leap into the flames?

No. Raises her arms. The ears of corn outlined against the brightness of the fire. Throws them in: two quick flares and they vanish. An immense roar from the villagers, a tremendous crashing discord from the musicians. The naked woman stumbles away from the fire, tottering, exhausted. Falls, landing with a thump on her left haunch, lies there sobbing. Priests and priestesses march into the darkness with stiff, pompous strides. The villagers simply fade away, leaving only the woman crumpled in the plaza. And a man coming toward her, a tall, bearded figure; Michael remembers seeing him in the midst of the mob when they were beating her. Lifts her now. Cradles her tenderly against him. Kisses her scratched breast. Runs his hand lightly over her belly, as though assuring himself that the child is unharmed. She clings close. He talks softly to her; the strange words drift across to Michael's cell. She replies, stammering, her voice thick with shock. Unbothered by her weight, the man slowly carries her away, toward one of the buildings on the opposite side of the plaza. All is still, now. Only the fire remains, crackling harshly, crumbling in upon itself. When after a long while no one appears, Michael turns away from his window and, stunned, baffled, throws himself on his blankets. Silence. Darkness. Images of the bizarre ceremony churn in his mind. He shivers; he trembles; he feels almost at the edge of tears. Finally he sleeps.

The arrival of breakfast awakens him. He studies the tray a few minutes before forcing himself to get up. Stiff and sore from yesterday's walking; every muscle protesting. Doubled up, he hobbles to the window: a heap of ashes where the fire had been, villagers moving about on their morning chores, the farming machines already heading toward the fields. He splashes water in his face, voids his wastes, looks automatically for the cleanser, and, not finding it, begins to wonder how he will tolerate the crust of grime that has accumulated on his skin. He had not realized before how ingrained a habit it was for him to get under the ultrasonic wave at the beginning of each day. He goes then to the tray: juice, bread, cold fruit, wine. It will do. Before he is finished eating, his cell door opens and a women enters, clad in the usual brief commune costume. He knows instinctively that she is someone of importance; her eyes have the clear cold light of authority, and her expression is an intelligent, perceptive one. She is perhaps thirty years old, and like most of these farming women her body is lean and taut, with supple muscles, long limbs, small breasts. She reminds him in some ways of Michael, although her hair is auburn and close-cropped, not long and black. A weapon is strapped to her left thigh.

"Cover yourself," she says briskly. "I don't welcome the sight of your nakedness. Cover yourself, and then we can talk."

She speaks the urbmon tongue! A strange accent, true, with every word cut short as if her sharp shining teeth have clipped its tail as it passes her lips. The vowels blurred and distorted. But unmistakably the language of his native building. Immense relief. Communication at last.

He pulls his clothing hastily on. She watches him, stony-faced. A tough one, she is. He says, "In the urbmons we don't worry much about covering our bodies. We live in what we call a post-privacy culture. I didn't realize—"

"You don't happen to be in an urbmon just now."

"I realize that. I'm sorry if I've given offense through my ignorance of your customs."

He is fully dressed. She seems to soften a bit, perhaps at his apology, perhaps merely because he has concealed his nudity. Taking a few steps farther into the room, she says, "It's a long time since we've had a spy from your people among us."

"I'm not a spy."

A cool, skeptical smile. "No? Then why are you here?"

"I didn't intend to trespass on your commune's land. I was just passing through, heading eastward. On my way toward the sea."

"Really?" As though he had said he had set out to walk to Pluto. "Traveling alone, are you?"

"I am."

"When did this marvelous journey begin?"

"Yesterday morning, very early," Michael says. "I'm from Urban Monad 116. A computer-primer, if that means anything to you. Suddenly I felt I couldn't stay inside that building any more, that I had to find out what the outside world was like, and so I arranged to get an egress pass and slipped out just before dawn, and started walking, and then I came to your fields and your machines saw me, I guess, and I was picked up, and because of the language problem I couldn't explain to anyone who I—"

"What do you hope to gain by spying on us?"

His shoulders slump. "I told you," he says wearily. "I'm not a spy."

"Urbmon people don't slip out of their buildings. I've dealt with your kind for years; I know how your minds work." Her eyes level with his. Cold, cold. "You'd be paralyzed with terror five minutes after you set out," she assures him. "Obviously you've been trained for this mission, or you'd never have been able to keep your sanity for a full day in the fields. What I don't understand is why they'd send you. You have your world and we have ours; there's no conflict, no overlapping; there's no need for espionage."

"I agree," Michael says. "And that's why I'm not a spy." He finds himself drawn to her despite the severity of her attitude. Her competence and self-confidence attract him. And if she would only smile she would be quite beautiful. He says, "Look, how can I get you to believe this? I just wanted to see the world outside the urbmon. All my life indoors. Never smelling fresh air, never feeling the sun on my skin. Thousands of people living on top of me. I'm not really well adjusted to urbmon society, I discovered. So I went outside. Not a spy. All I want to do is travel. To the sea, particularly. Have you ever seen the sea?...No? That's my dream—to walk along the shore, to hear the waves rolling in, to feel the wet sand under my feet—"

Possibly the fervor in his tone is beginning to convince her. She shrugs, looking less flinty, and says, "What's your name?"

"Michael Statler."

"Age?"

"Twenty-three."

"We could put you aboard the next courier pod, with the fungus shipment. You'd be back at your urbmon in half an hour."

"No," he says softly. "Don't do that. Just let me keep going east. I'm not ready to go back so soon."

"Haven't gathered enough information, you mean?"

"I told you, I'm not—" He stops, realizing she is teasing him.

"All right. Maybe you aren't a spy. Just a madman, perhaps." She smiles, for the first time, and slides down until she is squatting against the wall, facing him. In an easy conversational tone she says, "What do you think of our village, Statler?"

"I don't even know where to begin answering that."

"How do we strike you? Simple? Complicated? Evil? Frightening? Unusual?"

"Strange," he says.

"Strange in comparison to the kind of people you've lived among, or just strange, absolutely?"

"I'm not sure I know the distinction. It's like another world out here, anyway. I—I—what's your name, by the way?"

"Artha."

"Arthur? Among us that's a man's name."

"A-R-T-H-A."

"Oh. Artha. How interesting. How beautiful." He knots his fingers tightly. "The way you live so close to the soil here, Artha. There's something dreamlike about that for me. These little houses. The plaza. Seeing you walking around in the open. The sun. Building fires. Not having any upstairs or downstairs. And that business last night, the music, the pregnant woman. What was that all about?"

"You mean the unbirth dance?"

"Is *that* what it was? Some kind of"—he falters—"sterility rite?"

"To ensure a good harvest," Artha says. "To keep the crops healthy and childbirths low. We have rules about breeding, you understand."

"And the woman everybody was hitting—she got pregnant illegally, is that it?"

"Oh, no." Artha laughs. "Milcha's child is quite legal."

"Then why—tormenting her like that—she could have lost the child—"

"Someone had to do it," Artha tells him. "The commune has eleven pregnants, just now. They drew lots and Milcha lost. Or won. It isn't punishment, Statler. It's a religious thing: she's the celebrant, the holy scapegoat, the—the—I don't have the words in your language. Through her suffering she brings health and prosperity upon the commune. Ensuring that no unwanted children will come into our women, that all will remain in perfect balance. Of course, it's painful for her. And there's the shame, being naked in front of everyone. But it has to be done. It's a great honor. Milcha will never have to do it again, and she'll have certain privileges for the rest of her life, and of course everyone is grateful to her for accepting our blows. Now we're protected for another year."

"Protected?"

"Against the anger of the gods."

"Gods," he says quietly. Swallowing the word and

trying to comprehend it. After a moment he asks, "Why do you try to avoid having children?"

"Do you think we own the world?" she replies, her eyes abruptly fiery. "We have our commune. Our allotted zone of land. We must make food for ourselves and also for the urbmons, right? What would happen to you if we simply bred and bred and bred, until our village sprawled out over half of the present fields, and such remaining food as we produced was merely enough for our own needs? With nothing to spare for you. Children must be housed. Houses occupy land. How can we farm land covered by a house? We must set limits."

"But you don't need to sprawl your village out into the fields. You could build upward. As we do. And increase your numbers tenfold without taking up any more land area. Well, of course, you'd need more food and there'd be less to ship to us, that's true, but—"

"You absolutely don't understand," Artha snaps. "Should we turn our commune into an urbmon? You have your way of life; we have ours. Ours requires us to be few in number and live in the midst of fertile fields. Why should we become like you? We pride ourselves on *not* being like you. So if we expand, we must expand horizontally, right? Which would in time cover the surface of the world with a dead crust of paved streets and roads, as in the former days. No. We are beyond such things. We impose limits on ourselves, and live in the proper rhythm of our way, and we are happy. And so it shall be forever with us. Does this seem so wicked? We think the urbmon folk are wicked, for they will not control their breeding. And even *encourage* breeding."

"There's no need for us to control it," he tells her. "It's been mathematically proven that we haven't begun to exhaust the possibilities of the planet. Our population could double or even triple, and as long as we continued to live in vertical cities, in urban monads, there'd be room for everyone. Without encroaching on productive farmland. We build a new urbmon every few years, and even so the food supplies aren't dininishing, the rhythm of *our* way holds up, and—"

"Do you think this can continue infinitely?"

"Well, no, not infinitely," Michael concedes. "But for a long time. Five hundred years, maybe, at the present rate of increase, before we'd feel any squeeze."

"And then?"

"They can solve that problem when the time comes."

Artha shakes her head furiously. "No! No! How can you say such a thing? To go on breeding, letting the future worry about it—"

"Look," he says, "I've talked to my brother-in-law, who's a historian. Specializes in the twentieth century. Back then it was believed that everybody would starve if the world's population got past five or six billion. Much talk of a population crisis, etc., etc. Well, then came the collapse, and afterward things were reorganized, the first urbmons went up, the old horizontal pattern of land use was prohibited, and guess what? We found there was room for *ten* billion people. And then twenty. And then fifty. And now seventy-five. Taller buildings, more efficient food production, greater concentration of people on the unproductive land. So who are we to say that our descendants won't continue to cope with expanding population, on up to five hundred billion, a thousand billion, who knows? The twentieth century wouldn't have believed it was possible to support this many people on Earth. So if we worry in advance about a problem that may in fact never cause any trouble, if we unblessworthily thwart god by limiting births, we sin against life without any assurance that—"

"Pah!" Artha snorts. "You will never understand us. And I suppose we will never understand you." Rising, she strides toward the door. "Tell me this, then. If the urbmon way is so wonderful, why did you slip away, and go out wandering in our fields?" And she does not stay for an answer. The door clicks behind her; he goes to it and finds that she has locked it. He is alone. And still a prisoner.

A long drab day. No one comes to him, except the girl bringing lunch: in and out. The stench of the cell oppresses him. The lack of a cleanser becomes unbearable; he imagines that the filth gathering on his skin is pitting and corroding it. From his narrow window he watches the life of the commune, craning his neck to see it all. The farming machines coming and going. The husky peasants loading sacks of produce aboard a conveyor belt disappearing into the ground—going, no doubt, to the courierpod system that carries food to the urbmons and industrial goods to the communes. Last night's scapegoat, Milcha, passes by, limping, bruised, apparently exempt from work today; villagers hail her with obvious reverence. She smiles and pats her belly. He does not see Artha at all. Why do they not release him? He is fairly certain that he has convinced her he is no spy. And in any case can hardly harm the commune. Yet here he remains as the afternoon fades. The busy people outside, sweating, sun-tanned, purposeful. He sees only a speck of the commune: outside the scope of his vision there must be schools, a theater, a governmental building, warehouses, repair shops. Images of last night's unbirth

dance glow morbidly in his memory. The barbarism; the
wild music; the agony of the woman. But he knows that
it is an error to think of these farmers as primitive, simple
folk, despite such things. They seem bizarre to him, but
their savagery is only superficial, a mask they don to set
themselves apart from the urban people. This is a complex society held in a delicate balance. As complex as is
his own. Sophisticated machinery to care for. Doubtless
a computer center somewhere, controlling the planting
and tending and harvesting of the crops, that requires a
staff of skilled technicians. Biological needs to consider:
pesticides, weed suppression, all the ecological intricacies.
And the problems of the barter system that ties the
commune to the urbmons. He perceives only the surface
of this place, he realizes.

In late afternoon Artha returns to his cell.

"Will they let me go soon?" he asks immediately.

She shakes her head. "It's under discussion. I've
recommended your release. But some of them are very
suspicious people."

"What do you mean?"

"The chiefs. You know, they're old men, most of them,
with a natural mistrust of strangers. A couple of them
want to sacrifice you to the harvest god."

"Sacrifice?"

Artha grins. There is nothing stony about her now;
she is relaxed, clearly friendly. On his side. "It sounds
horrid, doesn't it? But it's been known to happen. Our
gods occasionally demand lives. Don't you ever take life
in the urbmon?"

"When someone threatens the stability of our society,
yes," he admits. "Lawbreakers go down the chute. In the

combustion chambers at the bottom of the building. Contributing their body mass to our energy output. But—"

"So you kill for the sake of keeping everything running smoothly. Well, sometimes so do we. Not often. I don't really think they'll kill you. But it isn't decided yet."

"When will it be?"

"Perhaps tonight. Or tomorrow."

"How can I represent any threat to the commune?"

"No one says you do," Artha tells him. "Even so, to offer the life of an urbmon man may have positive values here. Increasing our blessings. It's a philosophical thing, not easy to explain: the urbmons are the ultimate consumers, and if our harvest god symbolically consumed an urbmon instead—in a metaphorical way, taking you to stand for the whole society you come from—it would be a mystic affirmation of the unity of the two societies, the link that binds commune to urbmon and urbmon to commune, and—oh, never mind. Maybe they'll forget about it. It's only the day after the unbirth dance; we don't need any more sacred protection so soon. I've told them that. I'd say your chances of going free are fairly good."

"Fairly good," he repeats gloomily. "Wonderful." The distant sea. The ashy cone of Vesuvius. Jerusalem. The Taj Mahal. As far away as the stars, now. The sea. The sea. This stinking cell. He chokes on despair.

Artha tries to cheer him. Squatting close beside him on the tipsy floor. Her eyes warm, affectionate. Her earlier military brusqueness gone. She seems fond of him. Getting to know him better, as though she has surmounted the barrier of cultural differences that made him seem so alien to her before. And he the same with her. The separations dwindling. Her world is not his, but

186

he thinks he could adjust to some of its unfamiliar assumptions. Strike up a closeness. He's a man, she's a woman, right? The basics. All the rest is façade. But as they talk, he is plunged again and again into new awarenesses of how different she is from him, he from her. He asks her about herself and she says she is unmarried. Stunned, he tells her that there are no unmarried people in the urbmons past the age of twelve or thirteen. She says she is thirty-one. Why has someone so attractive never married? "We have enough married women here," she replies. "I had no reason to marry." Does she not want to bear children? No, not at all. The commune has its allotted number of mothers. She has other responsibilities to occupy her. "Such as?" She explains that she is part of the liaison staff handling urbmon commerce. Which is why she can speak the language so well; she deals frequently with the urbmons, arranging for exchanges of produce for manufactured goods, setting up servicing arrangements whenever the commune's machinery suffers a breakdown beyond the skills of the village technicians, and so forth. "I may have monitored your calls occasionally," he says. "Some of the nodes I prime run through the procurement level. If I ever get back home, I'll listen for you, Artha." Her smile is dazzling. He begins to suspect that love is blossoming in this cell.

She asks him about the urbmon.

She has never been inside one; all her contacts with the urban monads come via communications channels. A vast curiosity is evident in her. She wants him to describe the residential apartments, the transport system, liftshafts and dropshafts, the schools, the recreational facilities. Who prepares the food? Who decides what professions the children will follow? Can you move from one city to another? Where do you keep all the new people? How do you manage not to hate each other, when you must live so close together? Don't you feel like prisoners? Thousands of you milling about like bees in a hive—how do you stand it? And the stale air, the pale artificial light, the separation from the natural world. Incomprehensible to her: such a narrow, compressed life. And he tries to tell her about the urbmon, how even he, who chose to flee from it, really loves it. The subtle balance of need and want in it, the elaborate social system designed for minimal friction and frustration, the sense of community within one's own city and village, the glorification of parenthood, the colossal mechanical minds in the service core that keep the delicate interplay of urban rhythms coordinated—he makes the building seem a poem of human relationships, a miracle of civilized harmonies. His words soar. Artha seems captivated. He goes on and on, in a kind of rapture of narrative, describing toilet facilities, sleeping arrangements, screens and data terminals, the recycling and reprocessing of urine and feces, the combustion of solid refuse, the auxiliary generators that produce electrical power from accumulated surplus body heat, the air vents and circulation system, the social complexity of the building's different levels, maintenance people here, industrial workers there, scholars, entertainers, engineers, computer technicians, administrators. The senior citizen dorms, the newlywed dorms, the marriage customs, the sweet tolerance of others, the sternly enforced commandment against selfishness. And Artha nods, and fills in words for him when he leaves a sentence half finished to hurry on to the next, and her face grows flushed with excitement, as if she too is caught up in the lyricism of his account of the building. Seeing for the first time in her life that it is not necessarily brutal and antihuman to pack hundreds of thousands of people into a single structure in which they spend their entire lives. As he speaks he wonders whether he is not letting himself be carried away by his own rhetoric; the words rushing from him must make him sound like an impassioned propagandist for a way of life about which, after all, he had come to have serious doubts. But yet he goes on describing, and by implication praising, the urbmon. He will not condemn. There was no other way for humanity to develop. The necessity of the vertical city. The beauty of the urbmon. Its wondrous complexity, its intricate texture. Yes, of course, there is beauty outside it, he admits that, he has gone in search of it, but it is folly to think that the urbmon itself is something loathsome, something to be deplored. In its own way magnificent. The unique solution to the population crisis. Heroic response to immense challenge. And he thinks he is getting through to her. This shrewd, cool commune woman, raised under the hot sun. His verbal intoxication transforms itself into something explicitly sexual, now: he is communicating with Artha, he is reaching her mind, they are coming together in a way that neither of them would have thought possible yesterday, and he interprets this new closeness as a physical thing. The natural eroticism of the urbmondweller: everyone accessible to everyone else at all times. Confirm their closeness by the direct embrace. It seems like the most reasonable extension of their communion, from the conversational to the copulatory. So close already. Her eyes shining. Her small breasts. Reminding him of Micaela. He leans toward her.

Left hand slipping around her shoulders, fingers groping for and finding her nearer breast. Cupping it. Nuzzles the line of her jaw with his lips, going toward her earlobe. His other hand at her waist, seeking the secret of her one garment. In a moment she'll be naked. His body against hers, approaching congruency. Cunning experienced fingers opening the way for his thrust. And then.

"No. Stop."

"You don't mean that, Artha." Loosening the glossy red wrap now. Clutching the hard little breast. Hunting for her mouth. "You're all tensed up. Why not relax? Loving is blessworthy. Loving is—"

"*Stop it.*"

Flinty again. A sharp-edged command. Suddenly struggling in his arms.

Is this the commune mode of lovemaking? The pretense of resistance? She grasps at her wrap, pushes him with her elbow, tries to bring up her knee. He surrounds her with his arms and attempts to press her to the floor. Still caressing. Kissing. Murmuring her name.

"Get *off.*"

This is a wholly new experience for him. A reluctant woman, all sinews and bone, fighting his advances. In the urbmon she could be put to death for this. Unblessworthy thwarting of a fellow citizen. But this is not the urbmon. This is not the urbmon. Her struggles inflame him; as it is he has gone several days without a woman, the longest span of abstinence he can remember, and he is stiff, agonizingly erect, carrying a blazing sword. No finesse possible; he wants in, as quickly as it can be managed. "Artha. Artha. Artha." Primordial grunts. Her body pinned beneath him. The wrap off; as they fight he catches a glimpse of slender thighs, matted auburn delta.

The flat girlish belly of the unchilded. If he can only get his own clothes off somehow, while holding her down. Fighting like a demon. Good thing she wasn't wearing her weapon when she came in. Watch out, the eyes! Panting and gasping. A wild flurry of hammering fists. The salty taste of blood on his split lip. He looks into her eyes and is appalled. Her rigid, murderous gaze. The harder she fights, the more he wants her. A savage! If this is how she fights, how will she love? His knee between her legs, slowly forcing them apart. She starts to scream; he gets his mouth down on her lips; her teeth hunt for his flesh. Fingernails clawing his back.She is surprisingly strong. "Artha," he begs, "don't fight me. This is insanity. If you'll only—"

"Animal!"

"Let me show you how much I love—"

"Lunatic!"

Her knee suddenly in his crotch. He pivots, avoiding the worst of her attack, but she hurts him anyway. This is no coy game. If he wants to have her, he must break her strength. Immobilize her. Raping an unconscious woman? No. No. It has all gone wrong. Sadness over-whelms him. His lust suddenly subsides. He rolls free of her and kneels near the window, looking at the floor, breathing hard. Go on, tell the old men what I did. Feed me to your god. Naked, standing above him, she sullenly dons her wrap. The harsh sound of her breathing. He says, "In an urbmon, when someone makes sexual advances, it's considered highly improper to refuse him." His voice hollow with shame. "I was attracted to you, Artha. I thought you were to me. And then it was too late for me to stop myself. The whole idea that someone might refuse me—I just didn't understand—"

"What animals you all must be!"

Unable to meet her eyes. "In context, it makes sense. We can't allow explosive frustration-situations. No room for conflicts in an urbmon. But here—it's different, is it?"

"Very."

"Can you forgive me?"

"We couple with those we deeply love," she says. "We don't open for anyone at all who asks. Nor is it a simple thing. There are rituals of approach. Intermediaries must be employed. Great complications. But how could you have known all that?"

"Exactly. How could I?"

Her voice whiplashing with irritation and exasperation. "We were getting along so well! Why did you have to touch me?"

"You said it yourself. I didn't know. I didn't know. The two of us together—I could feel the attraction growing—it was so natural for me to reach out toward you—"

"And it was so natural for you to try to rape me when you felt me resisting."

"I stopped in time, didn't I?"

A bitter laugh. "So to speak. If you call that stopping. If you call that in time."

"Resistance isn't an easy thing for me to understand, Artha. I thought you were playing a game with me. I didn't realize at first that you were refusing me." Looking up at her now. Her eyes holding mingled contempt and sorrow. "It was all a misunderstanding, Artha. Can't we turn time back half an hour? Can't we try to put things together again?"

"I will remember your hands on my body. I will remember your making me naked."

"Don't carry a grudge. Try to look at it from my point

of view. The cultural gulf between us. A different set of assumptions in operation. I—"

She shakes her head slowly. No hope of forgiveness.

"Artha—"

She goes out. He sits alone in the dusk. An hour later, his dinner comes for him. Night descends; he eats with no interest in his food, nursing his bitterness. Engulfed by shame. Although he insists he was not entirely at fault. A clash of irreconcilable cultures. It was so natural for him. It was so natural. And the sadness. Thinking of how close they had come to be before it happened. How close.

Several hours after sundown they begin building a new bonfire in the plaza. He watches gloomily. She has gone to the village elders, then, to tell them of his attack on her. An outrage; they console her and promise vengeance. Now they will surely sacrifice him to their god. His last night of life. All the turmoil of his existence converging on this day. No one to grant a final wish. He'll die miserably, his body unclean. Far from home. So young. Jangling with unfulfilled desires. Never to see the sea.

And what's this, now? A farming machine being trundled up close to the fire, a giant upright thing, five meters high, with eight long, jointed arms, six many-kneed legs, a vast mouth. Some kind of harvester, maybe. Its polished brown metallic skin reflecting the fire's leaping red fingers. Like a mighty idol. Moloch. Baal. He sees his body swept aloft in the great clutching fingers. His head nearing the metal mouth. The villagers capering about him in rhythmic frenzy. Bruised swollen Milcha chanting ecstatically as he goes to his doom. Icy Artha rejoicing in her triumph. Her purity restored by his sacrifice. The priests droning. Please, no. No. Perhaps he's all wrong. Last night, the sterility rite, he thought they were punishing the pregnant one. And she was really the most honored one. But how vicious that machine looks! How deadly!

The plaza is full of villagers now. A major event.

Listen, Artha, it was merely a misunderstanding. I thought you desired me, I was acting within the context of my society's mores, can't you see that? Sex isn't a big complicated operatic thing with us. It's like exchanging smiles. Like touching hands. When two people are together and there's an attraction, they do it, because why not? I only wanted to give you pleasure, really. We were getting along so well together. Really.

The sound of drums. The awful skirling screeches of out-of-tune wind instruments. Orgiastic dancing is starting. God bless, I want to live! Here are the priests and priestesses in their nightmare masks. No doubt of it, the full routine. And I'm the central spectacle tonight.

An hour passes, and more, and the scene in the plaza grows more frenzied, but no one comes to fetch him. Has he misunderstood again? Does tonight's ritual actually concern him as little as did the one last night?

A sound at his door. He hears the lock turning. The door opens. The priests must be coming for him. So now the end is near, eh? He braces himself, hoping for a painless finish. To die for metaphorical reasons, to become a mystic link binding commune to urbmon—such a fate seems improbable and unreal to him. But it is about to befall him all the same.

Artha enters the cell.

She closes the door quickly and presses her back against it. The only illumination is the streaming firelight glaring through his window; it shows her to him with her face tense and stern, her body rigid. This time she wears her weapon. Taking no chances.

"Artha! I—"

"Quiet. If you want to live, keep your voice down."

"What's happening out there?"

"They prepare the harvest god."

"For me?"

"For you."

He nods. "You told them I tried to rape you, I suppose. And now my punishment. All right. All right. It isn't fair, but who expects fairness?"

"I told them nothing," she says. "It was their decision, taken at sundown. I did not cause this."

She sounds sincere. He wonders.

She goes on, "They will take you before the god at midnight. Just now they are praying that he will receive you gracefully. It is a lengthy prayer." She walks cautiously past him, as though expecting him to pounce on her again, and looks out the window. Nods to herself. Turns. "Very well. No one will notice. Come with me, and make no sound whatever. If I'm caught with you, I'll have to kill you and say you were trying to escape. Otherwise it'll be my life too. Come. Come."

"Where?"

"Come!" A fierce impatient whispered gust.

She leads him from the cell. In wonder he follows her through a labyrinth of passages, through dank subterranean chambers, through tunnels barely wider than himself, and they emerge finally at the back of the building. He shivers: a chill in the night air. Music and chanting floating toward him from the plaza. Artha gestures, runs out between two houses, looks in all directions, gestures again. He runs after her. By quick nervous stages they reach the outer edge of the commune. He glances back; from here he can see the fire, the idol, the tiny dancing figures, like images on a screen. Ahead of him are the fields. Above him the crescent sliver of the moon, the shining sprawl of the stars. A sudden sound. Artha clutches at him and tugs him down, under a clump of shrubs. Her body against his; the tips of her breasts like points of fire. He does not dare to move or speak. Someone goes by: a sentry, maybe. Broad back, thick neck. Out of sight. Artha, trembling, holds his wrists, keeping him down. Then at last getting up. Nodding. Silently saying the way is clear. She slips into the fields, between the burgeoning rows of tall, leafy plants. For perhaps ten minutes they trot away from the village, until his untrained body is gasping for breath. When she halts, the bonfire is only a stain on the distant horizon and the singing is drowned out by the chirping of insects. "From here you go by yourself," she tells him. "I have to return. If anyone misses me for long, they might suspect."

"Why did you do this?"

"Because I was unjust to you," she says, and for the first time since coming to him this evening she manages to smile. A ghost-smile, a quick flicker, the merest specter of the warmth of the afternoon. "You were drawn to me. There was no way for you to know our attitudes about such things. I was cruel, I was hateful—and you were only trying to show love. I'm sorry, Statler. So this is my atonement. Go."

"If I could tell you how grateful—"

His hand lightly touches her arm. He feels her quiver—in desire, in disgust, what?—and on a sudden insane impulse he pulls her into an embrace. She is taut at first, then melting. Lips to lips. His fingers on her bare muscular back. Do I dare touch her breasts? Her belly pressed to his. He has a quick wild vision of this afternoon's breach healed: Artha sinking gladly to the sweet earth here, drawing him down on her and into her, the union of their bodies creating that metaphorical link between urbmon and commune that the elders would have forged with his blood. But no. It is an unrealistic vision, however satisfying artistically. There will be no coupling in the moonlit field. Artha lives by her code. Obviously these thoughts have passed through her mind in these few seconds, and she has considered and rejected the possibilities of a passionate farewell, for now she slides free of him, severing the contact moments before he can capitalize on her partial surrender. Her eyes bright and loving in the darkness. Her smile awkward and divided. "Go, now," she whispers. Turning. Running back a dozen paces toward the commune. Turning again, gesticulating with the flats of her hands, trying to push him into motion. "Go. Go. What are you standing there for?"

Hurriedly through the moonsilvered night. Stumbling, lurching, tripping. He does not bother to pick a cautious route between the rows of growing things; in his haste he tramples plants, pushes them aside, leaves a swath of destruction by which, come dawn, he could readily be traced. He knows he must get out of the commune's territory before morning. Once the crop sprayers are aloft they can easily find him and bring him back to feed him to thwarted Moloch. Possibly they will send the sprayers out by night to hunt for him, as soon as they find that he has escaped. Do those yellow eyes see in the dark? He halts and listens for the horrid droning sound, but all is still. And the farming machines— will they go forth to track him down? He has to hurry. Presumably if he gets beyond the commune's domain he will be safe from the worshipers of the harvest god.

Where shall he go?

There is only one destination conceivable now. Looking toward the horizon, he sees the awesome columns of the Chipitts urbmons, eight or ten of them visible from here as brilliant beacons, thousands of windows ablaze. He cannot pick out individual windows, but he is aware of constant shiftings and flowings in the patterns of light as switches go on and off. The middle of the evening there. Concerts, somatic contests, glowduels, all the nightly amusements in full swing. Stacion sitting home, fearful, wondering about him. How long has he been gone? Two days, three? All blurred. The littles crying. Micaela distraught, probably quarreling mercilessly with Jason to ease her tension. While here he is, many kilometers away, newly fled from a world of idols and rites, of pagan dancing, of unyielding and infertile women. Mud on his shoes, stubble on his cheeks. He must look awful and smell worse. No access to a cleanser. What bacteria now breed in his flesh? He must go back. His muscles ache so desperately that he has passed into a discomfort beyond mere fatigue. The reek of the cell clings to his nostrils. His tongue feels furry and puffed. He imagines that his skin is cracking from exposure to sun, moon, air.

What of the sea? What of Vesuvius and the Taj Mahal?

Not this time. He is willing to admit defeat. He has gone as far as he dares, and for as much time as he can permit himself; now with all his soul he longs for home. His conditioning asserting itself after all. Environment conquering genetics. He has had his adventure; someday, god willing, he will have another; but his fantasy of crossing the continent, slipping from commune to commune, must be abandoned. Too many idols wait with polished jaws, and he may not be lucky enough to find an Artha in the next village. Home, then.

His fear ebbs as the hours pass. No one and nothing pursues him. He slips into a steady, mechanical rhythm of march, step and step and step and step, hauling himself robotlike toward the vast towers of the urban monads. He has no idea what time it is, but he supposes it must be past midnight; the moon has swung far across the sky, and the urbmons have grown dimmer as people go to sleep. Nightwalkers now prowl there. Siegmund Kluver of Shanghai dropping in to see Micaela, maybe. Jason on his way to his grubbo sweethearts in Warsaw or Prague. Another few hours, Michael supposes, and he will be home. It took him only from sunrise to late afternoon to reach the commune, and that was with much circuitous rambling; with the towers rising before him at all times he will have no difficulty going straight to his goal.

All is silence. The starry night has a magical beauty. He almost regrets his decision to return to the urbmon. Under the crystalline sky he feels the pull of nature. After perhaps four hours of walking he stops to bathe in an irrigation canal, and emerges naked and refreshed; washing with water is not as satisfying as getting under the ultrasonic cleanser, but at least he no longer need be obsessed with the layers of grime and corruption clinging to his skin. More springily, now, he strides along. His adventure already is receding into history: he encapsulates it and retrospectively relives it. How good to have done this. Tasting the fresh air, the dawn's mist, dirt under his fingernails. Even his imprisonment now seems a high excitement rather than an imposition. Watching the unbirth dance. His fitful, unconsummated love for Artha. Their struggle and their dream-like reconciliation. The gaping jaws of the idol. The fear of death. His escape. What man of Urbmon 116 has done such things?

This access of self-congratulation gives him strength that sends him plunging on, across the commune's unending fields, in renewed vigor. Only the urbmons seem to be getting no closer. A trick of perspective. His weary eyes. Is he heading, he wonders, toward 116? It would be a sad prank of topography to get turned about and come into the urban constellation at 140 or 145 or so. If, say, he is moving at an angle to his true course, the divergence could be immense by the end of his march, leaving him with a dreadful numbing hypotenuse to traverse. He has no way of knowing which of the urbmons ahead of him is his own. He simply goes onward.

The moon vanishes. The stars fade. Dawn is creeping in.

He has reached the zone of unused land between the commune's rim and the Chipitts constellation. His legs are ablaze, but he forces himself on. So close to the buildings that they seem to hang, unsupported, in midair. The formal gardens in view. Robot gardeners serenely going about their trade. Blossoms opening to the first light of day. Perfume drifting on the soft breeze. Home. Home. Stacion. Micaela. Get some rest before going back on the interface. Find a plausible excuse.

Which is Urbmon 116?

The towers bear no numbers. Those who live inside

them know where they live. Half staggering, Michael approaches the nearest building. Its flanks illuminated with radiant dawnlight. Looking up a thousand floors. The delicacy, the complexity, of its myriad tiny chambers. Beneath him the mysterious underground roots, the power plants, the waste-processing plants, the hidden computers, all the concealed wonders that give the urbmon its life. And above, rising like some immense vegetable growth, its sides marvelously intricate, a hatchwork of textures, the urbmon. Within the hundreds of thousands of interwoven lives, artists and scholars, musicians and sculptors, welders and janitors. His eyes are moist. Home. Home. But is it? He goes to the hatch. Holds up his wrist, shows the egress pass. The computer authorized to admit him on demand. "If this is Urbmon 116, open up! I'm Michael Statler." Nothing happening. Scanners scanning him, but all stays sealed. "What building is this?" he asks. Silence. "Come on," he says. "Tell me where I am!"

A voice from an invisible speaker says, "This is Urban Monad 123 of the Chipitts constellation."

123! So many kilometers from home!

But he can only continue. Now the sun is above the horizon and turning quickly from red to gold. If that is the east, then where is Urbmon 116? He calculates with a numbed mind. He must go east. Yes? No? He plods through the interminable series of gardens separating 123 from its eastern neighbor, and interrogates the speaker at the hatch. Yes: this is Urbmon 122. He proceeds. The buildings are set at long diagonals, so that one will not shade the next, and he moves down the center of the constellation, keeping careful count, while the sun climbs and swarms over him. Dizzy, now, with hunger and exhaustion. Is this 116? No, he must have lost count; it will not open for him. Then this?

Yes. The hatch slides back as he offers his pass. Michael clambers in. Waiting as the door rolls shut behind him. Now the inner door to open. Waiting. Well? "Why don't you open?" he asks. "Here. Here. Scan this." Holding up his pass. Perhaps some kind of decontamination procedure. No telling what he's brought in from outside. And now the door opens.

Lights in his eyes. A dazzling glare. "Remain where you are. Make no attempt to leave the entryway." The cold metallic voice nailing him where he stands. Blinking, Michael takes half a step forward, then realizes it might be unwise and stops. A sweet-smelling cloud engulfs him. They have sprayed him with something. Congealing fast, forming a security cocoon. The lights now go down. Figures blocking his path: four, five of them. Police. "Michael Statler?" one of them asks.

"I have a pass," he says uncertainly. "It's all quite legitimate. You can check the records. I—"

"Under arrest. Alteration of program, illicit departure from building, undesirable harboring of countersocial tendencies. Orders to immobilize you immediately upon your return to building. Now carried out. Mandatory sentence of erasure to follow."

"Wait a minute. I have the right of appeal, don't I? I demand to see—"

"Case has already been considered and referred to us for final disposition." A note of inexorability in the policeman's tone. They are at his sides, now. He cannot move. Sealed within the hardening spray. Whatever alien microorganisms he has collected are sealed in it with him. To the chute? No. No. Please. But what else did he expect? What other outcome could there be? Did he think he had fooled the urbmon? Can you repudiate an entire civilization and hope to slip yourself smoothly back into it? They have loaded him aboard some kind of dolly. Dim shapes outside the cocoon. "Let's get a detailed print of this on the record, boys. Move him toward the scanners. Yes. That's it."

"Can't I see my wife, at least? My sister? I mean, what harm will it do if I just talk to them one last time—"

"Menace to harmony and stability, dangerous counter-social tendencies, immediate removal from environment to prevent spreading of reactive pattern." As though he carries a plague of rebelliousness. He has seen this before: the summary judgment, the instant execution. And never really understood. And never imagined.

Micaela. Stacion. Artha.

Now the cocoon is fully hardened. He sees nothing outside it.

"Listen to me," he says, "whatever you're going to do, I want you to know that *I've been there*. I've seen the sun and the moon and the stars. It wasn't Jerusalem, it wasn't the Taj Mahal, but it was something. That you never saw. That you never will. The possibilities out there. The hope of enlarging your soul. What would you understand about that?"

Droning sounds from the far side of the milky web that contains him. They are reading him the relevant sections of the legal code. Explaining how he threatens the structure of society. Necessary to eradicate the source of peril. The words blend and mingle and are lost to him. The dolly begins to roll forward again.

Micaela. Stacion. Artha.

I love you.

"Okay, open the chute." Clear, unmistakable, unambiguous.

He hears the rushing of the tide. He feels the crash of the waves against the sleek shining sands. He tastes salt water. The sun is high; the sky is aglow, a flawless blue. He has no regrets. It would have been impossible ever to leave the building again; if they had let him live, it would be only under conditions of constant surveillance. The urbmon's million million watching eyes. A lifetime hanging on the interface. What for? This is better. To have lived a little bit, just once. To have seen. The dancing, the bonfire, the smell of growing things. And now he is so tired, anyway. Rest will be welcome. He feels a sense of movement. Pushing the dolly again. In and then down. Good-bye. Good-bye. Good-bye. Calmly descending. In his mind the leafy cliffs of Capri, the boy, the goat, the flask of cool golden wine. Fog and dolphins, thorns and pebbles. God bless! He laughs within his cocoon. Going down. Good-bye. Micaela Stacion. Artha. A final vision of the building comes to him, its 885,000 people moving blankfaced through the crowded corridors, floating upward or downward in the transportation shafts, jamming themselves into the sonic centers and the Somatic Fulfillment Halls, sending a myriad messages along the communications nexus as they ask for their meals, talk with one another, make assignations, negotiate. Breeding. Fruitful and multiply. Hundreds of thousands of people on interlocking orbits, each traveling his own little circuit within the mighty tower. How beautiful the world is, and all that is in it. The urbmons at sunrise. The farmers' fields. Good-bye.

Darkness.

The journey is over. The source of peril has been eradicated. The urbmon has taken the necessary protective steps, and an enemy of civilization has been removed.

7

This is the bottom. Siegmund Kluver prowls uneasily among the generators. The weight of the building presses crushingly on him. The whining song of the turbines troubles him. He feels disoriented, a wanderer in the depths. How huge this room is: an immense box far below the ground, so big that the globes of light in its ceiling are barely able to illuminate the distant concrete floor. Siegmund creeps along a catwalk midway between floor and ceiling. Palatial Louisville three kilometers above his head. Carpets and draperies, inlays of rare woods, the trappings of power, very far away now. He hadn't meant to come here, not this far down. Warsaw was his intended destination tonight. But somehow first here. Stalling for time. Siegmund is frightened. Searching for an excuse not to do it. If they only knew. The cowardice within. UnSiegmundlike.

He rubs his hands along the catwalk railing. Cold metal, shaky fingers. A constant throbbing boom running through the building here. He is not far from the terminus of the chutes that convey solid wastes to the power plant: discards of all kinds, old clothes, used data cubes, wrappers and packages, the bodies of the dead, occasionally the bodies of the living, coursing down the spiraling slideways and tumbling into the compactors. And moving thence on gliding belts into the combustion chambers. The liberation of heat for electrical generation: waste not, want not. The electrical load is heavy at this hour.

Every apartment is lit. Siegmund closes his eyes and receives a vision of Urban Monad 116's 885,000 people linked by an enormous tangle of wiring. A giant human switchboard. And I am no longer plugged into it. Why am I no longer plugged into it? What has happened to me? What is happening to me? What is about to happen to me?

Sluggishly he moves along the catwalk and passes out of the generating room. Entering a sleek-walled tunnel; behind its glossy paneled sides, he knows, run the transmission lines along which power flows toward the debooster circuitry. And here the reprocessing plant—urine pipes, fecal reconversion chambers. All the wondrous stuff by which the urbmon lives. No other human being in sight. The heavy weight of the solitude. Siegmund shivers. He must go up to Warsaw soon. Yet he continues to drift like a touring schoolchild through the utility center at the urbmon's lowest level. Hiding here from himself. The cold eyes of electronic scanners staring at him out of hundreds of shielded openings in floors and walls and ceilings. I am Siegmund Kluver of Shanghai, 787th floor. I am fifteen years and five months old. My wife's name is Mamelon, my son is Janus, my daughter is Persephone. I am assigned to work duty as a consultant in Louisville Access Nexus and within the next twelve months I will undoubtedly receive notice of my promotion to the highest administrative levels of this urban monad. Therefore shall I rejoice. I am Siegmund Kluver of Shanghai, 787th floor. He bows to the scanners. All hail. All hail. The future leader. Passing his hand nervously through his coarse bushy hair. For an hour now he has wandered about down here. You should go up. What are you afraid of? To Warsaw. To Warsaw.

He hears the voice of Rhea Shawke Freehouse, coming as though from a recording mounted at the core of his brain. *If I were you, Siegmund, I'd relax and try to enjoy myself more. Don't worry about what people think, or seem to think, about you. Soak up human nature, work at being more human yourself. Go around the building; do some nightwalking in Warsaw or Prague, maybe. See how simpler people live.* Shrewd words. Wise woman. Why be afraid? Go up. Go up. It's getting late.

Standing outside a NO ADMITTANCE hatch leading to one of the computer ganglia, Siegmund spends several minutes studying the tremor of his right hand. Then he hurries to the liftshaft and tells it to take him to the sixtieth floor. The middle of Warsaw.

Narrow corridors, here. Many doors. A compressed quality to the atmosphere. This is a city of extraordinarily high population density, not only because the inhabitants are so blessworthy in their fecundity, but also because much of the city's area is given over to industrial plants. Even though the building is much broader here than in its upper reaches, the citizens of Warsaw are pushed together into a relatively small residential zone. Here are the machines that stamp out machines. Dies, lathes, templates, reciprocators, positioners, fabrication plaques. Much of the work is computerized and automated, but there is plenty for human beings to do: feeding the conveyors, guiding and positioning, driving the fork-lifts, tagging the finished work for its destination. Late last year Siegmund pointed out to Nissim Shawke and Kipling Freehouse that nearly everything being done by human labor in the industrial levels could be handled by machines; instead of employing thousands of people in Warsaw, Prague, and Birmingham, they could set up a totally automated output program, with a few supervisors to keep watch over the inventory homeostasis, and a few maintenance men to handle emergencies, such as repairing the repair machines. Shawke gave him a patronizing smile. "But if they had no work, what would all those poor people do with their lives?" he asked. "Do you think we can turn them into poets, Siegmund? Professors of urban history? We deliberately devise labor for them, don't you see?" And Siegmund embarrassed by his naïveté. A rare failure, for him, of insight into the methodology of government. He still feels uncomfortable about that conversation. In an ideal commonwealth, he believes, every person should have meaningful work to do. He wishes the urban monad to be an ideal commonwealth. But yet certain practical considerations of human limitations interpose themselves. But yet. But yet. The make work in Warsaw is a blot on the theory.

Pick a door. Say, 6021. 6023. 6025. Strange to see the apartments bearing four-digit numbers. 6027. 6029. Siegmund puts his hand to the knob. Hesitates. A rush of sudden timidity. Imagining, within, a brawny hairy growling sullen working-class husband, a shapeless weary working-class wife. And he must intrude on their intimacies. Their resentful glare upon seeing his upper-level clothing. What is this Shanghai dandy doing here? Doesn't he have any regard for decency? And so forth. And so forth. Siegmund almost flees. Then he takes hold of himself. They dare not refuse. They dare not be sullen. He opens the door.

The room is dark. Only the nightglow on; his eyes adjust and he sees a couple on the sleeping platform and five or six littles on cots. He approaches the platform. Stands over the sleepers. His imagined portrait of the room's occupants altogether inaccurate. They could be any young married pair of Shanghai, Chicago, Edinburgh. Strip away the clothes, let sleep eradicate the facial expressions denoting position in the social matrix, and distinctions of class and city perhaps disappear. The naked sleepers are only a few years older than Siegmund—he maybe nineteen, she possibly eighteen. The man slender, narrow shoulders, unspectacular muscles. The woman trim, standard, agreeable body, soft yellow hair. Siegmund lightly touches her shoulder. A ridge of bone lying close beneath the skin. Blue eyes flickering open. Fear giving way to understanding: oh, a night-walker. And understanding giving way to confusion: the night-walker wears upper-building clothes. Etiquette demands an introduction. "Siegmund Kluver," he says. "Shanghai."

The girl's tongue passes hurriedly over her lips. "Shanghai? Really?" The husband awakes. Blinking, puzzled. "Shanghai?" he says. "What for, down here, huh?" Not hostile, just wondering. Siegmund shrugs, as if to say a whim, a fancy. The husband gets off the platform. Siegmund assures him that it isn't necessary for him to leave, that it'll be quite all right to have him here, but that kind of thing evidently isn't practiced in Warsaw: the arrival of the nightwalker is the signal for the husband to clear out. Loose cotton wrap already over his pale, almost hairless body. A nervous smile: see you later, love. And out. Siegmund alone with the woman. "I never met anybody from Shanghai before," she says.

"You haven't told me your name."

"Ellen."

He lies down beside her. Stroking her smooth skin. Rhea's words echo. *Soak up human nature. See how simpler people live.* He is so tightly drawn. His flesh mysteriously invaded by a spreading network of fine golden wires. Penetrating the lobes of his brain. "What does your husband do, Ellen?"

"He's on fork-lift now. Used to be a cabler, but he got hurt sheathing. The whiplash."

"He works hard, doesn't he?"

"The sector boss says he's one of the best. I think he's okay, too." A sniggering little giggle. "What floors are Shanghai, anyway? That's someplace around 700, isn't it?"

"761 to 800." Caressing her haunches. Her body quivers—fear or desire? Shyly her hand goes to his clothing. Maybe just eager to get him in and out and gone. The frightening stranger from the upper levels. Or else not accustomed to foreplay. A different milieu. He'd rather talk awhile first. *See how simpler people live.* He's here to learn, not merely to top. Looking around the room: the furnishings drab and crude, no grace, no style. Yet designed by the same craftsmen who furnish Louisville and Toledo. Obviously aiming for a lower taste. A prevailing film of grayness over everything. Even the girl. I could be with Micaela Quevedo now. I could be with Principessa. Or with. Or perhaps with. But I am here. He searches for probing questions to ask. To bring out the essential humanity of this obscure person over whom he one day will help to rule. Do you read much? What are your favorite screen shows? What sort of foods do you like? Are you doing what you can to help your littles rise in the building? What do you think of the people down in Reykjavik? And those in Prague? But he says nothing. What's the use? What can he learn? Impassable barriers between person and person. Touching her here and here and here. Her fingers on him. He is still soft.

"You don't like me," she says sadly.

He wonders how often she uses the cleanser. "Maybe I'm a little tired," he says. "So busy these days." Pressing his body against hers. The warmth of her possibly will resurrect him. Her eyes staring into his. Blue lenses over inner emptiness. He kisses the hollow of her throat. "Hey, that tickles!" she says, wriggling. He trails his fingers down her belly. To the core of her. Hot and moist and ready. But he isn't. Can't. "Is there anything special?" she asks. "If it isn't too complicated maybe I could." He shakes his head. He isn't interested in whips and chains and thongs. Just the usual. But he can't. His fatigue only a pretense; what cripples him is his sense of isolation. Alone among 885,000 people. And I can't reach her. Not even with this. Pushing the limp rod against her gate. The Shanghai swell, incapable, unmanned. Now she is no longer afraid of him and not very sympathetic. She takes his failure as a sign of his contempt for her. He wants to tell her how many hundreds of women he has topped in Shanghai and Chicago, and even Toledo. Where he is regarded as devilishly virile. Desperately he turns her over. His sweaty belly against her cool buttocks. "Listen, I don't know what you think you're doing, but—" Even this won't help. She squirms indignantly. He releases her. Rises, adjusts himself. Face blazing. As he goes to the door he looks back. She is sitting up wantonly, looking mockery at him. Makes a gesture with three fingers, no doubt a scabrous obscenity here. He says, "I just want you to know. The name I gave you when I came in—it isn't mine. That's not me at all." And goes hastily out. So much for soaking up human nature. So much for Warsaw.

He takes the liftshaft randomly to 118, Prague, gets out, walks halfway around the building without entering any apartment or speaking to anyone he meets; gets into a different liftshaft; goes up to 173 in Pittsburgh; stands for a while in a corridor, listening to the pounding of the blood in the capillaries of his temples. Then he steps into a Somatic Fulfillment Hall. Even at this late hour there are people making use of its facilities: a dozen or so in the whirl-pool tumbler, five or six prancing on the treadmill, a few couples in the copulatorium. His Shanghai clothes earn him some curious stares but no one approaches him. Feeling desire return, Siegmund moves vaguely toward the copulatorium, but at its entrance he loses heart and turns aside. Shoulders slumping, he goes slowly out of the Somatic Fulfillment Hall. Now he takes to the stairs, plodding up the great coil that runs the whole thousand-floor height of Urban Monad 116. He looks up the mighty helix and sees the levels stretching toward infinity, with banks of lights glittering above him to denote each landing. Birmingham, San Francisco, Colombo, Madrid. He grasps the rail and looks down. Eyes spiraling along the descending path. Prague, Warsaw, Reykjavik. A dizzying vortex; a monstrous well through which the light of a million globes drifts from above like snowflakes. He clambers doggedly up the myriad steps. Hypnotized by his own mechanical movements. Before he realizes it, he has climbed forty floors. Sweat drenches him and the muscles of his calves are bunching and knotting. He yanks open the doorway and lurches out into the main corridor. This is the 213th floor. Birmingham. Two men with the smirking look of night-walkers on their way home stop him and offer him some kind of groover, a small translucent capsule containing a dark, oily orange fluid. Siegmund accepts the capsule without a word and swallows it unquestioningly. They tap his biceps in a show of good fellowship and go on their way. Almost at once he feels nausea. Then blurred red and blue lights sway before his eyes. He wonders dimly what they have given him. He waits for the ecstasy. He waits. He waits.

The next thing he knows, the thin light of dawn is in his eyes and he is sitting in an unfamiliar room, sprawled out in a web of oscillating, twanging metal mesh. A tall young man with long golden hair stands over him, and Siegmund can hear his own voice saying, "Now I know why they go flippo. One day it just gets to be too much for you. The people right up against your skin. You can feel them. And—"

"Easy. Back it up a little. You're overloading."

"My head is about to explode." Siegmund sees an attractive red-haired woman moving around in the far corner of the room. He is having difficulty focusing his eyes. "I'm not sure I know where I am," he says.

"370th. That's San Francisco. You're really sectioned off, aren't you?"

"My head. As if it needs to be pumped out."

"I'm Dillon Chrimes. My wife, Electra. She found you wandering in the halls." His host's friendly face smiling into his. Strange blue eyes, like plaques of polished stone. "About the building," Chrimes says. "You know, one night not too long ago I took a multiplexer and I *became* the whole crotting building. And really flew on it. You know, seeing it as one big organism, a mosaic of thousands of minds. Beautiful. Until I started to come down,

213

and on the downside it struck me as just an awful hideous beehive of a place. You lose your perspective when you mess your mind with chemicals. But then you regain it."

"I can't regain it."

"What's the good of hating the building? I mean, the urbmon's a real solution to real problems, isn't it?"

"I know."

"And most of the time it works. So it's a sterilizer to waste your time hating it."

"I don't hate it," Siegmund says. "I've always admired the theory of verticality in urban thrust. My specialty is urbmon administration. Was. Is. But suddenly everything's all wrong, and I don't know where the wrongness is. In me or in the whole system? And maybe not so suddenly."

"There's no real alternative to the urbmon," Dillon Chrimes says. "I mean, you can jump down the chute, I guess, or run off to the communes, but those aren't sensible alternatives. So we stay here. And groove on the richness of it all. You must just have been working too hard. Look, you want something cold to drink?"

"Please. Yes," Siegmund says.

The red-haired woman puts a flask in his hand. As she leans toward him, her breasts sway out, tolling like fleshy bells. She is quite beautiful. A tiny spurt of hormones within him. Reminding him of how this night had begun. Nightwalking in Warsaw. A girl. He has forgotten her name. His failure to top her.

Dillon Chrimes says, "The screen's been broadcasting an alarm for Siegmund Kluver of Shanghai. Tracers out for him since 0400. Is that you?"

Siegmund nods.

"I know your wife. Mamelon, right?" Chrimes shoots a glance at his own wife. As if there is a jealousy problem here. In a lower tone he says to Siegmund, "Once when I was doing a performance in Shanghai I met her on a nightwalk. Lovely. That cool grace of hers. A statue full of passion. Probably very worried about you right now, Siegmund."

"Performance?"

"I play the vibrastar in one of the cosmos groups." Chrimes makes ecstatic keyboard gestures with his fingers. "You've probably seen me. How about letting me put through a call to your wife, all right?"

Siegmund says, "A purely personal thing. A sense of coming apart. Or breaking loose from my roots."

"What?"

"A kind of rootlessness. As though not belonging in Shanghai, not belonging in Louisville, not belonging in Warsaw, not belonging anywhere. Just a cluster of ambitions and inhibitions, no real self. And I'm lost inside."

"Inside what?"

"Inside myself. Inside the building. A sense of coming apart. Leaving pieces of me all over the place. Films of self peeling away, drifting off." Siegmund realizes that Electra Chrimes is staring at him. Appalled. He struggles for self-control. Sees himself stripped down to the bone. Spinal column exposed, the comb of vertebrae, the oddly angular cranium. Siegmund. Siegmund. Dillon Chrimes' earnest, troubled face. A handsome apartment. Polymirrors, psychedelic tapestries. These happy people. Fulfilled in their art. Plugged into the switchboard. "Lost," Siegmund says.

"Transfer to San Francisco," Chrimes suggests. "We

don't push hard here. We can make room. Maybe you'll discover artistic talent. You could write programs for the screen shows, maybe. Or—"

Siegmund laughs harshly. His throat is furry. "I'll write this show about the hungry rung-grabber who gets almost to the top and decides he doesn't want it. I'll—no, I won't. I don't mean any of this. It's the groover talking out of my mouth. Those two slipped me a filther, that's all. You'd better call Mamelon." Getting to his feet. Trembling. A sensation of being at least ninety years old. He starts to fall. Chrimes and his wife catch him. His cheek against Electra's swaying breasts. Siegmund manages a smile. "It's the groover talking out of my mouth," he says again.

"It's a long dull story," he tells Mamelon. "I got into a place where I didn't want to be, and somehow I took a capsule without knowing what I was taking, and everything got confused after that. But I'm all right now. I'm all right."

After a day's medical absence he returns to his desk in Louisville Access Nexus. A pile of memoranda awaits him. Much need of his services by the great men of the administrative class. Nissim Shawke wants him to do a follow-up reply to the petitioners from Chicago, on that business of asking for freedom to determine the sex of one's offspring. Kipling Freehouse requests an intuitive interpretation of certain figures in next quarter's production-balance estimates. Monroe Stevis is after a double flow-chart showing attendance at sonic centers plotted against visits to blessmen and consolers: a psychological profile of the populations of six cities. And so on. Picking his brains. How blessworthy to be useful. How wearying to be used.

He does his best, laboring under his handicap. A sense of coming apart. A dislocation of the soul.

Midnight. Sleep will not come. He lies beside Mamelon, tossing. He has topped her, and still his nerves rustle in the darkness. She knows he is awake. Her soothing hand roams him. "Can't you relax?" she asks.

"It gets harder."

"Would you like some tingle? Or even mindblot."

"No. Nothing."

"Go nightwalking then," she suggests. "Burn up some of that energy. You're all wired up, Siegmund."

Held together by golden thread. Coming apart. Coming apart.

Go up to Toledo, maybe? Seek consolation in Rhea's arms. She always is helpful. Or even nightwalk Louisville. Drop in on Nissim Shawke's wife Scylla. The audacity of it. But they were trying to push me onto her at that party, Somatic Fulfillment Day. Seeing whether I had the blessmanship to deserve promotion to Louisville. Siegmund knows he failed a test that day. But maybe it is not too late to undo that. He will go to Scylla. Even if Nissim's there. See, I have the requisite amorality! See, I defy all bounds. Why should a Louisville wife not be accessible to me? We all live under the same code of law, regardless of the inhibitions of custom that we have lately imposed upon ourselves. So he will say if he finds Nissim. And Nissim will applaud his bravado.

"Yes," he tells Mamelon. "I think I'll nightwalk."

But he remains on the sleeping platform. Some minutes go by. A failure of impulse. He does not want to go; he pretends to be asleep, hoping Mamelon will doze. Some minutes more. Cautiously he opens one eye, slit-wide. Yes, she sleeps. How beautiful she is, how noble even while asleep. The fine bones, the pale skin, the jet-black hair. My Mamelon. My treasure. Lately he has felt little desire even for her. Boredom born of fatigue? Fatigue born of boredom?

The door opens and Charles Mattern comes in.

Siegmund watches the sociocomputator tiptoe toward the platform and silently undress. Mattern's lips are tightly compressed, his nostrils flaring. Signs of yearning. His penis already half erect. Mattern hungers for Mamelon; something has been developing between them over the past two months, Siegmund suspects, something more than mere nightwalking. Siegmund hardly cares. Just so she is happy. Mattern's harsh breathing loud in the room. He starts to awaken Mamelon.

"Hello, Charles," Siegmund says.

Mattern, caught by surprise, flinches and laughs nervously. "I was trying not to wake you, Siegmund."

"I've been up. Watching you."

"You might have said something, then. To save me all this stealthing around."

"I'm sorry. It didn't occur to me."

Mamelon is awake now too. Sitting up, bare to the waist. A stray coil of ebony hair passing deliciously across her pink left nipple. The whiteness of her skin illuminated by the faint glow of the nightlight. Smiling chastely at Mattern: the dutiful female citizen, ready to accept her nocturnal visitor.

Siegmund says, "Charles, as long as you're here, I can tell you that I've got an assignment to do that'll involve working with you. For Stevis. He wants to see if people are spending more time than usual with blessmen and consolers, and less in sonic centers. A double flow-chart that—"

"It's late, Siegmund." Curtly. "Why don't you tell me about it in the morning."

"Yes. All right. All right." Flushing, Siegmund rises from the sleeping platform. He does not have to leave, even with a nightwalker here for Mamelon, but he does not want to stay. Like a Warsaw husband, granting a superfluous and unasked privacy to the other two. He hurriedly finds some clothing. Mattern reminds him that he's free to remain. But no. Siegmund leaves, a little wildly. Almost running down the hall. I will go up to Louisville, to Scylla Shawke. However, instead of asking the liftshaft to take him to the level where the Shawkes live, he calls out a Shanghai floor, 799. Charles and Principessa Mattern live there. He does not dare risk attempting Scylla while he is in this jangled state. Failure could be costly. Principessa will do. A tigress, she is. A savage. Her sheer animal vigor may restore his well-being. She is the most passionate woman he knows, short of Mamelon. And a good age, ripe but not overripe. Siegmund halts outside Principessa's door. It strikes him that it is somewhat bourgeois, something of a pre-urbmon thing, for him to be seeking the wife of the man who is now with his own wife. Nightwalking should be more random, less structured, merely a way of extending the range of one's life-experiences. Nevertheless. He nudges the door open. Relieved and dismayed to hear sounds of ecstasy from within. Two people on the platform: he sees arms and legs that must be Principessa's, and, covering her, emitting earnest grunts, is Jason Quevedo, thrusting and pumping. Siegmund quickly ducks out. Alone in the corridor. Where to, now? The world is too complicated for him tonight. The obvious next destination is Quevedo's apartment. For Micaela. But no doubt she will have a visitor too. Siegmund's forehead begins to throb. He does not want to roam the urbmon endlessly. He wants only to go to sleep. Night-walking suddenly seems an abomination to him: forced, unnatural, compulsive. The slavery of absolute freedom. At this moment thousands of men roam the titanic building. Each determined to do the blessworthy thing. Siegmund, scuffing at the floor, strolls along the corridor and halts by a window. Outside, a moonless night. The sky ablaze with stars. The neighboring urbmons seeming farther away than usual. Their windows bright, thousands of them. He wonders if it is possible to see a commune, far to the north. The crazy farmers. Micaela Quevedo's brother Michael, the one who went flippo, supposedly visited a commune. At least so the story goes. Micaela still brooding about her brother's fate. Down the chute with him as soon as he stuck his head back inside the urbmon. But of course a man like that can't be permitted to resume his former life here. An obvious malcontent, spreading poisons of dissatisfaction and unblessworthi-ness. A hard thing for Micaela, though. Very close to her brother, she says. Her twin. Thinks he should have had a formal hearing in Louisville. He did, though. She won't believe it, but he did. Siegmund remembers when the papers came through. Nissim Shawke issuing the decree: if this man ever returns to 116, dispose of him at once. Poor Micaela. Something unhealthy going on, maybe, between her and her brother. I might ask Jason. I might.

Where shall I go now?

He realizes that he has been standing by the window for more than an hour. He stumbles toward the stairs and jogs down twelve levels to his own. Mattern and Mamelon lie sleeping side by side. Siegmund drops his clothing and joins them on the platform. Coming apart. Dislocation. Finally he sleeps too.

The solace of religion. Siegmund has gone to see a blessman. The chapel is on the 770th floor: a small room off a commercial arcade, decorated with fertility symbols and incrustations of captive light. Entering, he feels like an intruder. Never any religious impulses before. His mother's grandfather was a Christer, but everyone in the family assumed it was because the old man had antiquarian instincts. The ancient religions have few followers, and even the cult of god's blessing, which is officially supported by Louisville, can claim no more than a third of the building's adult population, according to the last figures Siegmund has seen. Though perhaps things are changing lately.

"God bless," the blessman says, "what is your pain?"

He is plump, smooth-skinned, with a round complacent face and cheerily shining eyes. At least forty years old. What does he know of pain?

"I have begun not to belong," Siegmund says. "My future is unraveling. I am coming unplugged. Everything has lost its meaning and my soul is hollow."

"Ah. Angst. Anomie. Dissociation. Identity drain. Familiar complaints, my son. How old are you?"

"Past fifteen."

"Career profile?"

"Shanghai going on Louisville. Perhaps you know of me. Siegmund Kluver."

The blessman's lips go taut. The eyes veil themselves. He toys with sacred emblems on his tunic's collar. He has heard of Siegmund, yes.

He says, "Are you fulfilled in your marriage?"

"I have the most blessworthy wife imaginable."

"Littles?"

"A boy and a girl. We will have a second girl next year."

"Friends?"

"Sufficient," Siegmund says. "And yet this feeling of decomposition. Sometimes my skin itchy all over. Films of decay drifting through the building and wrapping themselves about me. A great restlessness. What's happening to me?"

"Sometimes," the blessman says, "those of us who live in the urban monads experience what is called the crisis of spiritual confinement. The boundaries of our world, that is to say our building, seem too narrow. Our inner resources become inadequate. We are grievously disappointed in our relationships with those we have always loved and admired. The result of such a crisis is often violent: hence the flippo phenomenon. Others may actually leave the urbmon and seek a new life in the communes, which, of course, is a form of suicide, since we are incapable of adapting to that harsh environment. Now, those who neither go berserk nor separate themselves physically from the urbmon occasionally undertake an internal migration, drawing into their own souls and, in effect, contracting as a response to the impingement of adjacent individuals on their psychic space. Does this have any meaning for you?" As Siegmund nods doubtfully, the blessman goes smoothly on, saying, "Among the leaders of this building, the executive class, those who have been propelled upward by the blessworthy drive to serve their fellow men, this process is particularly painful, bringing about as it does a collapse of values and a loss of motivation. But it can be easily cured."

"Easily?"

"I assure you."

"Cured? How?"

"We will do it at once, and you will go out of here healthy and whole, Siegmund. The way to health is through kinship with god, you see, god being considered in our view the integrative force giving wholeness to the universe. And I will show you god."

"You will show me god," Siegmund repeats, uncomprehending.

"Yes. Yes." The blessman, bustling around, is busy darkening the chapel, switching off lights and cutting in opaquers. From the floor sprouts a cup-shaped web-seat into which Siegmund is gently nudged. Lying there looking up. The chapel's ceiling, he discovers, is a single broad screen. In its glassy green depths an image of the heavens appears. Stars strewn like sand. A billion billion points of light. Music issues from concealed speakers: the plashy plinks of a cosmos group. He makes out the magical sounds of a vibrastar, the dark twangs of a comet-harp, the wild lurches of an orbital diver. Then the whole group going at once. Perhaps Dillon Chrimes is playing. His friend of that dismal night. Overhead the depth of the perceptive field is deepening; Siegmund sees the orange glint of Mars, the pearly blaze of Jupiter. So god is a light-show plus a cosmos group? How shallow. How empty.

The blessman, speaking over the music, says, "What you see is a direct relay from the thousandth floor. This is the sky over our urbmon at our present moment. Look into the black cone of night. Accept the cool light of the stars. Open yourself to the immensity. What you see is god. What you see is god."

"Where?"

"Everywhere. Immanent and all-enduring."

"I don't see."

The music is turned up. Siegmund now is surrounded by a cage of heavy sound. The astronomical scene takes on a greater intensity. The blessman directs Siegmund's attention to this group of stars and to that, urging him to merge with the galaxy. The urbmon is not the universe, he murmurs. Beyond these shining walls lies an awesome vastness that is god. Let him take you into himself and heal you. Yield. Yield. Yield. But Siegmund cannot yield. He wonders if the blessman should have given him some sort of drug, a multiplexer of some kind that would make it easier for him to open himself to the universe. But the blessman scoffs at the idea. One can reach god without chemical assistance. Simply stare. Contemplate. Peer into infinity. Search for the divine pattern. Meditate on the forces in balance, the beauties of celestial mechanics. God is within and without us. Yield. Yield. Yield. "I still don't feel it," Siegmund says. "I'm locked up inside my own head." A note of impatience enters the blessman's tone. What's wrong with you, he seems to be saying. Why can't you? It's a perfectly good religious experience. But it is no use. After half an hour Siegmund sits up, shaking his head. His eyes hurt from staring at the stars. He cannot make the mystical leap. He authorizes a credit transfer to the blessman's account, thanks him, and goes out of the chapel. Perhaps god was somewhere else today.

The solace of the consoler. A purely secular therapist, relying heavily on metabolic adjustments. Siegmund is apprehensive about seeing him; he has always regarded those who have to go to a consoler as somehow defective, and it pains him to be joining that group. Yet he must end this inner turmoil. And Mamelon insists. The consoler he visits is surprisingly young, perhaps thirty-three, with a pinched, bleak face and frosty, ungenerous eyes. He knows the nature of Siegmund's complaint almost before it is described to him. "And when you attended this party in Louisville," he asks, "what effect did it have on you to learn that your idols weren't quite the men you thought they were?"

"It emptied me out," Siegmund says. "My ideals, my values, my guiding images. To see them cavorting like that. Never having imagined they did. I think that's where all the trouble started."

"No," says the consoler, "that's merely where the trouble surfaced. It was there before. In you, deep, waiting for something to push it up into view."

"How can I learn to cope with it?"

"You can't. You'll have to be sent into therapy. I'm going to turn you over to the moral engineers. You can use a reality adjustment."

He is afraid of being changed. They will put him into a tank and let him drift there for days or weeks, while they cloud his mind with their mysterious substances and whisper things to him and massage his aching body and alter the imprinting of his brain. And he will come forth healthy and stable and different. Another person. All his Siegmundness lost along with his anguish. He remembers Aurea Holson, whose number came up in the lottery for the stocking of the new Urbmon 158, and who did not want to go, and who was persuaded by the moral engineers that it would not be so bad to leave her native urbmon. And came forth from her tank docile and placid, a vegetable in place of a neurotic. Not for me, Siegmund thinks.

It will be the end of his career, too. Louisville does not want men who have had crises. They will find some middle-rung post for him in Boston or Seattle, some tepid minor administrative job, and forget about him. A formerly promising young man. Full reports on reality adjustments are placed each week before Monroe Stevis. Stevis will tell Shawke and Freehouse. Have you heard about poor Siegmund? Two weeks in the tank. Some sort of breakdown. Yes, sad. Very sad. We'll drop him, of course.

No.

What can he do? The consoler has already made up the adjustment request and filed it with one of the computer nodes. Sparkling impulses of neural energy are traveling through the information system, bearing his name. Time is being cleared for him on the 780th floor, among the moral engineers. Soon his screen will tell him the hour of his appointment. And if he does not go to them, they will come for him. The machines with soft rubbery pads on their arms, gathering him up, pushing him along.

No.

He tells Rhea of his predicament. Not even Mamelon knows yet, but Rhea. He can trust her. His best interests at heart. "Don't go to the engineers," she advises.

"Don't go? How? The order's already in."

"Have it countermanded."

He looks at her as though she has recommended demolition of the Chipitts urbmon constellation.

"Pull it out of the computer," she tells him. "Get one

226

of the interface men to do it for you. Use your influence. Nobody'll find out."

"I couldn't do that."

"You'll go to the moral engineers, then. And you know what that means."

The urbmon is toppling. Clouds of debris swirl in his brain.

Who would arrange such a thing for him?

Micaela Quevedo's brother worked in an interface crew, didn't he? But he's gone now. There must be others within his grasp, though. When he leaves Rhea, Siegmund consults the records in the access nexus. The virus of unblessworthiness already at work in his soul. Then he realizes he doesn't even need to use his influence. Merely make it a matter of professional routine. In his office he taps out a data requisition: status of Siegmund Kluver, remanded for therapy on 780th floor. Instantly comes the information that Kluver is due for therapy in seventeen days. The computer does not withhold data from Louisville Access Nexus. The presumption exists that anyone who asks, using the equipment in the nexus, has the right to do so. Very well. The vital next step. Siegmund instructs the computer to yank the therapy assignment for Siegmund Kluver. This time there is a bit of resistance: the computer wants to know who authorizes the yanking. Siegmund meditates on that for a moment. Then inspiration comes. The therapy of Siegmund Kluver, he informs the machine, is being canceled by order of Siegmund Kluver of the Louisville Access Nexus. Will it work? "No," the machine may say, "you can't cancel your own therapy appointment. Do you think I'm stupid?" But the mighty computer *is* stupid. Thinking with the speed of light but unable to cross the gaps of intuition. Does Siegmund Kluver of Louisville Access Nexus have the right to cancel a therapy appointment? Yes, certainly; he must be acting on behalf of Louisville itself. Therefore let it be canceled. The instructions flicker through the proper node. No matter whose appointment it is, as long as authority to cancel can be attributed properly. It is done. Siegmund taps out a data requisition: status of Siegmund Kluver, remanded for therapy on 780th floor. Instantly comes the information that Kluver's appointment for therapy has been canceled. His career is safe, then. But he is left with his anguish. There is that to consider.

This is the bottom. Siegmund Kluver prowls uneasily among the generators. The weight of the building presses crushingly on him. The whining song of the turbines troubles him. He feels disoriented, a wanderer in the depths. How huge this room is.

He enters apartment 6029, Warsaw. "Ellen?" he says. "Listen, I've come back. I want to apologize for the last time. It was all a tremendous mistake." She shakes her head. She has already forgotten him. But she is willing to accept him, naturally. The universal custom. Her legs parted, her knees flexed. Instead he kisses her hand. "I love you," he whispers, and flees.

This is the office of Jason Quevedo, historian, on the 185th floor, Pittsburgh. Where the archives are. Jason sits before his desk, manipulating data cubes, as Siegmund enters. "It's all here, isn't it?" Siegmund asks. "The story of the collapse of civilization. And how we rebuilt it again. Verticality as the central philosophical thrust of human congruence patterns. Tell me the story, Jason. Tell me." Jason looking at him strangely.

"Are you ill, Siegmund?" And Siegmund: "No, not at all. How perfectly healthy I am. Micaela's been explaining your thesis to me. The genetic adaptation of humanity to urbmon life. I'd like more details. How we've been bred to be what we are. We happy many." Siegmund picks up two of Jason's cubes and fondles them, almost sexually, leaving fingerprints on their sensitive surfaces. Tactfully Jason takes them from him. "Show me the ancient world," Siegmund says, but as Jason slips a cube into the playback slot, Siegmund goes out.

This is the great industrial city of Birmingham. Pale, sweating, Siegmund Kluver watches machines stamping out machines. While slumped and sullen human handlers supervise the work. This thing with arms will help in next autumn's harvest at a commune. This dark glossy tube will fly above the fields, spraying insects with poison. Siegmund finds himself weeping. He will never see the communes. He will never dig his fingers into the rich brown soil. The beautiful meshing ecology of the modern world. The poetic interplay of commune and urbmon for the benefit of all. How lovely. How lovely. Then why am I weeping?

San Francisco is where the musicians and artists and writers live. The cultural ghetto. Dillon Chrimes is rehearsing with his cosmos group. The thunderous web of sounds. An intruder. "Siegmund?" Chrimes says, breaking his concentration. "How are you getting along, Siegmund? Good to see you." Siegmund laughs. He gestures at the vibrastar, the comet-harp, the incantator, and the other instruments. "Please," he murmurs, "keep on playing. I'm simply looking for god. You don't mind if I listen? Maybe he's here. Play some more."

On the 761st floor, Shanghai's bottom level, he finds Micaela Quevedo. She does not look well. Her black hair is dull and stringy, her eyes are bitter, her lips are clamped. Seeing Siegmund in midday startles her. He says quickly, "Can we talk awhile? I want to ask you some things about your brother Michael. Why he left the building. What he hoped to find out there. Can you give me any information?" Micaela's expression grows even harder. Coldly she says, "I don't know a thing. Michael went flippo, that's all that matters. He didn't explain himself to me." Siegmund knows that this is untrue. Micaela is concealing vital data. "Don't be unbless-worthy," he urges. "I need to know. Not for Louisville. Just for myself." His hand on her thin wrist. "I'm thinking of leaving the building too," Siegmund confides.

He halts at his own apartment on the 787th floor. Mamelon is not there. As usual, she is at the Somatic Fulfillment Hall, enhancing her supple body. Siegmund records a brief message for her. "I loved you," he says. "I loved you. I loved you."

He meets Charles Mattern in a Shanghai hallway. "Come have dinner with us," the sociocomputator says. "Principessa's always happy to see you. And the children. Indra and Sandor talk about you. Even Marx. When's Siegmund coming again, they say? We like Siegmund so much." Siegmund shakes his head. "I'm sorry, Charles. Not tonight. But thanks for asking." Mattern shrugs. "God bless, we'll get together soon, eh?" he says, and strolls away, leaving Siegmund in the midst of the flow of pedestrian traffic.

This is Toledo, where the pampered children of the administrative caste make their homes. Rhea Shawke Freehouse lives here. Siegmund does not dare pay a call on her. She is too perceptive; she will understand at once that he is in a terminal phase of collapse, and undoubtedly will take preventive action. But yet he must make some move in her direction. Siegmund pauses outside her apartment and tenderly presses his lips to the door. Rhea. Rhea. Rhea. I loved you too. He goes up.

Nor does he make any visits in Louisville, though it would please him to see some of the masters of the urbmon tonight, Nissim Shawke or Monroe Stevis or Kipling Freehouse. Magical names, names that resonate in his soul. Best to bypass them. He goes directly to the landing stage on the thousandth floor. Stepping out on the flat breeze-swept platform. Night, now. The stars glittering fiercely. Up there is god, immanent and allenduing, floating serenely amidst the celestial mechanics. Below Siegmund's feet is the totality of Urban Monad 116. What is today's population? 888,904. Or some such. +131 since yesterday and +9,902 since the first of the year, adjusted for the departure of those who went to stock the new Urbmon 158. Maybe he has the figures all wrong. It hardly matters. The building is athrob with life, at any rate. Fruitful and multiplying. God bless! So many servants of god. Shanghai's 34,000 souls. Warsaw. Prague. Tokyo. The ecstasy of verticality. In this single slender tower we compress so many thousands of lives. Plugged into the same switchboard. Homeostasis, and the defeat of entropy. We are well organized here. All thanks to our dedicated administrators.

And look, look there! The neighboring urbmons! The wondrous row of them! Urbmon 117, 118, 119, 120. The fifty-one towers of the Chipitts constellation. Total population now 41,516,883. Or some such. And east of Chipitts lies Boshwash. And west of Chipitts is Sansan. And across the sea is Berpar and Wienbud and Shankong and Bocarac. And more. Each cluster of towers with its millions of encapsulated souls. What is the population of our world now? Has it reached 76,000,000,000 yet? They project 100,000,000,000 for the not too distant future. Many new urbmons must be built to house those added billions. Plenty of land left though. And they can put platforms on the sea.

To the north, on the horizon, he imagines he can see the blaze of a commune's bonfires. Like the flash of a diamond in sunlight. The farmers dancing. Their grotesque rites. Bringing fertility to the fields. God bless! It is all for the best. Siegmund smiles. He stretches forth his arms. If he could only embrace the stars, he might find god. He walks to the very edge of the landing stage. A railing and a force-field protect him against the vagrant gusts of wind that might hurl him to his death. It is very windy here. Three kilometers high, after all. A needle sticking into god's eye. If he could only spring into the heavens. Looking down as he floats past, seeing Chipitts below, the rows of towers, the farmland surrounding them, the miraculous urban rhythm of verticality plotted against the miraculous commune rhythm of horizontality. How beautiful the world is tonight. Siegmund throws his head back. Eyes shining. And there is god. The blessman was right. There! There! Wait, I'm coming! Siegmund mounts the railing. Teeters a little. Currents of wind buffeting him. He has risen above the protective force-field. It seems almost as though the whole building is swaying. Think of the body heat that 888,904 human beings under the same roof must generate. Think of the waste products they daily send down the chute. All these linked lives. The switchboard. And god watching over us. I'm coming! I'm coming. Siegmund flexes his knees, gathers his strength, sucks air deep into his lungs. And sails toward god in a splendid leap.

Now the morning sun is high enough to touch the uppermost fifty stories of Urban Monad 116. Soon the building's entire eastern face will glitter like the bosom of the sea at daybreak. Thousands of windows, activated by the dawn's early photons, deopaque. Sleepers stir. Life goes on. God bless! Here begins another happy day.